Praise for *Pocketful of Pearls*

"Absorbing and poignant. With a deft hand, Bates examines how our Lord's unfailing grace can set even the most broken spirits free."

—Deborah Bedford, author of *Remember Me*

"This is a book that resonates in the heart. I literally couldn't put it down."

—Ciji Ware, bestselling author of
A Light on the Veranda and *Island of the Swans*

Praise for *A Sounding Brass*

"Readers will appreciate that things are a little topsy-turvy, with spiritual insights coming from unexpected places."

—*Publishers Weekly*

"*A Sounding Brass* grabbed me on page one . . . I couldn't put it down. A great read for a rainy day or any day."

—Lyn Cote, author of
the Women of Ivy Manor series

OVER
HER
HEAD

A NOVEL

Shelley Bates

New York   Boston   Nashville

This book is a work of fiction. Names, characters, places, and incidents are the product of the author's imagination or are used fictitiously. Any resemblance to actual events, locales, or persons, living or dead, is coincidental.

FaithWords

Hachette Book Group USA

237 Park Avenue

New York, NY 10169

Visit our Web site at www.faithwords.com.

Book design by Fearn Cutler de Vicq

Printed in the United States of America

First Edition: May 2007

10 9 8 7 6 5 4 3 2 1

The FaithWords name and logo are trademarks of Hachette Book Group USA.

Library of Congress Cataloging-in-Publication Data

Bates, Shelley.

   Over her head : a novel / Shelley Bates.—1st ed.

      p. cm.

   ISBN-13: 978-0-446-69493-3

   ISBN-13: 0-446-69493-3

   1. Housewives—Fiction. 2. Mothers and daughters—Fiction. 3. Pennsylvania—Fiction. I. Title.

PS3602.A875O94 2007

813'.66 —dc22   2006037376

For the kids in my life:
Kailey, Derrik, Spencer, Joshua, and Sarah

Acknowledgments

First of all, my thanks go to my teenage informants, Kailey Senft and Anna Lekomtseva, whose honesty and humor were a gift as they reminded me of what it was like to be fourteen.

Thanks go to Debrah Williamson, Diana Duncan, Tina Novinski, and Catherine Mulvany, for their help with nailing the story down.

Thank you to Captain Robert Dixon and to Lieutenant Chris Forrester of the Santa Clara County Coroner's Office, for all the information and the tour of the facility on a busy Monday morning . . . a tour that included thirteen bodies and a homicide.

Thank you to Angelique Bagley, Marriage and Family Therapist, who gave me all the information I needed about post-traumatic stress syndrome and how it would affect a teenager in Anna Hale's situation.

Thank you to Jennifer Jackson, my agent, and Anne Goldsmith, my editor at FaithWords, both of whom encourage me to "go deeper."

As always, love and thanks go to my parents, Dan and Carol, who are a constant source of joy as they discover a new world, and to my husband, Jeff, who makes it possible for me to write and not cook.

And lastly, my respect and thanks go to R.V., who will never know how much her life has touched mine. The events of this book, while they were inspired by her reality, are entirely fictional.

I love to hear from readers. You can visit me on my Web site, http://www.shelleybates.com, or drop me a note at shelley@shelleybates.com.

OVER
HER
HEAD

If it had not been the Lord who was on our side, when men rose up
    against us:
Then they had swallowed us up quick, when their wrath was kindled
    against us:
Then the waters had overwhelmed us, the stream had gone over our
    soul:
Then the proud waters had gone over our soul.

—PSALM 124:2-5 (KJV)

Chapter One

*E*ven in *November,* when the trees were skeletal and the ground covered in dead leaves and puddles, the jogging trail by the river was still Laurie Hale's favorite place to run. Not that she was wild about physical fitness—it was just that something had to be done about an hourglass figure that had drooped into more of a pear shape. She simply could not go up to a size sixteen on her next trip to the mall, and that was final.

There are barriers in every woman's life beyond which she will not go, and a size sixteen was Laurie's.

Besides, jogging got her out of the house. Going to Curves would do the same, but she'd still be in a gym with people she knew from church and Anna's and Tim's schools. What Laurie liked best about jogging by the river was simply that she was alone. With a ten-year-old son and a fourteen-year-old daughter, who could blame her for taking extreme measures in order to get a little peace and quiet?

So what if her sweats were a shrunken pair of her husband Colin's and her shoes were from the local discount store? No one was out here at seven thirty on a winter morning. The executive types had already come and gone, taking the commuter train from the Glendale station into Pittsburgh and leaving the trails to the winter birds, squirrels, and slightly chunky moms.

Laurie's legs were beginning to ache at the end of her mile. She wasn't much of a goal setter, but if she had to set one, it would be getting back to the parking lot without keeling over and dying of oxygen deprivation. She'd nearly reached the half-way point where she turned around—where the Susquanny River widened a little and a sandbar had built up. Often the herons would gather there to pick over what the river had tossed up, or to spear minnows on their way past in the shallows. The kids had loved to play there in the summer. Someone had tied a rope swing into a tree, and they'd drop off it into the deep pool scooped out close to the bank.

But now the swing was as frozen and lifeless as the tree that supported it, waiting for the sun and the return of the children.

There must have been some high water recently. A log had washed up onto the sandbar, and crows were walking around it like car salesmen sizing up a new deal. There were clothes draped over it, too. *Good grief. Surely someone hasn't been swimming?* It had to be forty-five degrees out there.

Laurie jogged a little closer, taking one of the offshoot trails closer to the bank. Maybe it wasn't a log, after all. Maybe someone had tossed a bag of old clothes off the bridge instead of taking them to the Salvation Army like normal people did. But weren't those branches sticking out? And was that an animal trapped under it? With brown fur?

The river trail, though beautiful and scenic, didn't change much. That was why Laurie liked it. She didn't have to watch out for hazards because she knew where they all were, and she could pay attention to seasonal changes in the scenery without worrying about falling flat on her face.

So anything different meant a little investigation was in order. Maybe there would be identifying marks among the clothes to tell her who the litterbug was. She'd march right down to the

Glendale sheriff's office and wake up her cousin Nick or one of the other—

Good heavens.

Laurie slid down the bank and landed upright by sheer luck. She squinted against the sparkle of the sun on the water and focused on the pile on the sandbar.

Not fur. Hair. Dark brown, short-cropped hair with a pink streak dyed into it, now drying and rimed with sand.

A green jacket. Jeans.

Bare feet. Slender, pale feet, so cold they were gray.

Laurie let out her breath with a whoosh and then couldn't get it back again. Her lungs and heart felt as though they were being squeezed tight with sheer horror.

"Oh, no. No." Crablike, she scrambled sideways up the bank, her gaze fixed on the sandbar. "It can't be."

Maybe it wasn't. Maybe the life hadn't yet left that pitiful, damp body on the sand. Maybe there was still something she could do.

She yanked her cell phone out of her pocket and dialed 911.

Chapter Two

Shut up. Keep it down low.

EXHIBIT 1

TRANSCRIPT   11/07 07:43:57
MASTER TAPE 203

DISPATCHER: County Communications.
UNID FEMALE: I'm—there's a—there's a girl. In the
    river. Please send someone, quick.
DISPATCHER: Please state your name, ma'am.
U/F: Laurie. Laurie Amelia Hale. I'm Nick
    Tremore's cousin. He's in the sheriff's office.
    Please, do we need to waste time on this? She
    might still be alive.
DISPATCHER: Ms. Hale, please give me your
    location.
HALE: I'm on the jogging trail next to the river.
    [gasps] About half a mile south of the commuter
    parking lot. The one at the train station.
DISPATCHER: Are you in need of assistance, Ms.
    Hale?
HALE: No, it's not me. There's a girl on the

sandbar in the river. She needs help—don't you
get it? I think she might be dead.
DISPATCHER: Please calm down, ma'am. Is anyone
with you?
HALE: No. [Subject is weeping.]
DISPATCHER: I'm sending a marked unit and an
ambulance now. Please wait there so they can
find you, ma'am.
HALE: Tell them I'll meet them in the commuter
lot. Tell them to hurry.
END TRANSCRIPT   11/07 07:45:32
                    TAPE 203

*PLEASE BE THERE. Please don't be in a meeting. Please have your
phone on you and not in a jacket hanging on a chair somewhere.*

After the third ring, Colin answered. "Hey, Lor. What's up?"

"This is terrible." Her voice climbed the scale and she worked
to bring it under control. "You won't believe it."

"What? Was there an accident? Are you okay? The kids?"

"No, no. The kids are in school, and I'm—" Her voice broke
and she cleared her throat. "I'm down by the river. They told me
to stay here until they had time to get a statement."

"You were in an accident? Was anyone hurt?"

Controlling the emotions was like building a muscle. The
more you used it, the stronger you got. "No, and no. I was on my
run this morning and found a—a body." *That sounds so cold.* "A
girl, in the river. Nick and his guys and the coroner are here."

Static crackled in her ear as this information bounced
off a satellite somewhere in the atmosphere and reached her
husband.

"Laurie, are you sure it's not just some drunk sleeping it off
under the bridge?"

"Nobody sleeps under the bridge in November, Colin. And we're half a mile downstream from it. It was a girl, around the same age as Anna, I think. Maybe a little younger. She was washed up on the sandbar across from where the rope swing is. I saw her from the jogging trail."

This unembellished recital of facts seemed to convince him, and the unflappable president of Susquanny Home Supply melted into Colin the normal husband. "Are you all right? It must have been a shock to find—her . . ."

The nice deputy who'd responded to the scene with Nick had used the same word. *Shock.*

"I'm fine. I'm going straight home as soon as they're done with me, though. My knees are a bit wobbly still."

"I don't doubt they are. Want me to come and get you?"

He had a staff meeting at nine, and they both knew it. "No, no. I'll see you at home."

She closed the phone and clipped it to the stretchy waistband of her sweats.

The kind deputy, whose name she'd already forgotten, climbed the riverbank and angled up the slope to where she stood on the jogging trail. Below them, on the bar, two men in navy blue jackets, who had arrived in a white van with "Keystone Removal Services" discreetly lettered on the side, zipped up the plastic bag containing the girl's body, hoisted it with a man on each end, and sloshed through the shallows to the bank.

The tears that she couldn't seem to control welled up again, and she focused on the deputy, trying to concentrate.

"Feel up to giving a statement now, Mrs. Hale?" he asked.

She nodded. "Mind going down to the station? It's a lot warmer down there, and we could scare up some coffee for you. Nick should be done here in a couple of minutes, and he'll go over what happened with you."

She was beginning to wonder if she'd ever be warm again. The ambulance driver had brought her a blanket, but the chill was the kind that only hot soup and a long hug could drive away.

Much to her relief, Nick didn't ask her to sit in the back of the police car like a criminal. Instead, she sat up front, where the blast from the heater turned her cheeks fire-engine red, but didn't do anything to dispel those deep-seated tremors inside her.

The Glendale sheriff's department wasn't very big—just a couple of offices for the sergeants and the sheriff, and an open area with workstations for the four deputies behind the main counter. Her statement consisted of a few paragraphs on the green-ruled report form. What was there to say, after all?

I went jogging at seven thirty. I found the girl at seven forty. For once, my cell phone was charged and on me, and I dialed 911.

So simple. And she was going to be having nightmares about it for months. Maybe even years.

Lord, please block the sight of that poor girl lying on the sand out of my mind.

"Nick, what will happen now?"

"It's too early to say. When we find out who it is, the coroner will notify the parents."

Laurie felt her control waver again. She could just imagine what that might be like. A stranger on your doorstep, telling you your child was dead.

She shook her head at herself. Colin was always telling her that her imagination tended to run away with her. There were some things a person just couldn't think about and still keep functioning.

"You don't look so good, Laurie." Nick leaned over and rubbed her shoulder. "Come on. Let me give you a ride home."

"Don't be silly. It's not even half a mile. And I didn't finish my run."

"Quit being brave. It's me, remember? The guy who beat up Melvin Hartzheim for you in third grade."

As he'd probably planned, the tension in her shoulders relaxed. "And all because he said he had a crush on me. Good thing your methods changed later on. I'd never have been able to get a date."

It was a relief to be able to take refuge in silly memories, the kind that only family hung on to for years and years. That poor little girl on the sandbar had probably had friends and cousins and people she laughed with. Maybe someone had even beat up a bully for her once. But all that was over now—cut short before it had even really blossomed.

She had to stop thinking like this or she really would break down again.

Nick dropped her off in front of the house. When she'd closed the door of the police sedan, he leaned over and rolled down the window.

"Make yourself a hot cup of tea, okay? And take it easy for the rest of the day. You still look a little shell-shocked."

She nodded and fingered the keys in the pocket of her jacket. "Thanks, Nick. I owe you for looking after me."

He shrugged and flashed Auntie Lou's lopsided grin at her. "Your tax dollars at work."

With a wave he drove off, and Laurie let herself into the house. They'd moved in here when Anna was born—their dream home, the one she didn't plan to leave until they pried the keys out of her age-spotted hands. The lots on their street were big and the trees were old, like the houses. Theirs had the typical Pennsylvania shape, with steep gables, thick stone walls, and ten-foot ceilings with plaster medallions around the light fixtures. When the owner of the building company had retired and Colin had been promoted to president five years ago, they'd remodeled the kitchen. It had taken months to transform the dark, damp lean-to that had been added in the twenties into a clean, light-filled area where people liked to congregate, but it had been worth every minute.

A cup of stale coffee was still waiting in the pot for her to get back from her run. She poured it down the sink and then glanced at the phone. *You are not going to call the junior high to ask if Anna is in class and okay.*

Because of course Anna was okay. In fact, she was probably just heading off to second-period math. If Laurie called, it would do nothing but embarrass her daughter, and then they'd all have to deal with the fallout when she got home from school.

Was the drowned girl's mother thinking of calling, too?

No, that wasn't possible. The coroner's voice had carried, and she'd heard him mention that the girl had probably died in the middle of the night. So somewhere there was a frantic mother whose daughter had not come home. Who wouldn't be in homeroom, or going to first period. Somewhere, a woman was probably calling in a missing-persons report.

But if that was the case, wouldn't Nick have known about it? Laurie made a mental note to call him at home tonight to find out if one had been filed.

Then she stopped herself.

This is none of your business. The police will look after it. And a few

days from now, you'll read the details in the paper, send up a prayer for
the parents, and go on with your life. This is some other mother's tragedy.
It has nothing to do with you.

Laurie frowned as her troubled thoughts took on Colin's
practical tone. Practicality in one's husband was a wonderful thing a lot of the time, but it was just a fact that she and
Colin saw the world differently. Sometimes that was good, such
as during the kids' homework, when he supervised math and
grammar. But her brain didn't run on the narrow track of rules
and structure. Her skills were the kind that encouraged them
to think about what the holes and the mountain really meant in
Louis Sachar's novel, or why the table of stone broke when Aslan
came back to life.

But sometimes Colin's practicality wasn't good. He would
give the shirt off his back to a needy person, or front a customer
some scrap lumber for free, but to listen to that person's troubles made him uncomfortable. Colin never borrowed trouble.
He spent his energy trying to make sure it stayed as far away as
possible. This meant the insurance was always paid up, their cars
went in for maintenance on the exact date recommended by the
manufacturer, and there was always gas in the generator in the
garden shed, in case the power went out.

But there was more to life than gas and insurance. There
was sorrow, and joy, and sharing the highs and lows of life. And
sometimes there were things she could only share with her
women friends—the ones she'd found in her Bible study group.
On Mondays, Wednesdays, and Fridays, she job-shared as an
administrative assistant in the literature department at Murdo
University, a private college that sat on the hill on the other side
of the highway. But Thursdays were the highlight of the week,
when her Bible study group sipped Maggie's apricot tea and

drank from the water of life as they made their way through—this month—the Psalms.

Half an hour after Nick had dropped her off, she showered, and still feeling that chill that just wouldn't wear off, she walked six doors down, tapped on the door, and stepped into the Lessers' living room. She closed the door quietly behind her and pushed the "door dog" back into its place along the bottom, where its long knitted body kept the drafts out.

Besides Maggie, half a dozen women were already there. The sound of their voices settled like a blanket of comforting normalcy around her shivering soul.

And then the chatter died away.

"Laurie, good heavens, look at your face. Are you all right?" Maggie took her coat and slid an arm around her shoulders. "Laurie?"

The study was held at Maggie's house to encourage her in her sometimes halting Christian walk, but Laurie led it by tacit understanding. Everyone was used to looking to the members of her family to lead things in Glendale—and they'd been doing so since Great-great-grandpa Tremore had brought the railroad through here when the town wasn't much more than a clearing in the woods.

She had to pull it together, even though her spirit felt bruised and her mind was like a frightened bird, unable to settle on anything for more than a minute. All she wanted to do was unload the whole morning's story on the group, to share it so that maybe the horror would dissipate. Talking it over would bring normalcy back. She hoped.

Laurie glanced from one concerned face to the next. Natalie, Maggie, Cammie, Mary Lou, Donna, and Janice. Her spine stiffened a little.

Janice Edgar was the incumbent mayor's wife, and if there was anyone who could make Laurie Tremore Hale, of the Glendale Tremores, feel not only fat, but also not very bright, it was she. Not that she tried to, of course. She was unfailingly pleasant and always had a perfectly chosen word in season. But despite this, around Laurie she always seemed stiff and proud. She was tall and slender, and her blonde pageboy fell in perfect parentheses on either side of her face. Laurie's mahogany-brown mane did whatever it pleased unless she braided it tightly in a French braid, where it lay down the center of her back and sulked between her shoulder blades.

Janice was the type that presided over mayoral teas. Laurie was the type that organized them—and never the twain should meet. Until a few weeks ago, when Pastor Dayton suggested that Laurie invite Janice to prayer group.

With Janice here, she absolutely could not fall apart. Maybe that was a blessing. "I'm fine. Thanks." She gave Maggie's hand a grateful squeeze. "Does anyone know if Tanya Peizer and Debbie Jacks are coming?"

"Debbie and Jeff went to his mother's," Donna Carter said. "She's going into the hospital in Pittsburgh for some tests."

"And Tanya?"

Tanya was fairly new to their group, and they hadn't quite gotten to the point of friendship. Friendliness, yes, but not friendship. When the other women, most of whom Laurie had known all her life, shook their heads and looked blank, she said, "I'll give her a call when I get home. See if she needs anything." Sometimes a person needed nothing more than encouragement, or sometimes something more substantial, such as a casserole, or a hand getting the housework done.

Tanya was a single mom, and she lived in that eyesore of a

new subsidized apartment complex next to the big discount store on the far side of town. Laurie often felt guilty when she looked at Tanya, who barely held things together and was dealing with a teenager who, from all accounts, was quite a handful. She did what she could, though. It was Laurie who had been behind the cook-in after prayer group last month, where they'd each brought a freezable dish or a plastic container full of snacks and loaded them all into Tanya's beat-up Honda. Over her teary protests, mind you, but she'd still driven away with it all in the end.

Laurie tried to get her brain working along normal lines. She needed to start the study. She needed to open with prayer. But instead, her knees buckled and she landed in one of the living room chairs, more by accident than design, and began to cry.

"Laurie!"

Cammie slid into a chair next to her and pressed a tissue into her hand. Maggie poured a cup of steaming tea and offered it. The rest of the group pulled their chairs in, as if they could offer comfort just by leaning closer.

Laurie knew she was distressing them, but she couldn't help it. What had happened that morning was sitting inside her like a pipe bomb, ready to explode.

"I need you to do something for me," she managed at last, after blowing her nose and wiping her eyes.

"Of course," Maggie said. "Please drink some of this. Tell us. It's got to be something awful. I knew the minute you walked in."

Laurie took a deep breath. "I need you to pray for me. When I was jogging this morning, something awful did happen." She paused. "I found a body."

Silence.

"It was a girl. Probably in Anna's class. She looked about that age."

"Who?" Cammie said. "Who was it?"

Laurie took a sip of tea, then another. "I don't know. I called 911 right away and they sent an ambulance. But of course it was too late. Then I had to go down to the sheriff's office and give a statement."

The group of women clustered around her. "Oh, Laurie, how horrible. No wonder you're so upset."

It felt so good. No statements of logic, just love and the concern of sisters in Christ surrounding her with warmth. She told them what little she knew, and she even refrained from embellishing the story with speculation and educated guesswork, in case someone might think she was being too dramatic.

When she was finished, from the edge of the little group, Janice spoke up. The voice that Laurie had heard on television, confident and persuasive on whatever civic point she was making, was soft and hesitant now.

"Should we pray?" Janice's fingers riffled the top corner of her Bible's pages, over and over. "For the family, I mean. Whoever they are. Some poor mother needs to be lifted up before God right now, don't you think?"

I should have thought of that. Immediately Laurie felt like an attention hog, guilty of asking for her own support when what she should have done was ask the group to pray for the unknown woman.

"That's exactly what we should do," she said.

"Janice, maybe you could lead us?" Maggie suggested. "And maybe you could put in a word for Laurie, too."

Laurie would have thought that Janice would jump at the chance to lead in this intimate little group the way she led out there in public life. Or that she'd take charge and delegate to someone who had known Laurie and Tanya longer, such as Cammie or Mary Lou. But instead, she hesitated, looked around as though she were trapped, and then nodded at last.

"All right." Laurie could hardly hear her. Janice's face had gone completely white. She closed her eyes with that resigned look that people got when they were about to dive off the highest platform at the community pool.

"Father God, thank you for the strength we've received as a result of this time here with you. We pray for our sister Laurie and ask that you give her the strength to move on after this experience. And please, Father—" Her voice broke, and she swallowed. "Please give your strength to this girl's mother and her family. Lift them up with the hope that is in you, and wrap your love around them so they'll know they can get through it. Be with them as they grieve, and remind them that you lost your Son, too. Amen."

When Laurie opened her eyes, Mary Lou said, "We need to find out who it was and see if we can do something for them."

Laurie spoke up. "My cousin Nick is investigating. But the family has to be notified before they announce anything. It might be in the papers tomorrow."

"I'll find out." Janice's voice firmed, and beneath her pale skin Laurie glimpsed the mayor's wife. The one with connections.

Well, Laurie had connections, too. She was just going to have to lean on Nick a little. After all, she had found the poor child's body, so she should be the one to take the lead in helping the bereaved family through this terrible time.

Chapter Three

To group: Budz
From: JohnnysGrrl

5-o found her. Shut up.

*T*he thing *Nick* liked most about the folks who worked in the county coroner's office was their sense of humor. He supposed that it was a defense mechanism more than anything— you had to find a way to regain your emotional balance when you were faced with the sometimes grisly end result of simply being human.

As he was about to do today.

He paused at the door and pulled a pair of blue paper booties out of the receptacle next to it. He snapped the fragile protection over his shoes and then donned a white apron. He looked like the guy behind the meat counter at the local grocery—if you didn't count the uniform and the radio clipped to his shoulder.

Lisa Nguyen looked up when he pushed open the door. Her white overalls were still spotless, which meant he was on time and she wouldn't threaten him with her rose loppers for being late to the autopsy.

He had a healthy respect for a woman who had a pair of rose loppers and wasn't afraid to use them.

"I could have done without this today." She waited for him to snap on a pair of latex gloves and take his place at the end of the table on which the girl's body lay. "She can't be much older than my Jessica. Makes me think about things I usually manage to block."

"She was fourteen." He schooled himself to impassivity as he looked down at the girl. Her eyes were closed, all expression wiped away by the finality of death. Her smooth oval face had a chin he could imagine might get pretty stubborn, but her mouth, which had been outlined in some dark lipstick, now worn away, held a heartbreaking innocence. "Some days the thought of being a parent scares me."

"It should." As gently as if the girl had merely been sleeping, Lisa touched her cheek. "You risk your heart every single day. I hope I never have to face what this poor child's mother is facing right now." She glanced up at him. "If we get too cavalier about death in this job, it's time to find another one."

On the basis of the school ID in a folder in her back pocket, the coroner himself had gone out to notify her next of kin. The girl's clothes and any jewelry she'd worn had already been processed by the technician, and were bagged and waiting in the property closet for her family to pick up.

There were bags in that closet that had been there for years. Maybe the families had never been able to face that final duty. Or maybe there were no families to come. But there they sat, those sad plastic bags holding the last things in which a human being had seen value.

Nick thought of the coroner going out to find one of these families. He supposed he should be thankful for small mercies. His experience in informing parents that their kid had been picked up for reckless driving wasn't quite the same as the coroner's having to tell them their child would never come home.

As the deputy first at the scene, though, it was his job to watch the autopsy and hear the preliminary findings. He glanced around the antiseptic room with its three autopsy bays, racks of tools, white linoleum, and bright, no-nonsense lighting.

Aha. There it was.

A metal bucket sat under a workbench about three feet away. Just in case. He stood a little straighter. As a point of pride he'd make sure he didn't use it, but still, he felt better knowing it was there.

Lisa made notes in a spiral notebook as she worked, but directed comments over her shoulder to him. "There's a lot of lividity in the thighs and chest, and grains of sand everywhere in her clothing. Was she found lying on her stomach?"

"Yes. On a sandbar in the middle of the river." The contents of his initial report remained vivid in his mind. "Her feet were bare when she was found. She might have been abducted from her bedroom, though she was fully dressed."

"Impact with the water and any time in the current could have forced her shoes and socks off," Lisa said. "It's not likely she was an abductee—she was wearing a jacket and a scarf was knotted around her neck. Her clothes weren't damaged much. Given the riverbed and the brush along the banks, I could speculate that whatever happened to her happened fairly close to where she was discovered."

"Maybe she fell or jumped off the bridge."

"Now *that* I should be able to tell you pretty shortly. But in my experience, jumpers take off their coats before they go in. Heaven knows why."

"Any ideas about time of death?"

"Uh, last night?"

"Very funny."

"Nick, you know this isn't *CSI*. We can't pinpoint it to the hour. Not to mention that the temperature of the water makes my thermometer readings meaningless."

"Ballpark?"

Lisa sighed. "Ballpark—last night. No earlier." She hovered over the girl's head and touched her cheek, this time to indicate the injuries rather than mourn. "Bruising here, too, consistent with a blow. A slap, maybe. Uh-oh." Her fingers, gloved in thin latex, moved through the girl's hair. "This is nasty. Skull fracture. A deep one. I'll know more when I examine her brain."

Nick glanced at the bucket, then away.

He hung on to his cool as Lisa completed the external exam and moved on to the part with the rose loppers. "This is interesting." After thirty minutes of careful work, Lisa's white overalls were covered in stains. "Water in the lungs. Means she was breathing when she went in. We have a couple of ounces here. I'll tell you in a couple of minutes whether the skull fracture happened before, after, or during."

Nick concentrated on the bucket for the next few minutes, until Lisa spoke again.

"You okay, Deputy?"

He nodded.

"You sure? 'Cause I can give you all the details in my report."

"Thanks, but I need the preliminary findings today. We had a report of a disturbance on the Susquanny Bridge last night, and I think it might have been connected to our girl here."

"Is Forrest on it?"

"As we speak." In their county, the coroner's investigators

processed the crime scene, not the cops. They had specialized training—and an eye for minuscule detail that often meant the difference between securing or losing a conviction. "Depending on what he finds up there, we might have a homicide on our hands, not just an accident."

"Well, from the look of the marks on her face, and what seems to be finger-shaped bruising on her chest, I'd say the chances are pretty good."

Nick winced as the whine of the Stryker saw drowned out her voice. Lisa made a series of notes, then glanced at him again. "Water in the cranial cavity, too. So the blow to the head happened before she went in. And it's a funny shape."

"Yeah?" He risked a look.

She opened her thumb and forefinger into an L, then pointed. "See this? A right angle. Blunt trauma, like from the corner of a brick, only bigger."

He thought for a second. "Have you ever been up on that bridge? Maybe when you were a kid and wanted to try diving in?"

She gave him the kind of look big sisters have given clueless little brothers for millennia, and shook her head. "Do I look like I have a death wish? Besides, I didn't grow up here. My folks moved out to the San Joaquin Valley in California when they left Vietnam. Not a lot of bridges you'd want to jump off out there."

"It's like a rite of passage around here. Anyway, what I was getting at is that the undercarriage of the bridge is made of these big wood beams." He made a square in the air with his hands. "Twelve by twelve at least. Would this"—he indicated the angle-shaped depression—"be consistent with one of those beams?"

Lisa nodded. "I'd say yes. Look at this." She indicated a discolored area on the brain where the dura mater had been pierced and shredded. "Subdural hematoma. Lots of blood. Whatever hit her, it rendered her unconscious immediately. I'd say Forrest ought to know soon, if he hasn't examined the area already."

"I'll drive out there myself as soon as we're done."

"For your purposes, we are." Lisa pulled her mask down over her chin, so that it hung around her neck. "My preliminary findings are that the cause of death is drowning, precipitated by blunt trauma to the head, sometime in the last twelve hours. That good enough for you?"

"As my grandma says, it's good enough to be going on with. Thanks, Lisa."

"No problem. It surprises me to get a case like this. Mostly all we get are indigents and traffic fatalities. This is a little uglier."

"If we're talking homicide, it's going to get a lot uglier."

"Job security," Lisa quipped and turned back to the body. "Come on, darling," she said softly. "Let's finish up, take our organ samples, and put you back together for your family, okay?"

Nick left her to it. He passed the bucket without giving it a look, removed the apron and booties, and tossed them in the HazMat bin. Then he walked with measured steps out the back doors and into the coroner's gated parking lot behind the building.

And that's where he lost this morning's bagel and peanut butter, one orange, and four cups of coffee.

The unmarked SUV belonging to the coroner's investigator was already parked on the bridge when Nick pulled up twenty minutes later. He waved to the guy pulling traffic duty on the afternoon shift. The bridge was down to one lane around the cones and crime-scene tape, and the deputy guided people past.

Nick made a turn in the parking lot of the Stop-N-Go and pulled up behind the gray 4x4. There was no sign of Forrest, but a security line was tied to a strut, and it was taut where it ran over the rail.

He leaned over. "Hey down there! It's Nick."

Ten or twelve feet below, Forrest looked up and sketched a salute with the small knife in his right hand. "Hey." Tethered to the rail for safety, he balanced on one of the joists that supported the roadbed, where creosote and decades-old bird droppings had permeated the wood.

"Lisa told me I'd find you out here. Got anything?"

"You mean besides a bad need for a hot cup of coffee? Man, I am claiming hazard pay for this. The wind comes howling under here like you wouldn't believe. I think my butt is frostbit."

"Quit complaining. It's good for you to get off the phone and out into the field once in a while."

"Been lucky, I guess. Not a lot of homicide going on in this county. Not like Pittsburgh. I couldn't get away from there fast enough."

Nick glanced down at the heavy beam that seemed to be the focus of Forrest's equipment. "Homicide?"

The investigator nodded. "Not conclusive until I talk to Lisa, but definitely suspicious." Carefully, he loosened a wide sliver of wood from the end of the beam, and slipped it into an evidence bag. Then he stretched up to hand it to Nick.

The bit of wood was stained with a dark, sticky substance, and even without a magnifier, Nick could see hair embedded in it.

Forrest handed up his heavy-duty digital Canon EOS, then

hefted himself up to road level and over the rail before he un-snapped the security line. "Over there." He nodded at the plank decking a few feet away that formed the walkway for pedestri-ans next to the asphalt, directly over the beam. "Scuff marks and blood. If she'd been a jumper, there would have been foot-prints on the rail, nice and clean. But it looks like a scuffle took place."

Nick glanced at the Stop-N-Go at the far end of the bridge. "I'll talk to the staff at the store and see if anyone saw anything." He leaned over and looked down, past the beam to the water swirling thirty feet below. "So she gets pushed or someone lands a blow. Hits her head on the beam hard enough to fracture her skull—and lights out. Lands in the water unconscious and drowns."

Forrest nodded. He finished coiling his line and stripped off his gloves. "Sounds about right, from what we can see here. What does Lisa say?"

"Cause of death is drowning, precipitated by blunt trauma to the head."

"Question is, who pushed her, and did they mean to do it?"

"That is the question, all right."

Shoving his equipment into the back of the SUV, Forrest spoke over his shoulder. "That's why I didn't go into police work, see. It's my job to find out how. It's *your* job to find out why and who."

And he would. The memory of that still face, the long-lashed eyes closed in permanent sleep, was probably going to haunt Nick long after he found the person responsible for leaving her that way.

～

The elementary school's classes ended at 2:45, which meant that if Tim didn't have band practice, or if he and his buddies didn't find some piece of architecture to try their skateboards on, he hit the front door at home by 3:15. Today, Laurie's hug had a little more force behind it than usual, and she took a moment to thank God that her baby was home, alive and well.

"Mom, you're squishing me."

She released him and he tossed his backpack onto the floor by the door on his way into the kitchen.

"I'm just glad to see you, that's all."

To the ten-year-old mind this was probably just motherly weirdness, since, after all, they saw each other day in and day out. But Laurie felt better for having said it. In fact, she was going to start saying it a lot more after this.

At four o'clock she glanced at the clock on the microwave. Anna would be home any second, and she needed to make a decision. Should she ask her if any of her classmates were missing? Should they discuss the girl's death in a family enclave? Because of course she had to tell her kids before anyone asked them about it in the hallway at school.

Which, she supposed, was pretty much a decision. She'd bring it up when they'd eaten supper, before they scattered. A quiet word with Colin beforehand would ensure he didn't spill the beans before she was ready.

Her next glance at the clock in the living room said it was 4:15. Anna was probably walking home with a gaggle of her friends and dawdling in front of some boy's house. Or maybe they'd stopped in at the drugstore to try out makeup.

When the alarm clock in her bedroom, where she was folding laundry, said ten to five, Laurie could stand it no longer. She dropped Colin's underwear back in the basket and grabbed her cell phone.

Where r u?
Love, mom

A minute later, her cell jingled.
Kates. Home soon.

Soon? "Soon" had once meant two minutes, but since Anna had hit fourteen, it sometimes meant two hours.
Dinner 5:15. Home now.

No reply. Laurie went downstairs to put more tomatoes in the marinara sauce, and by the time she got them stirred in, Anna was pushing open the front door.

"Hi, sweetie."

"Mom, can I ask you a favor?" Anna dropped her coat on the floor next to the hall tree instead of hanging it up like a civilized person, went straight to the fridge, and pulled out a packet of string cheese.

"Sure. What?"

"Can you not ding me when I'm late like I'm a little kid? It's totally embarrassing to get a call in front of your friends and have it be your mom."

Laurie bit back her first response and kept her tone calm. "I'll be happy to, when you text me and let me know you'll be late. Until then, you get dinged."

Anna rolled her eyes and headed out of the kitchen.

"What were you doing?" Laurie called after her. "Hanging with the kids?"

But Anna was already halfway up the stairs and pretended not to hear her.

Laurie sighed and stirred the sauce more out of habit than because it needed it. She'd read more books on parenting adolescents than she could count. She was patient, supportive, and positive about self-image. She gave advice on the rare occasions when Anna asked for it, and on a lot of occasions when she didn't, but she always tried to couch it in noncritical terms.

Anna did not seem to appreciate this maternal care one bit. What happened to teenagers? Did they drink some evil potion that turned them into careless, scatterbrained, inconsiderate half humans?

No, she took that back. Anna had beautiful moments, when her big blue eyes would fill with tears over the poverty suffered by the kids in the Bolivian mission schools the church supported, or she'd go out of her way to help a friend struggling with a school project. But she had her share of ugly moments, too, and sometimes it was all Laurie could do not to turn her over her knee—if she could have. Anna was nearly as tall as she was. Thank goodness she'd taken after Colin, for which they could both be grateful.

When Colin came home from work a few minutes later, she put the water for the spaghetti on to boil and followed him up to their room.

He hung up his trousers and his tie, put his shirt in the hamper, and pulled on his jeans and a comfortable T-shirt. Then he turned to her and held out his arms. "Hey."

She leaned against his chest, grateful for his strength and the tight circle of his arms. "Hey."

"You all right?"

"I am now. Bible study helped a lot."

"I'm glad to hear it."

"We need to talk to the kids about it, though. Once we've finished eating."

He held her a little away from him so he could look into her eyes. "Is that necessary, Lor?"

She nodded. "It's going to be all over the school tomorrow, and my name will be in the papers. Think how you'd feel if your mom had been involved and she didn't bother to tell you."

"Their mom isn't 'involved.'"

"Colin, you know I am. I discovered the poor little thing."

"But you make it sound as though you have some part to play in this. You don't. Yes, you found the girl. But that's as far as it goes."

She pulled away and bent to pick up the stack of his underwear where she'd dropped it earlier. "I know."

"I'm just saying, keep to the facts."

"Like I wouldn't? What, do you think I'm going to lie? To make up things to make me sound more important than I am?"

She didn't need to do that kind of thing. She never *tried* to hog the spotlight or take over in situations. It just seemed to happen, as though people wanted her to be out in front.

"Of course not, sweetheart." He pulled her to him and she tried to relax against his chest once more. A fight was the last thing she wanted. "Look, say what you need to say to prepare them. Then if it upsets them, I'll step in."

"Okay."

So, even though she was dying to jump right in and ask the kids if they'd heard anything as soon as they'd said grace, she held it in until everyone had finished eating.

"Hang on a minute, sweetie." Laurie smiled at Anna as she slid sideways out of her chair. "I want to talk to you and Tim."

"I didn't do anything," her youngest said immediately from across the table.

Thank you, Lord, for my baby's innocence. "What's that, a pre-emptive strike?"

"I'm just saying," he said, and she heard the echo of Colin's voice.

"This has nothing to do with either of you. But something happened this morning that we need to talk about."

Tim and Anna slid back into their chairs. Tim's eyes lit up now that his innocence had been established. Anna was interested, too, but in front of her little brother it was no doubt cooler to look as though she didn't care.

As she'd promised Colin, Laurie stuck to bare facts as she outlined what had happened that morning. "So," she concluded, "I wanted you guys to know, in case it's in the papers tomorrow and the other kids come to you asking questions. Now you know as much as I do."

"I bet I can find out who it was," Tim said with the macabre interest of childhood.

"Right, Sherlock," Laurie said. "You just let Nick and the other cops do their jobs. They have to notify next of kin first."

"What's that?"

"The girl's family. Her kin," Colin said.

Anna hadn't moved during the whole recital. In fact, her face had gone white and she looked as though she was about to cry.

Laurie reached across the table for her hand. "Sweetie, are you okay? I know this is shocking. We'll all pray for the family tonight, even though we don't know who they are yet. It's probably not anybody you know."

Her daughter turned a horrified, teary glare on her. "Like

that's supposed to make me feel better?" She pushed her chair back and ran out of the dining room. Her sneakered feet pounded on the stairs, and a few seconds later a door slammed like a sonic boom at the far end of the house.

Laurie traded glances with Colin. "Better let me talk to her," he said. "In a little while."

But when he slipped into their room later that night, it didn't look as though talking had done much good. Laurie took off her reading glasses and put them on top of the book she'd picked up to prevent herself from putting her ear to her daughter's door.

"Any luck?"

He shrugged and shook his head. "It's clear she's upset about it, but she won't say a word. She's such a softhearted kid."

"Maybe I should try. My best friend died of a staph infection when we were kids."

"That's different. This could be foul play. Has anyone thought of that?"

"In Glendale?" Laurie shook her head. "It's more likely the poor kid was struggling with depression and decided to end it all. Or maybe she was goofing around and there was an accident."

"Nobody is going to jump off the bridge, even on a dare, at this time of year." Colin folded his jeans and T-shirt and sat on the edge of the bed.

"She didn't have to jump. She could have been bird-watching or daydreaming. She could have slipped on those wet boards and hit her head. Anything is possible."

Her husband gazed at the rug. "It's pointless to speculate. Whatever we're supposed to know will come out in the papers." He glanced up. "You going to pray?"

Together, they knelt. Laurie often thought that this time

as a couple, alone at God's feet, was the most beautiful few minutes of her day. But tonight there was someone else in the room with them. Someone who didn't even have a face. Yet. Again, she prayed for the girl's mother. Prayer usually calmed her, set her at peace for the night. But in the dark, Laurie lay and wondered about the bereaved family. Who were they? What were they thinking right now? Had they even been notified yet?

And most important of all, were they part of a social fabric the way she was? Laurie tried to imagine getting through such a horrible time without support. It would be like trying to cross a desert without water or shelter or transportation. The simple fact was, her life was knit so tightly with those in her family, in Bible study group, in the leadership of Glendale Bible Fellowship that she couldn't even imagine living a different way. Her friendships had started in kindergarten—and her kids' friendships started that way, too. She was so used to joining her mom and aunts in organizing benefits and events for church and school that she'd practically learned leadership by osmosis. And by the time she'd earned her degree at Murdo, she'd begun to realize that Colin was more than the lanky kid who had played on the high-school basketball team and sang tenor in the row behind her family's at church. Marrying him and working to put him through his MBA before the babies came had just seemed a natural extension of a life she'd established without really thinking much about it.

For the most part, she loved her life. Unfortunately, somewhere out there was a poor woman who would never be able to say that again.

In the morning, Laurie looked at Anna closely when she came downstairs. She touched her daughter's forehead under the curve of her bangs.

"Did you sleep okay, honey?" Anna's skin was cool, but her eyes were shadowed, as though she hadn't slept at all.

Anna nodded, and Laurie frowned. Anna was a sound sleeper—so sound that if she didn't have to get up to go to school, she'd be out cold from ten at night until ten in the morning.

"You've got dark circles under your eyes."

"Thanks, Mom, I needed that." She refused to meet Laurie's gaze.

"If something is bothering you, it might help to talk about it. Maybe tonight, after supper."

"Nothing's bothering me. Have you seen my backpack?"

"It's by the door, where it always is, and your lunch money is in it. Do you have all your books?"

"I think so."

"You'd better know so. Double-check. Sweetie, I lost someone when I was your age. Maybe it's time I shared that with you. We'll talk about it tonight, okay?"

"Okay, Mom." She pounded back up the stairs, returning with her math notebook and stuffing it into the backpack.

Laurie herded both kids out to the van, which was warming up in the driveway, and dropped the subject while she drove them to school. But as she watched Anna join a group of girls and make her way across the lawn to the main doors, she nibbled her lower lip.

Laurie needed to find a way to break through this new reluctance to talk so she could give her daughter some comfort.

Maybe it wasn't the discovery of the girl's body at all. Maybe something else was going on that she felt she needed to keep from her mother, like a crush or a clique being mean to her. If Laurie shared her own loss with Anna, it might break down her reticence and help them find some common ground.

Her decision made, Laurie drove up the hill to the university and tried to concentrate on work. On her break from collating handouts on the significance of metaphor for one of the creative-writing profs, she cruised the staff room in search of the morning paper. They didn't get it at the house because both the English department and Susquanny Home Supply took it, and there was no point in putting out a few dollars a month when you could read it at work for free.

GIRL'S BODY FOUND

The story had made the front page, with an enlargement of a school picture showing a teenage girl with a lot of eye makeup and a heartbreaking sincerity in her smile. Laurie gathered up the paper and took it back to her cubicle to read in private.

> A morning jog is part of local community leader Laurie Hale's routine, but yesterday's discovery was anything but routine. Hale discovered the body of Lincoln High freshman Miranda Peizer, 14—

Peizer? As in Tanya Peizer? Laurie caught her breath as her gaze raced down the column.

> —in the Susquanny River about half a mile downstream from the bridge. According to the Glendale sheriff's of-

fice, the young woman's body had sustained multiple contusions, but it is unclear yet whether they were the result of her trip downriver or injuries sustained before she entered the water. When asked for comment, Deputy Sheriff Nicholas Tremore stated, "The family has been notified. We're investigating all avenues at this point and not ruling anything out." If Miranda Peizer's death turns out to be the result of foul play, it will be the first homicide in Glendale since the murder of attorney Reginald Holzing in 1996.

Laurie sat back, her breath bottling up in her chest.

Miranda Peizer. *Oh, no. Surely not.*

She grabbed the phone and dialed Maggie. "Have you seen the paper this morning?" she asked as soon as her friend picked up the phone. "The front page?"

"Who hasn't seen it?"

"The girl, Maggie. Miranda Peizer. Is that—"

"Isn't it just awful? Poor, poor Tanya. She had so much trouble with her. She told me once she caught Randi smoking pot when she was only eleven."

"Is anybody with her? Maggie, she's in our study group. We have to do something."

"I've called over there, but the answering machine keeps picking up."

"I'll take some sick time and get out of here early. I'll pick you up at two and we'll go over, okay?"

"See you then."

Laurie could hardly concentrate as two hundred and forty interminable minutes dragged past. Fortunately, the day wasn't all that heavy—the most complicated thing she had to do was a couple of updates to the lit department's Web page. At two o'clock she practically ran out the door and kept her foot on the gas as she negotiated the winding quarter-mile drive and then the back roads over to her neighborhood.

Maggie was watching at her front window, and in a couple of minutes they were heading down the highway to the newer part of Glendale.

Tanya lived in one of the units in a new building, but Laurie had her doubts about the construction of the place. The walls seemed flimsy and the view was, well, the Wal-Mart parking lot. At least it was convenient when Tanya had to do a run for socks and school supplies.

Would have been convenient. *Oh, Tanya,* she thought.

The building had no security—just an exterior staircase, like a motel. A woman Laurie had never seen before answered the door of the second-floor apartment.

"We're friends of Tanya's, from her Bible study group," Laurie explained. The woman looked to be in her mid-fifties and wore her hair cropped short, as though she had recently undergone chemotherapy and it was beginning to grow back in. "Is she home?"

The woman didn't smile. "I'm Patty. I live next door. Yes, she's home. The poor thing has no one to sit with her."

If you're such good friends, how come it's taken you this long to show up? Laurie heard the unspoken accusation clearly.

"We just found out the girl who drowned was Tanya's daughter." Why was she explaining herself to this nasty woman? "We brought some supper for her. Does she have any family? Is anyone coming?"

"If they are, no one's told me. I'm glad you're here. I've got things to do."

"Thank you for being with her." Laurie put as much sincerity into her voice as she could. "If you want to take a break, we can sit with her for a while, and try to find out what's going on."

Without a word, the woman grabbed a coat off a chair next to the door and pushed past them.

"Just who I'd want with me at a time like this," Maggie whispered as she closed the door.

They found Tanya passed out on the bed, a quilt over her and a bottle of prescription tablets on the nightstand. Laurie took one look around the eight-by-ten bedroom and made a few decisions.

"Don't wake her up. Sleep is probably a blessing right now. We can't do much, but one thing we can do is pick this place up." She glanced at Maggie. "Would you take a stab at those dishes in the sink? I'll do this room and the living room and get started on the laundry. I think I have enough quarters in my purse for a load of whites, anyway. You certainly can't face the world if you don't have any clean underwear."

"Good plan."

Maggie headed into the kitchen, carrying a casserole dish in two pot holders, and Laurie got to work. Tanya didn't seem to have many clothes, and most of them were on the floor. Laurie sorted some into a laundry pile and hung some of them up in the tiny closet. Shoes went on the closet floor in a neat row, and a number of scattered paperback novels were placed in a stack on the dresser.

Laurie pushed open the door of Randi's room and came out of housemother mode with a jolt. The bed was unmade and clothes—a purple camisole, a black skirt, several pairs of stockings in colors that hurt the eyes—lay draped on the bed and on the chair in front of the student desk. On the bulletin board above the desk, pictures, concert notices, tickets, and other minutiae of a teenager's life were tacked with push pins. Huge posters of scary-looking rock bands were tacked to the walls with blissful disregard for the apartment's security deposit.

The room needed a cleanup in the worst way, but Laurie backed out and closed the door gently. The mess was all that Tanya had left. When she was able to deal with it, she could grieve her daughter's death as she folded the camisole and the skirt and put away books and magazines. If Laurie and Maggie did it, Tanya wouldn't see it as a favor. She'd see it as an insensitive invasion of the relationship between herself and Randi— whatever that had been.

Laurie piled the laundry into the half-full basket she found in the bathroom and made her way downstairs to the laundry room. Once she had that going, she took on the living room. Tanya didn't have much in the way of clutter, other than clothes. Laurie supposed that when you moved a lot, you kept your possessions to a bare minimum. Clothes. Cookware. Something to sit on. Practically everything here would fit in the back of a pickup.

When the Hales had moved into their dream house, it had taken an entire Allied van and a solid week of work. Laurie had decided then and there that they were never moving again. And there was no reason to. Everything she and Colin loved and needed was right here.

Except for the occasional big night out in Pittsburgh, like seeing a play or going to a Penguins game, or, in Anna's case, a major shopping trip, they hardly ever left town.

"Now what?" With the dishes done and all four feet of counter spotless, Maggie joined her in the living room. "Leave a note and be on our way?"

Something rustled behind them, and both Laurie and Maggie turned.

Tanya Peizer swayed in the hallway, her face so pale it was nearly green. Her hair was matted down on one side, as if she'd been asleep for hours. Laurie's breath caught at the haunted expression in her eyes, as if she knew something was wrong, but couldn't quite remember what.

"What are you guys doing here?" she croaked. "Has Randi done something wrong?"

Chapter Four

Those were the last coherent words Tanya said. And it was a good thing, too, because Laurie's brain had frozen up with horror and she wouldn't have been capable of even a comforting but vague reply. She and Maggie got Tanya back into bed, and the young woman slid back into unconsciousness as abruptly as she'd come out of it.

"That was close." Maggie glanced at Laurie as they gave the apartment a final check. "She knows, right? That Randi's gone?"

"The paper said she was told. But if the doctor gave her a sedative, she probably doesn't remember, and thank goodness for that. We need to organize people to sit with her. And we should find out who's making arrangements for the funeral, too."

"I'll stay till suppertime," Maggie said. "Ben can look after the kids till then."

"Okay, you organize a roster and call everyone in study group, and I'll get ahold of Cale Dayton."

It was easier to handle a crisis when you had a plan. As Laurie drove away from the apartment complex, half her brain concentrated on the drive home and the other half on dialing their pastor on her cell.

"Cale, it's Laurie," she said. "We've just been to see Tanya Peizer. Did you hear that it was her daughter I—who was found in the river?"

"I read it in the paper," he said. "I've been calling over there but got no answer. Have you seen her? How is she?"

"Sedated." Laurie's tone was wry as she made a left turn and sped down the county road. "And who can blame her? Maggie and I are organizing a roster of people to sit with her. I don't think she realizes what's happened yet—or her brain isn't letting her realize it. But when the shock and the drugs wear off, she'll need help."

"Thank you for spearheading this." His bass voice rumbled through her cell phone. "I should have known you'd already be on it."

"The thing is, we don't know if she has any family. Have they been told? And I assume you're taking the funeral . . ."

"To my knowledge, she doesn't have family. Sophie and I have gone over there a couple of times in the past few months, and she never mentioned any relatives. There were no pictures. I think there's an ex-husband somewhere, though."

"I'll get Maggie to find out. There has to be an emergency contact number in the apartment. Probably in her purse. Or maybe we could call the school and see if there's a name in Randi's file."

"As for a funeral, we'll need to contact the police about—about when Randi's body will be released."

Laurie digested this for a second. "What do you mean, released?"

"In case it's being . . . you know. Treated as a suspicious death."

Colin had said something about that, too. "That's ridiculous. The poor girl had an accident."

"I guess the police are taking everything into account. We'll need to know what's going on there before we do anything else."

Poor Tanya. Laurie's very next call was going to be to Nick. "Thanks, Cale. I'll talk to you later."

She rang off and dialed her cousin, who was not where he was supposed to be when she needed him. "Nick, it's Laurie," she told his voice mail. "Pastor Dayton tells me Randi's body might not be released for a funeral because you guys might be treating it as a suspicious death. I'm on my way home from Tanya Peizer's place now, and trust me, we don't want to drag this out any longer than we have to. The poor woman is sedated, and it would be great if the funeral were over before the prescription runs out. Call me."

But he didn't. Laurie kept her phone clipped to her waistband while she oversaw Tim's homework and made dinner. Afterward, she checked it to make sure the charge hadn't run down. What was the matter with that guy? He always returned her calls. It was a lucky thing she wasn't lying in the street with a broken leg, trying to call him for help.

Nick never did call back. Instead, he and his partner Gil Schwartz turned up on the doorstep at ten minutes after seven. Laurie could tell right away he wasn't there to sell tickets for the policemen's annual Christmas ball.

"Laurie, can we talk to Anna for a minute?" He and Gil stood a little awkwardly in the foyer, the crowns of their caps and the shoulders of their jackets misted with rain that had just begun to fall.

She gaped at him a little stupidly while her brain rearranged her expectations to line up with reality.

"Aren't you here to answer my page?" She'd assumed he'd been driving by and figured it was just as easy to stop in as it was to call.

"No. I got it, but that's not why we're here. Is Anna home?"

"Of course she's home. But what do you need to talk to her about?"

Colin came out of his office and smiled at Nick and Gil, both of whom were men like him—practical, sensible, and handy with a hammer in their off-hours.

"Hey, guys. What's up?"

"They want to talk to Anna," Laurie said before Nick could open his mouth.

"We should call her, then." He loped up the stairs to do that very thing instead of something sensible, like finding out why first.

"It's okay, Laurie," Nick assured her over the murmur of voices upstairs. "We just need to ask her a couple of questions about Miranda Peizer."

"She didn't hang around with her, if that's what you mean," Laurie said. "Not that I know of, anyway." And she would have known. Tanya would have said something at Bible study about their daughters being friends. It had mattered deeply to her that Randi find nice kids to hang around with, though it seemed she didn't really know how to go about making sure it happened. She worked two jobs, and keeping up with a teenager like Randi seemed to be a full-time job in itself.

Anna thumped down the stairs in her stocking feet, her dad behind her, giving the odd impression that he was cutting off an escape route. Anna wore fraying cargo pants and a camisole under a plaid flannel shirt. She also wore a set, wary expression that Laurie had never seen before. She came to a slow stop on the bottom step, and instead of flying into Nick's arms the way she usually did, Anna looked at him as if he were about to whip out the handcuffs.

"Hey, kiddo," Nick said easily. "Gil and I need to talk to you for a sec."

She retreated one step, eyeing him as though she were searching for an ulterior motive. "Why?" With one foot, she felt for the next step.

"It's okay, sweetie," Colin assured her. "No big deal."

"No." She turned an appealing gaze on her dad. "Daddy, I don't want to."

Laurie blinked. "Anna, don't be silly. Go into the living room and offer your cousin a seat."

"There's nothing to worry about," Nick said. "We're just gathering information right now, and we hope you can help us."

This seemed to reassure her a little, but she still looked spooked as she led the way into the living room. Laurie followed.

"Mom." Anna flopped into the easy chair that sat kitty-corner from the couch. "They want to talk to *me*."

"*Not you—my mom, who is always hogging the spotlight,*" Laurie heard. Why did everyone think that?

"I can't imagine anything that Nick couldn't say in front of Dad and me," she said easily and made herself comfortable on the love seat.

Nick and Gil folded themselves onto the edges of the couch cushions, and Colin leaned on the mantel while the fire snapped and popped in a silence that was unusual in their talkative family.

"You or your husband need to be here, anyway, Mrs. Hale," Gil said, getting down to business. "We wouldn't interview a person under sixteen without a parent or guardian present."

"What exactly are you interviewing her for? She hardly knows—knew—Randi Peizer." If they didn't answer that question soon, she was going to abandon politeness and give her cousin the kind of healthy whack upside the head that had done wonders for his cooperation when he'd been a little boy.

Anna's smooth forehead creased under her bangs. "I don't know anything about Randi."

"Well, you might be surprised at what could help us. How

well did you know her?" Nick said, as if Laurie hadn't just told him.

Anna shrugged and the wary look settled on her features again. "Not very. She's in third-period science with me, and last-period phys ed."

"Did you talk with her much?"

"Uh-uh."

"Why not?"

Anna's clear gaze fell to the carpet. "Well, she's new. And . . ."

"And?"

"And she's kind of a . . . the kids don't—didn't—like her very much."

"Why not?"

"She's a poser." At the two cops' blank looks, she expanded. "You know, she says stuff that it's obvious she hasn't done to look cool, like she said she was in a gang in Columbus. And she met some lame rock star and was friends with his daughter. Stuff like that." She paused a moment. "That's where she got her nick-name. Poser. You know. Instead of Peizer."

Laurie thought of poor Tanya, working fourteen-hour days to keep their heads above water, and her daughter making up a life that sounded exciting and cool so she could survive the first year of high school.

She wondered if Randi had known it wasn't working, that the other kids had seen right through her and despised her for it.

"So when was the last time you saw Randi?" Gil asked.

Anna raised her eyebrows and turned down the corners of her mouth in an expression that said, Who knows? "I don't remem-ber. We had phys ed on Tuesday, so she was there, probably."

"What about Wednesday? Did you see her that day?"

Anna shrugged and shook her head. "I don't know. I don't keep tabs on people."

"And you're not really friends, so you wouldn't pay attention," Laurie put in.

"Yeah."

"So what did you do Wednesday night?" Nick asked.

The night Randi had been killed. *Wait a minute.* "We had supper, Anna did her homework, we watched TV, and we went to bed," Laurie said. "What are you—"

"Lor," Colin said in a warning tone.

"Please let Anna answer the question, Mrs. Hale," Gil said. His tone was polite, but Laurie bristled anyway.

"It's a ridiculous question! Where do you think she was?" Laurie lifted her arms to encompass the room where they sat, and by extension, their home.

"Lor," Colin said again, a little louder this time.

"What?" she snapped. Couldn't he see what they were implying?

"Calm down, Laurie," Nick said. "We're trying to establish a time line here. And trying to figure out where everyone was Wednesday night."

"Everyone who? Who all are you talking to?"

"At this point it seems like everyone in the high school," Gil said, obviously trying to lighten the mood.

"But why?"

"A clerk at the Stop-N-Go by the bridge says there was a big gang of teenagers hanging around there at about ten thirty that night. It's significant that Randi's body turned up the next morning. We're trying to establish whether the two events are connected."

"Whether they are or not, it has nothing to do with Anna."

Laurie knew she sounded like an angry bear defending her cub. Nick should have known better than to even bother coming here. They were a good family. They always tried to do the right thing, to pitch in and help when there was a need, to be good examples in the community. Why, Colin hadn't even had a traffic ticket in twenty years. And as far as Anna and Tim went, you couldn't find better kids. They were loyal, got good grades, had lots of friends.

Why would he think he needed to bother interviewing his own cousin?

"Probably not," Nick said gently, "but Anna, you still need to confirm for us about that night."

"Mom already told you," Anna said, glancing at her mother and back at Nick. Her blue eyes were huge, and she was pale. "I was right here. We watched *The Planet's Funniest Animals* and then I went to bed."

"And you can corroborate that?" Nick looked from Laurie to Colin.

Laurie sucked in a breath. "Of course I can. For heaven's sake, Nick, you almost sound like you doubt her word." She waited for him to laugh and say of course he didn't, but he was writing in his notebook and didn't look up.

"So. One down, two hundred to go. Do you guys want a hot chocolate or coffee?" She felt compelled to hint that they were on the cops' side. The good guys. They were family, too. This was just a formality so it wouldn't look as though Nick was playing favorites as he went around town doing his interviews.

Nick and Gil got to their feet. "No thanks, Mrs. Hale," Gil said. "We just had about a gallon of coffee at the station, and we have a pretty long list of kids to talk to yet tonight."

Colin saw them to the door and closed it behind them. Anna jumped to her feet.

"Hang on, sweetie." He put an arm around her shoulders and guided her back to the couch. "I want to make sure you're okay."

"Sure, I'm okay." She wriggled out from under his arm, scooted over into the corner of the couch, and grabbed one of the matching pillows. She hugged it to her chest the way she did when they watched *The Princess Diaries*. "Why wouldn't I be?"

"It's not every day the cops come by asking where you were on the night of a crime," Laurie said in a voice that wobbled a little, as if she were about to either giggle or weep with relief now that it was over. "Fortunately, it was just a fact-finding mission. Not . . . anything else."

"I didn't do anything. I don't *know* anything."

"I know, honey. But it's Nick's job to make sure they cover everything—especially if they think it might be murder."

"Who's being murdered? What did I miss?" Tim slid down the banister and landed in the foyer with a thump. "Was that Nick?"

"Timothy Lucas Hale, how many times have I told you not to do that?"

"I was in a hurry, Mom. How come you didn't call me? Sometimes he lets me turn the siren on in the cop car."

"He didn't want to see you, loser."

"Anna, don't call your brother that."

"I s'pose he wanted to see *you*, Anna Banana Breath. Did Brendan O'Day or Kyle Edgar finally call the cops on you for stalking them?"

Laurie opened her mouth to lay down the law, but before she could say a word, Anna leaped to her feet. She swung the couch cushion at Tim with killing force and knocked him to his knees on the carpet.

"Ow! Mom!"

"Anna!"

Their daughter ignored their simultaneous exclamations, stormed up the stairs, and slammed herself into her room.

Laurie turned to Colin, her eyes wide with disbelief. "My turn to talk to her." Teenage irritability was one thing, but they weren't a family of hitters. Anna needed to get that clear and apologize to her brother.

She marched upstairs and didn't wait for a response to her knock. The soft glow of the lamp on the bedside table fell across the carpet and illuminated Anna as she lay on the bed with her back to the door, sketching furiously on a pad.

"Anna."

"I'm not going to apologize." The words were sullen, and she didn't even turn to speak over her shoulder.

Laurie let it pass. She also swallowed the urge to rain down her fear and anger on her daughter's head, and spoke quietly instead. "I'm worried about you. Why would you hit your brother like that? You're not four years old anymore."

"He needs it."

"Nobody needs to be knocked off their feet with a couch cushion." She sat on the edge of the mattress and began to rub soothing circles on Anna's back. The flannel shirt was fuzzy and warm, her daughter's shoulder blades sharp and defensive under her palm. "Want to talk about what's wrong?"

"Nothing's wrong." On the pad of drawing paper, a fairylike creature with huge eyes, a tiny waist, and gossamer wings was taking shape. Another of Anna's manga people.

"I think there is. We all go through stuff when we're teenagers. School stuff, family stuff. It makes it better to talk about it. Get some perspective, you know?"

"I have lots of perspective."

In the soft light, Laurie made a face, but didn't let the wryness reach her tone. "I know. I'm proud of you for the way you usually handle things. But this thing with Randi Peizer . . . it might be more than you can handle."

"What thing?" Anna blacked in the pupils of the fairy's eyes with fierce concentration.

"Her death, sweetie. Losing a classmate, even one you didn't know very well, can be hard. People are supposed to die when they're old, not when they're fourteen and haven't even started to live yet."

Silence, except for the swoop of the pen. Laurie kept up the slow rhythm of her palm. As a baby, Anna had loved to have her back rubbed.

"When I was a teenager," she began in a once-upon-a-time tone, "I had a best friend named Sharon. We had the same classes, did ballet together, got part-time jobs delivering papers together. Then she got sick."

"What with?"

"Just an infection. A simple staph infection, like when Tim had strep throat last winter. But Sharon's system didn't handle it well, and she was staying with relatives because her parents had split up. They didn't catch it in time with antibiotics, and Sharon died."

"Your best friend?" Anna abandoned the pen in mid-stroke, turned over, and looked into her mother's face, her brow wrinkling with distress. "She died? Really?"

Laurie nodded. "The rest of that school year I had to do everything alone. No partner for biology lab. No one to walk to the ballet studio with. No one to deliver papers with. We had done everything together, you see, which meant that practically every minute of the day, I missed her."

"Wow."

"It was like there was this big space beside me all the time where she used to be. And even after she'd been gone a long time, the space didn't go away. It just traveled around with me, reminding me of her."

"What did you do?"

"I went to church, went to school, hung out with the cousins and my youth group. That space beside me began to shrink after a while, until finally it was small enough for me to put it in my heart and tuck it away for good."

"You still miss her?"

Laurie nodded. "As you guys would say, we were tight."

Anna's eyes clouded. "But I wasn't tight with Randi. I hardly knew who she was."

"I know. But her empty space will still be felt at school, won't it? Traveling around from class to class?"

"But nobody's going to put her in their heart. She didn't have any friends."

"It would be pretty sad to have only one person in the world—like her mom—left to remember her, wouldn't it? It would be nice if there was a little place in your heart for her, too."

"Maybe," Anna conceded and picked up the pen.

"So if you can do that, maybe you can say sorry to your brother. Because I know he has a big place in your heart, no matter how much you guys complain and argue with each other."

Anna glanced over her shoulder. "You're grasping now, Mom."

Laurie leaned over and kissed her. "You'd miss him if he was gone."

"Yeah, like zits."

If her sense of humor was reestablishing itself, maybe it was time to go a little deeper. "Getting back to what I said about Sharon, you see that it's okay to grieve, and okay to move on as well, don't you?"

"Yeah."

"Sometimes our emotions can scare us, maybe make us feel as if we can't handle them. Then we lie awake at night thinking all kinds of things that maybe aren't even real. Are you struggling with that?"

"No." Anna turned a page and began a fresh drawing. "I was up late studying, that's all. Math is really hard this year."

"So things at school are all right, then. You've got lots of friends, right?" The pen faltered for a split second, and Anna turned the page again and started over. "Anna? Is everything okay with you and your girlfriends?"

"Sure."

"Then how come you just messed up that drawing?"

With a sigh, Anna put the pen down and rolled over. "Because I can't concentrate with you hovering over me."

"We were having a talk."

"You were talking, you mean. You're always talking. You hardly ever give me a chance to say anything."

Laurie sat back and stared at her. What had she just spent the last ten minutes doing, if it wasn't encouraging her to talk? "I'm giving you the chance now, sweetie. I honestly want to know how it's going at school. About your friends. How you're feeling about Randi. All of it."

"Why? Why now, all of a sudden?"

"Because you're not sleeping, that's why, and you whacked your brother with a pillow, and Nick was here on official business. These things are not normal. That's why I'm concerned."

Anna's eyes closed briefly, as if she were marshaling her resources. When she opened them again, Laurie realized her little girl wasn't so little anymore. There was a reticence, an adult sense of reserve seeping into her gaze that Laurie hadn't seen before. The gaze of a young woman who wasn't going to spill everything to her mother the way a child would, with complete confidence that Mommy would know how to solve any problem she brought to her.

"Everything's fine at school, Mom. Math is kind of a pain, but I'll sweat it out. My friends are cool. You know them. Kelci, Michelle, Jaimi."

"Are they the popular girls?"

Anna pulled her chin in and frowned. "Popular? What does that have to do with anything?"

"Well, you know." Laurie shrugged. "We all want to have lots of friends."

"Mom," Anna sighed, "just because you were homecoming queen in nineteen eighty whatever, doesn't mean I want to be like that."

"What's wrong with being homecoming queen? It was fun. And you might not care now, but when you're seventeen I bet you will."

"I doubt it. I don't care about being popular. Popular girls are—" She stopped.

"What? They're what?" Anna shrugged and went back to her drawing. Laurie sensed that she'd been on the edge of saying something important. "Anna?"

"They're not who I want to be."

How could any normal girl not want to be popular and well-liked and join all kinds of clubs and activities? High school had been the most fun years of Laurie's life. She couldn't imagine a young girl having that kind of opportunity and turning it down.

But then, as Anna had pointed out, she was not Laurie, and never had been.

"What do you want to be? How can I help?"

"That's just the thing, Mom. You can't help. If you do, you'll just take over and make me do stuff I don't want to do."

Laurie blinked at the sudden needle of pain that pricked her heart. "When did I ever do that?"

"You always do it. You pushed me to be in the choir at church even though I can't really sing. You talked me into being a counselor last year at Camp Victory when all I wanted to do was go swimming and canoeing and stuff."

"Being a counselor is a great way to learn leadership, Anna. You aren't going to do that falling out of a canoe."

"Mom, you just don't get it. What if I don't want to be a leader? What if I just want to be a kid and fall out of a stupid canoe if I feel like it? At least it would be my own decision."

How could a fourteen-year-old make the kinds of decisions that would set her on the right track for the future? Anna didn't have the tools yet. That's what parents were for, wasn't it? To guide their children in the way they should go, as the Bible said.

Frankly, it hurt that Anna could lie here and coldheartedly reject the things that Laurie had been trying to teach her. Leadership and the ability to get along with others were fine qualities. Necessary qualities. As she'd proven herself.

"Mom? Do you hear what I'm saying?"

"I hear you," she said around the hurt. "We should talk about this some more."

"That always means you still want me to agree with you."

"For heaven's sake, Anna, what's wrong with agreeing with me?" she exploded, then lowered her voice. "You're saying that learning to be a leader and having everyone like you are bad things."

"I'm not saying that, Mom," Anna said with exaggerated patience. "I'm saying that you need to let me decide what I want to do and how I want to handle things. I'm fourteen."

And that was it, wasn't it? Fourteen. No longer a child, and adulthood a long way off.

"You can trust me," Anna persisted.

"Of course I can," Laurie said automatically. And she did. But sometimes you needed more than trust to hang on to.

She kissed Anna good night and heard the scratch and swoop of the pen begin again as she closed the door behind her.

Then she went into her bedroom and dropped to her knees next to the bed.

Help me with Anna, Lord. We talked, but I still don't know what's bothering her. It can't be just math. Please give Anna an open heart and give me the ability to listen. Is she right, Lord? Do I talk and push too much? You've helped me to be a good mother, Lord, and you've given me good kids. Help me now that Anna's getting more independent. Give me wisdom.

And trust, Lord. Give me trust.

～

To group: Budz
From: JohnnysGrrl

Here comes 5-0. Be EZ. Stay cool.

～

SUSQUANNY COUNTY SHERIFF'S OFFICE

CASE NUMBER: 07-201
REPORTING OFFICER: N. Tremore, badge #78512
DATE: November 12, 2007
TIME: 21:46
SUMMARY: Investigating officers Tremore and
   Schwartz followed up on information given
   by Harim Saur, employee at the Stop-N-Go
   convenience store located at the west end of
   the Susquanny River Bridge. Saur reports that
   around 10:30 p.m. on Wednesday, November 7,
   he saw a "large gang of kids" hanging around
   the bridge. Because of the time of night and
   the distance from the store, he could not
   see clearly, but he had the impression that
   "something was going on."
   To rule out or include this activity in the
death of Miranda Peizer, officers canvassed
the students at Lincoln High School. Most deny
being out on the night of November 7 and can
be vouched for by their parents. Some were
working at part-time jobs; these were verified.
The individuals who cannot verify their
movements or who have given an alibi that was
subsequently contradicted by verbal statements
are as follows:

   Kate Parsons
   Michelle Gibson
   Anna Hale
   Kelci Platt
   Morgan Williams
   Kyle Edgar
   Brendan O'Day
   Rose Silverstein

Jaimi Silverstein
Keisha Jones

ACTION:The above subjects will be interviewed
    again. Victim's mother, Tanya Peizer, should
    also be interviewed but is unavailable at this
    time due to her state of mind in bereavement.
    Report to follow.

Chapter Five

*N*ick *Tremore stood* at the front door of the apartment and checked his notebook. Number 202, the home of the victim's mother.

This wasn't going to be easy.

He knocked, and when no one answered after a few seconds, knocked again. Through his boots, he felt a small vibration, as though something heavy had fallen somewhere at the back of the unit, and his instincts kicked in. He tried the door and to his surprise, the knob turned under his hand.

"Mrs. Peizer?" he called. "It's Deputy Tremore from the sheriff's office. I left a couple of messages on your phone. Can I come in?"

A sound that might have been a reply came from a bedroom. He stepped in and closed the door behind him.

"Mrs. Peizer? Are you okay?"

A small woman with hair halfway between blonde and red appeared in the hallway, holding what looked to be a rope of some kind in her hands.

"They had runs in them," she said, and looked down at what he now realized were a pair of stockings. "I sent her to school with runs in her hose."

Aw, man. Nick had plenty of experience with women—the kind he was related to and the kind he chose for himself—but he'd never gone one-on-one with a grieving mother before.

"Maybe she put holes in them on purpose," he offered. "Like the kids do with their jeans."

The tears that had been swimming in her eyes overflowed and streaked her cheeks. "Not Randi." She made a gulping sound. "They were a statement for her. These were her favorites."

"Uh, maybe I should come back another time." He glanced around the tiny apartment. "Isn't there supposed to be someone with you?" Hadn't Laurie said that she and her church ladies were watching out for her?

Tanya twisted the black hose between her fingers, and Nick had a sudden flash of what exactly a person in despair could do with something like that. He resisted the urge to pull them out of her hands and put them somewhere safe.

"Cammie left a while ago." Thin shoulders drooped. "She told me not to think about cleaning up Randi's room yet, but I had to." She looked up at him as though he were about to haul her in for it.

Inside him, something twisted, hard.

"Mrs. Peizer, please, sit down."

She let him lead her over to the couch, where she sat and wrung the hose between her hands, over and over. "Not Mrs.," she finally said. "I never married Randi's dad." A quick glance sideways at him. "That was before I became a Christian."

He didn't want to hear about ex-husbands or Christians. He was surrounded by them—Christians, not ex-husbands. His mother and aunts never lost an opportunity to parade yet another prospective wife in front of him, and she was invariably a member of some church or another. His brothers had done the right thing and married fine, upstanding girls, producing fine, upstanding families. He supposed he was the black sheep, although going into law enforcement like his uncle probably wasn't the best rebellion he could have come up with.

And now here was another one. How was her faith going to get her through this?

"Ms. Peizer—"

"My name is Tanya."

At least the tears had stopped trickling down her cheeks.

"I'd like to ask you some questions about Randi," he said gently, grateful for small mercies. "If you feel up to it."

"I took those pills Patty gave me, but they just made me sick. Reality is hard to face right now, but it's better than turning into a zombie." She touched her scalp. "I hurt my head."

Too bad he couldn't arrest this Patty person for loaning out her pharmaceuticals. "Let me look."

She leaned away from his attempt to part her hair. "I'm okay. It was yesterday. Janice looked at it."

To cover the unwanted gesture, which had been as automatic as picking up Tim after a tumble from his bike, Nick pulled out his notebook.

"We're interested in Randi's movements during the last week of—last week," he amended. "But especially Wednesday."

"Why? Nothing is going to change." Her eyes were bleak. "God gave her to me and he must not have thought I was doing a very good job, because he took her back."

No way was he going to get into that kind of theological quagmire. "We're not sure it was an accident," he said. "Are you sure you're up for this?"

With the sleeve of her shirt, she wiped her face. "I don't have much choice, do I?"

"Yes, you do. You can tell me to go away. But the sooner we act, the sooner we can find out the truth."

"I wish you *would* go away."

He closed the notebook and shifted his weight to his feet. He should send Gil to do this. Gil had a better bedside manner.

"I wish it would all go away," Tanya went on as if he hadn't moved, "but it won't, so I have to get on with it. Please tell me why you don't think it was an accident."

He sank back onto the couch, and a spring gouged him in the hip. He moved over a little.

"The clerk at the convenience store said there were a bunch of kids on the bridge, and it looked like something was going on. Then Randi turned up on the sandbar the next day. The one event may have nothing to do with the other, but in case they do, I need to have a picture of her movements leading up to Wednesday night. Maybe something will tell me what could have happened."

Tanya shrugged. "She did what she always does. She went to school. She went to the mall. She hung out with her friends."

According to Anna Hale, nobody much liked her. Who were these friends? "Do you know their names?"

"Kate's one of them. And Kelci—with an *i*." She glanced at his notebook, as if to check he had the spelling right. "And let's not forget the man of the hour, Brendan O'Day. I wanted to meet him."

"Why?"

Another sideways glance, wryly. "Not the parent of a teenage girl, huh?"

"Not a parent. Not married." Not even close, and happy to keep it that way, thanks.

"I think he was her boyfriend. I wanted to do the mom thing, you know? Meet him, get to know him. But it never seemed to happen. She always had somewhere else to be, and I always had to work."

Brendan O'Day was the captain of the junior varsity basketball team and was pegged for some Ivy League school in the future, according to his proud father, who hung out with one of Nick's brothers. Nick had his doubts that he was going out with Randi Peizer, who was new in town, lived in subsidized housing, and wasn't well-liked. But, he supposed, stranger things had happened.

"Why don't you walk me through the events of Wednesday?" he suggested. "Start with when the two of you woke up."

"We had scrambled eggs for breakfast, and I dropped her off at school on my way to work."

"Where do you work?"

"Depends on the day. On Wednesday I have early shift at the university. I drive the shuttle bus around the campus. Then from two till six I work swing at Susquanny Home Supply. I'm a cashier."

Which didn't leave a whole lot of time for meeting her daughter's friends.

"What did Randi do that day?"

"She gets out of school at three. I called her at four and she was at the mall with Kate and the other girls."

She might have been at the mall, but Kate had said in their interview the other night that she had dance class until five and had been there with all the other ballerinas. Randi, it appeared, was as good at spinning yarns as her mother was at believing them.

Or maybe this slender, hunched-over woman just needed to believe in something good in her life. The picture of Randi at the mall, having fun with other girls her age, must have been too appealing to resist.

"What about when you got home? Was she there?"

Tanya shook her head. "She called and said she was staying with one of the girls to eat supper and study, and she'd be home around eight."

"And was she?"

"I don't know. I grabbed the extra hours—a mistake, because I wound up not getting home until ten. The store closes at nine, and then we cash out."

"And she wasn't here." She was on the bridge, doing—what?

"No."

"What did you do?"

"I called her cell and left a message."

"She didn't answer?"

"I thought she was inside somewhere. Sometimes it doesn't work in certain buildings. So I—" She stopped. "I—" Her breathing shortened, became a series of gasps. "I'm sorry."

"That's okay. Take your time."

Her breath hitched. "I meant to call over to Kate's—to see if she was there—but I was so tired—I just shut my eyes for a second and—and—"

Aw, no. Nick rubbed a cold hand over his face and wished he'd left while he'd had the chance.

"And the next thing I knew, it was morning and a man who said he was the coroner was on the doorstep—and he said—he—" The last word ended on a wail and Nick found himself dropping his notebook beside him on the couch and folding Tanya Peizer into a hug while she cried.

What kind of God lets a girl die while her exhausted mother sleeps? he asked silently as she shook against his chest.

Of course there was no answer to that question.

There were answers to the mystery of what had happened to

Randi Peizer before the river carried her away, though. And he was going to find them.

To Group: GBFWomensBible
From: all.hale@hotmail.com

Hey girls,

Thanks to Maggie and Cammie, we've helped Tanya get through the first couple of days. We need to stick with her through the funeral and probably afterward. Can you all zip me a note and let me know what evenings you'll be able to park the kids with your DH in order to go over to her place for a couple of hours? I want to draw up a roster so no one person has to spend too much time away from her own family. Also, let me know if you can make dishes for her freezer or throw a few extra groceries in your cart next time you're at the market. I know we're all busy, but our sister needs us.

Thanks, as always!

Laurie

Sunday morning, Laurie walked into church with to-do lists and schedules and menu plans on a neat list in her tote bag, with enough copies for everyone in the Bible study group. Cammie, she saw right away, had picked up Tanya and made sure she got to the service. Laurie knew for a fact that staying in that apartment, alone and grieving, was not going to start her on the road to recovery. Simply being in the place where others could help her would be a balm to her soul and the best thing she could do for herself.

Cammie stuck to Tanya like a burr during the service, where Cale Dayton preached on the healing power of love. At the end, he announced that the memorial service for Randi would be Tuesday afternoon at four.

"Tanya has requested that Randi's remains be cremated," he explained, "so we'll have a memorial service and celebration of her life. We'll hold it right here, after school, so her classmates can attend as well."

When the service was over, people crowded around to offer condolences and help. Tanya looked a little like a drowning woman, glancing right and left as if she were hoping that the sea would part and she could escape. Laurie made her way to her side and made sure that people who were serious about their offers of help got their names on the roster for either food or time.

This was one of the reasons she loved Glendale Bible Fellowship—brotherly love translated itself into action here. Nobody had to be asked first. No one who had a need ever went without, whether it was as practical as making supper for a bereaved family, or as spiritual as praying for someone who was struggling.

Tanya gripped her arm. "Laurie, please, can we go?" Tears streaked her face, and fine hair that would have been curly if it had been styled a little better was coming out of its knot.

"Of course, sweetie. I'm just going to finish up with these folks. Cammie, can you take Tanya home?"

The two women made their way to the door and escaped into the chilly morning. The weatherman had predicted snow by mid-afternoon, and you could really feel it if you were standing near the door.

Thanks to the list and the schedule, someone would be with Tanya whenever she needed it—whether keeping her company during her hours off, or pulling out a frozen dish and putting it in the oven, or picking up scrapbooking materials for Randi's memory book.

It turned out that Tanya was a lapsed scrapbooker, and creating the pages of the album on Monday turned out to be a kind of therapy. Fortunately, Mary Lou and Debbie were scrapbookers, too, and by the time people had begun to gather for the service on Tuesday, the album was finished and displayed on a miniature podium, where people could look through it before they entered the sanctuary.

At the front, Randi's ninth-grade picture had been enlarged and mounted, and stood on an easel between two elevated baskets of roses and lilies. Three members of the high-school band played flute, piano, and clarinet onstage, and the melody of "Amazing Love" floated through the sanctuary.

Anna's phone rang just as Colin ushered them all up the aisle.

"Turn that off!" Laurie whispered. Anna knew better than that. The whole family automatically turned off their phones on the way to church every Sunday. Today should have been no different.

Anna glanced at the text message and thumbed the little phone off, then dropped it in her denim messenger bag. As they sat in their usual pew five rows back on the left side, Laurie heard sniffles and the stifled sound of weeping as the church filled.

Cale opened the service with a eulogy that was as short as Randi's life had been. His text was 1 John 4:10: "Herein is love, not that we loved God, but that he loved us . . ." Laurie glanced over at Tanya and hoped that she was able to take it in. God's love was active. And so was theirs, right there in the church. Tanya might not be able to see it now, but some day she would, and the care all around her would comfort her.

Then, one by one, Randi's classmates got up and walked to the podium. Kate Parsons moved with the confidence and assurance of the social leader that Laurie wished Anna would be. Even after their uncomfortable conversation of the other night, she still had hopes. People grew and changed—and a fourteen-year-old changed her mind a dozen times a day.

Kate's father, Neil, was a lawyer, and as far as Laurie knew, his appearance in church today was a first. His wife, Noreen, came once in a while, but she'd declined to join their study group even though they'd invited her more than once.

Tears rolled down Kate's perfect skin as her soft voice filled the church, mourning the loss of a schoolmate "who dressed like a real original" and who "is remembered every day." Brendan O'Day spoke next, and a girl called Rose Silverstein, both of whom Laurie had not met personally, but whose parents she knew by reputation. Everyone knew Brendan O'Day's father— he was as full of bombast as the furniture crates in his warehouses. He ran the Hawthorne House chain from its head office in Pittsburgh, selling reproductions of English country-house interiors to people who thought they deserved them. She couldn't stand Jack O'Day, but he and Colin sat on the church board, and she was as sweet as southern tea whenever they met.

Tanya didn't get up. Laurie was glad that Mary Lou and Debbie had worked with her on the scrapbook—it formed the record of Randi's life that Tanya was too shattered to say out loud.

During the last hymn, Laurie and her team slipped downstairs to the multipurpose room and got the coffeepots going and the trays of cake and cookies and sliced fruit laid out on the tables. It didn't take long for the room to fill once the memorial was over. Cammie made sure Tanya had a comfortable place to sit and brought her a plate full of food, heavy on the protein.

Cammie was not a nutritionist for nothing.

Laurie laid a paper doily over a round plastic serving tray and began to arrange her famous pecan tarts on it. On the other side of the table, Natalie Martinez moved a tray of coconut squares from the meat table onto the one that held sweets, and said to Maggie Lesser, "I hear the police are making their rounds."

"I know," Maggie said. "I just talked to Joyce Silverstein. I can't tell you how glad I am that my Kevin's only in fourth grade. You have to hand it to Rose, though." She glanced at the other end of the long table, where the teenagers were piling their paper plates high with sweets. "Interrogated one night and eulogizing her friend the next. That's character."

"Why are they interrogating Rose? She babysits for us. She's the last person who would be involved in . . . something like this."

Natalie stole a mini cherry cheesecake. "They're interrogating everybody. No one is exempt, apparently." She glanced around her. "Rose. Kate. Even Anna Hale."

A skinny man in tight jeans and a silk shirt stepped in front of Laurie, and she restrained herself from pushing him out of the way.

While she waited impatiently for him to move so she could join her friends, Natalie went on: "Who'd ever have thought something like this would happen in our town? Especially among kids we all know."

"How do we really know what they're thinking?" Maggie asked. "With all this TV violence and sex and shootings in the schools . . . man," she said on a sigh. "High school isn't what it was when we were young, that's for sure. But still, you'd think you'd be able to write some kids off the suspect list. Anna, for instance. Or Kyle Edgar or Kelci Platt."

The skinny guy finally stopped filling his plate with desserts, and Laurie pushed past him.

"I don't know," Natalie went on as Laurie came up behind her, "sometimes the quiet types are the worst. I mean, Anna is a lovely kid, but in a murder investigation you can't rule anyone out. Still waters run deep, if you know what I mean."

Laurie could stand it no longer. Natalie's tone had Anna clothed in jailhouse orange and manacles by sundown. "Come on, Nat," she said as she joined them. "We have to stand behind our kids, don't we?"

She couldn't help a little internal smile of satisfaction at Natalie's guilty start. That would teach her to talk behind people's backs.

"Of course we do," Natalie said. She made a quick recovery, Laurie would give her that. "I'm just saying that Anna, like so many of these other kids, is a deep person. Teenagers don't put it all out there like younger kids do. They keep secrets."

"Not about this. Anna was completely up front with Nick and Gil when they came by. I'm sure the others were, too."

Nick and Gil. She used their first names deliberately. These women could use a reminder that the investigating officer was family. The Hales and Tremores didn't harbor criminals. They brought them to justice.

"I'm sure she was," Maggie said. "But I heard that Anna was one of the ones on the bridge that night."

"You heard wrong," Laurie replied. "Anna has already explained that she was at home and in bed. Who is saying this?"

Maggie shrugged. "I can't remember. There's so much talk going around."

"Well, I hope you set them straight. It's just . . . ridiculous, that's all."

Natalie and Maggie looked at one another. What? What did that look mean? Why were they even entertaining for one second the thought that Anna had been involved in any way? They'd all known one another for most of their lives. Maggie had babysat Anna herself, times without number, and Laurie had done the same for her three kids.

These women were her friends. If they couldn't defend Anna, the least they could do was not pass on gossip about her.

Laurie was drawing a breath to tell them so, when Maggie gripped her arm. "Laurie. Is that—?"

She followed Maggie's gaze to the skinny man, who was sharing his plate of dessert with an equally skinny girl with mousy brown hair and talking to Kate Parsons and Brendan O'Day.

"Who? The guy in the silk shirt?"

"Yes!" She sounded breathless. "Isn't that Jimmy Tyler? You know, the lead singer of Wolf?"

Natalie stared. "I haven't heard anything of them in twenty years. They used to be as big as Led Zeppelin and Aerosmith and bands like that in the seventies, didn't they?"

Laurie was not ready to talk about aging rock singers. "His daughter was a friend of Randi's, apparently."

"Really? Rose said something about that, but I didn't think it was true. Come on, Nat. Let's go talk to him."

"Are you kidding?" But Natalie let Maggie drag her over, and Laurie gave up. She'd talk to them later, or maybe bring it up at Bible study. They had to stick together, to believe in each other, or where would they be? Gossiping around town and hurting one another, that's where.

She turned and practically ran into Janice Edgar. "Oops." She took the other woman's forearms to steady her. Fine wool crepe by some high-end designer crumpled under her fingers. "Sorry about that."

"Not to worry." Janice glanced over at Natalie and Maggie, who had taken Jimmy Tyler the plate of coconut squares. "I see the news of our visiting celebrity is out."

"Anna told the police that Randi had made him up." Laurie took one of her own tarts to fortify herself. "Apparently not. No one could make up clothes like that."

Janice's attention swung to her abruptly. "The police came to talk to Anna?"

"Sure. They said they had two hundred teenagers on the list. Practically everyone at the high school. Kyle, too?"

"Unbelievable, isn't it?"

At least she believed in her son, even if others didn't. Laurie felt the first flicker of affinity with Janice.

"Unbelievable or not, I'm glad Anna isn't involved," she admitted. "We have enough on our plate with helping Tanya survive this."

Janice's face wavered, and then steely control seemed to bring her features back to their usual smiling calm. "I'm glad you know Anna had no part in it. I wish I could say the same."

Chapter Six

To group: Budz
From: JohnnysGrrl

Someone's talking. Better not B u. Nice funeral huh? How bout that Jimmy Tyler? Ha ha.

*N*ick *didn't consider* himself a type A kind of guy. He didn't fly off the handle; he thought things through. He never leaped to conclusions, and he liked clean evidence and orderly thinking. He'd seen the results of road rage a time or two, and that had even cured him of any urges he might have had toward reckless driving.

But orderly thinking wasn't doing him any good today. Not after he'd received Lisa Nguyen's e-mail with her written preliminary findings and the attached zip file full of digital photographs of Randi's autopsy.

Between those and Forrest Christopher's investigation of the crime scene on the bridge, the sequence of events had become clear. But even if she had been pushed, and had gone over either accidentally or by design, why had no one jumped in to help, why had no one called 911? If Randi had still been breathing when she went under, maybe she could have survived.

He glanced again at the photograph of her skull. Maybe.

The list of teenagers on the bridge was now part of the permanent record in his brain. Nobody was admitting to seeing anything. Kate Parsons and her little crew of two, Rose Silverstein and Kelci Platt, had bought sodas and chocolate bars at the Stop-N-Go and stopped to talk to Kyle Edgar, Brendan, and another boy named Morgan Williams. According to them, the conversation hadn't lasted more than half an hour or so. Kate thought she'd seen Anna Hale and another girl talking to Randi under the trees, but Kyle said he hadn't seen Anna since their last class, earlier in the day.

Nick was a little more inclined to believe Kyle than Kate, especially when Anna had said she was at home in bed. In that case, who had really been talking to Randi under the trees? He'd be extremely interested in interviewing that person.

He'd also be interested in getting a straight story about what had happened to Randi between talking under the trees and falling into the river, because every statement in this folder said something different.

Were kids really that scatterbrained and unobservant? Or were they just all lying through their orthodontically perfect teeth?

He printed the report and the photographs and slid them into the case folder. With the funeral today, it was only a matter of time before Randi's mother would be asking for answers. It was Nick's job to provide them.

Too bad he didn't have any at the moment. Just a boatload of new questions.

Those teenagers held the key. One or all of them were hiding the truth about what happened. He was just going to have to lean harder on them, and sooner or later somebody would crack.

In the church activity room, Laurie stared at Janice Edgar.

"Kyle was there?"

The poor woman. It was bad enough having the police come to visit and hint that your child might be involved when someone had died. But to actually know that he might be prosecuted— she couldn't bring herself to think about it.

Janice took a sip from her cup of tepid tea, and seemed to swallow with difficulty. "So he told Nick."

"What else did he say?"

"That Kate was there, and that other girl who spoke today."

"Rose. Who else?"

Janice lifted an eyebrow. "Why do you want to know? Anna wasn't there, according to Kyle."

"No, for which I'm thanking God as we speak. But surely one of them must have seen something."

"Apparently not." She would have said more, but Tanya touched Laurie's arm and they both turned to her.

"Laurie, I can't handle this," Tanya whispered. "I need to go home."

"I'll take you," Janice offered instantly.

Laurie would just as soon have taken Tanya home herself and made sure she was all right before Debbie Jacks came on duty that evening, but then who would take care of getting all this food put away and the activity room cleaned up?

"Thanks, Janice," she said. "I'll talk with you later. Before Bible study on Thursday, okay?"

Janice gave her a surprised look, but murmured something in the affirmative before she and Tanya made their way out of the room. Well, maybe she'd deserved it. She and Janice weren't exactly on "I'll give you a call for any old reason" terms. But that could change. She wanted to know what Kyle knew.

She wasn't sure exactly why—but there was this knot of anxiety growing inside her, and something had to be done about it. If she could find out something—any detail—about that night, then maybe it would dissipate.

Laurie didn't indulge much in self-examination. She didn't have a therapist or spend her energy figuring out how to self-actualize. Frankly, she didn't have the time. Getting Colin and the kids from one end of a day to the other didn't leave much time for contemplating her navel, and any free time she did have went to the church or even to herself in a rare hour alone to read.

So she didn't bother examining the roots of the little knot under her breastbone. She just went with what her instincts told her—that information about that night would help, and the more facts she had, the safer she'd feel.

Safe from what?

Well, that was the silly part. Anna had done nothing wrong. Her family was safe, and there was nothing to be afraid of. But she trusted her instincts. Colin didn't put much store in instincts—they were too close to what he called "that ESP nonsense." But they hardly ever led her wrong.

When the mourners had thinned to just a trickle of die-hards who were there because they didn't often get the opportunity to socialize and enjoy a good spread at the same time, Laurie and her team—down to just Cammie and Mary Lou now—began to clean up. The leftover cookies and squares would be perfect for the worship team's music rehearsal the following night, along with the soda, so that all went into the fridge.

The kitchen had a cooking area, with stove, sink, and refrigerator. A long staging counter with a pass-through opening on one side faced the multipurpose room, with storage cupboards beneath it. Laurie was on her knees putting minarets of paper cups back in their space when she heard her name on the other side of the pass-through.

"I don't think Laurie knows that."

She froze. Her legs tensed as she got ready to pop to her feet and say, "Knows what?"

But then she recognized the voice of Sophie Dayton, the pastor's wife, who would probably clam up if she did that. So she stayed on her knees and closed the cupboard door as quietly as she could.

"Brendan swears Anna was there, too." Aha. Nancy O'Day.

Sophie's tone was gentle but honest. "It's not likely Brendan is going to lie about that. He's been very up-front about being out that night."

"Why shouldn't he be?" Nancy seemed to bristle a little. Well, using the word *lie* in connection with her child would make Laurie bristle, too. "He's got nothing to hide. He didn't do anything wrong."

"None of them did. I'm sure it was all an accident or a suicide and the police are being overly cautious. Even treating it like a murder investigation. Not that it is," she said hastily. "Just treating it that way."

"They should treat it carefully. That's their job. Pass me one of those pecan tarts, would you? I've been holding out all afternoon, and I just can't anymore."

Their voices faded to the other side of the room and then out the door. Laurie stood, wishing she'd had the courage to stand up. At least there were two people who stuck up for Brendan the way she'd wished her friends would have stuck up for Anna.

Brendan, who didn't deserve people sticking up for him.

Who was putting the word out that Anna had been on the bridge that night. Putting her in danger. Laurie could practically feel the hackles rise on the back of her neck. She'd had just about enough of people spreading lies about her daughter. But she wasn't the police. Other than solving the investigation herself, how was she going to make them stop?

No one was with Tanya Peizer at the mortuary, which puzzled Nick a little, considering the army of loving and efficient women who had surrounded her up until now. Maybe she'd slipped her handlers and come to do this on her own. Maybe he should butt out and find another time to talk to her.

It wasn't strictly necessary that he tell her in person about what Lisa and Forrest had found. A copy of Lisa's report would come to the mailbox at apartment 202 in due time, in all its stark and ugly detail. But somehow he couldn't bring himself to put this fragile woman through reading something like that when he had the means to break it to her kindly, as a compassionate but impartial officer of the law.

This wasn't Pittsburgh, where an officer might not see the family of a homicide victim unless he chose to go to the funeral. This was Glendale, where he knew nearly everyone, from the drunks he put in the slammer to sleep it off before they drove home, to the kids he coached in Little League every summer. If he had the power to do someone a kindness, then he did it simply because he could—and today's errand fell into that category.

He sat in what the funeral business called the "meditation room," which resembled the waiting room of a doctor's office but with comfortable chairs and no magazines. When Tanya came out, he expected to see her carrying an urn, but her hands were empty. A worn brown leather purse swung from her left shoulder.

She looked a little surprised when he got to his feet. "Deputy Tremore."

"You can call me Nick. Everybody else does."

Her gaze took in his khaki uniform, badge, utility belt, and the radio on his shoulder. "Nick, then. Do you have more questions for me?"

Her skin was so pale it made her reddish hair look as though it were burning. Dark smudges hung below her eyes, as though sleep was something she chased every night and failed to catch.

His insides squeezed with compassion. Coming here had been the right decision.

"No, no questions," he said, and her shoulders dipped a little, as though she had exhaled a sigh of relief. "I did want to talk about something, though, so the woman in the apartment next to yours told me where you'd gone."

She led the way outside into the blustering wind, buttoning a duffle coat cut to look like the kind sailors wore. It was pea green and a little tattered at the cuffs and collar. Navy surplus, probably.

"This might take a while," he said when she paused by his vehicle. "I have the preliminary findings about Randi's death."

This time her shoulders really did sag. "I can't do this," he thought he heard her murmur, but the wind had kicked up a flurry of leaves in the parking lot, and the sudden whisper scratched out her words.

On impulse, he went around and opened the passenger door of the police vehicle. "Come on. Let's go for a ride."

Instead of following him, she stepped back. "Down to the station?"

"No, no. Just for a ride. I think better when I'm driving, and you'll have a little privacy." He glanced at the door of the mortuary, where a black limo was pulling up. "More than we'll get here, anyway."

"All right." She climbed in and he closed the door behind her, then went around the front and got in. It took about five minutes to get to the edge of town, and then they were headed east into the Pennsylvania hills, now covered in the bare skeletons of trees.

"Where are we going?" She didn't look at the bleak scenery, but at the radio, the rifle rack, the GPS, and the computer system angled around him.

"There's a place I know about eight miles away. I used to ride there on my bike as a kid. It has a nice view and my cousins couldn't find me."

"Isn't Laurie your cousin?"

"Yeah, but she's five years older than me. When you're eight, you don't want your teenage girl cousin acting like your mother and bossing you around."

"That sounds like Laurie."

"Nothing's changed. But people need to be organized, and she happens to be good at it."

"She makes sure I have company all the time. Not that I'm not grateful," she said hastily, glancing at him. "At first I hated to be alone, and the memorial service was awful. But now that those things are over, I want to breathe a little bit and feel like I can grieve. I didn't want anyone with me during the"—her voice broke—"the cremation. I wanted to cry without anyone thinking they had to make me feel better."

He paused, feeling for the right words. "I think they're afraid you'll hurt yourself," he said quietly. "Like with the pills."

She shifted and fussed with the seat belt. "I flushed them days ago. Patty meant well, but I wasn't thinking straight when I took them." Another glance his way. "You're not going to arrest her for giving them to me, are you? She wanted to help."

He shook his head. "I had a little chat with her after I talked with you, and it didn't take long to realize she was honestly trying to do right. But she won't be doing it again, that's for sure."

He signaled and turned off the highway, taking a narrow road that wound up the side of a hill. In a few minutes—a distance that had taken him an hour of pumping and puffing on his bike—he pulled over where the road widened a little.

"Is this it?" she said doubtfully. "I think you've brought me up here under false pretenses."

If this had been any other woman, he might have thought she was flirting. But Tanya was dead serious.

"We have to walk a little way. Not far." Belatedly, he checked to see what she had on her feet. Sneakers. Good.

Only a few hundred feet of trees and brush separated the road from a place he remembered as being a kind of refuge. Collars of dirty snow stood around the bases of the trees in the deepest shade, but as they cleared the trees and emerged onto the south-facing cliff, it was dry and almost warm. Provided you had a good coat. At least the wind had died down.

"Over here." He helped her up a tumble of limestone boulders and then settled on one that was nearly level. This natural bench was where he'd done his daydreaming as a kid.

"You came all the way out here on your bike?" Her profile looked very young and almost wistful as she gazed out over the valley. Glendale lay off to their right, the highway snaking through the bare trees, following the course of the Susquanny.

"Sure."

"Didn't your mom tell you not to?"

"I never told her about it. Never told anyone. I used to pick her flowers up here and bring them home in my backpack, and she never asked me where I got them."

"I always asked Randi where she went. She might not have liked it, but she always told me."

Told you something. Maybe not the truth.

"We had pretty good communication," she went on, "considering we mostly saw each other at breakfast and at night. I wanted her to know she could tell me anything. Heaven knows I've done a ton of stuff I'm not proud of. She probably couldn't make any mistakes I haven't made myself."

The cold air moving down the side of the hill stirred the curls on her forehead. She'd pinned her hair back into a twist for the trip to the mortuary—a touch of formality, a show of respect for her daughter's last journey.

Unexpectedly, his throat closed up on whatever inane comment he'd been about to make, and he cleared it roughly.

"Sorry," she said. "I didn't mean to babble. You had something you wanted to tell me."

He frowned. Trust him to break a mood. "No. I mean, you weren't babbling. Talking about Randi is natural."

"Talking about the coroner's findings isn't."

"I can do it another time. I'd rather listen to you reminisce about her."

"On my tax dollars? I don't think so." For a moment, he thought a smile might soften the words, but she gazed at the river instead, the corners of her eyes pinched with pain. He braced himself. What he had to say was not going to make this any better.

As gently as he could, he summarized what Lisa had told him. By the end, Tanya's cheeks were glassy with tears.

Yeah. A real pro at ruining a mood, a view, and a whole blasted day.

He didn't even have a tissue on him. She dug in her pocket, found a tattered one, and blew her nose. "Is that everything?" she said when she could finally speak.

"Not quite. But we can leave the rest for another time."

"No." She took a deep, shaky breath. "If I have to have this in my head for the rest of my life, you might as well give it all to me. I just can't bear . . ." The word trailed off into tears, and a flock of brown sparrows who had been investigating the rock below them took off in alarm. "Bear thinking of her in pain and me not being there."

One crumb of comfort. It was all he had, and he offered it with eagerness, as if it would make up for the rest. "She wasn't in pain, Tanya. When she went in, I mean."

The sobs jerking her body under the ugly green coat seemed to slacken as she tried to listen. "How do you know?"

How could he say this without inflicting even more agony? "Because Forrest Christopher is the coroner's investigator, and he told me. When I went up on that bridge he was already there, going over it, taking evidence, taking pictures. He found blood and hairs on one of the horizontal support beams that stick out under the roadbed, ten or twelve feet down. They matched Randi's."

"That doesn't sound good."

"The protruding end of the beam matches the fracture in Randi's skull. It means that when she fell, she hit her head on it and it knocked her out. So she would have been unconscious when she went into the water."

And wouldn't have known she was drowning.

The words hung, heavy and cold and unsaid, in the air between them.

"But what I want to know is, what made her fall?"

"That makes two of us." His tone was grim and very low. "Forrest said that if she'd been trying to stand on the railing, to jump off voluntarily, there would have been muddy footprints on it, or marks in the frost that morning."

She shot him a glance. "Randi would never do that."

How could he put this gently? "Well, it looks like she didn't. Forrest found scuff marks on the deck of the bridge right above the support beam, as if there was a struggle. We're treating it as suspicious. I'm going to find out what happened—I promise you."

There didn't seem to be very much to say after that. The wind kicked up again, and when he saw her shiver, he hustled her back to the still-warm police car. Neither of them said a word as he drove her to the mortuary's parking lot, where her little hatchback sat.

He caught her eye and nodded toward the building. "When will they be . . . finished?"

She gathered her purse and put her hand on the door. "In a day or two. They said they'd call me. I want to take her home with me until I decide whether to scatter her ashes or not."

"Ah. Well." He wasn't sure what to say. "Thanks for tolerating me this afternoon. I'm sorry to be the bearer of ugly news."

"It's not your fault." Her gaze fixed on her car, as if she couldn't wait to get out of the police vehicle and away from him. He could hardly blame her. "I'd rather hear it from a human

being than get it in a report in the mail. I probably wouldn't understand it, and that would frustrate me even more."

"I'm glad." That hadn't come out right. "Well, not that we
had to have this conversation, but that I—um—"

Her nod was brisk, and she climbed out of the car. "I know
what you meant. Thanks for the ride."

Before he could say one more stupid thing, she bumped the
door shut with her hip and climbed into her own vehicle. There
was nothing else he could do for her except follow her home at
a discreet distance, to make sure she got there safely.

As he waited behind her at the traffic light, he could see her
silhouette shake through the rear window, her hands gripping
the wheel as though it were a life preserver. It was a miracle she
made it back to the apartment. He waited out on the street until
the door of unit 202 closed before he let the communications
center know he was back in service.

It didn't happen very often, but there were days when he
really hated his job.

Chapter Seven

To: KelciP
From: JohnnysGrrl

    Hows little bro, K-girl? He OK? No broken bones? No accidents?

I think we should get Anna some counseling."

Laurie had taken advantage of a break between getting off work and picking up the kids, and dropped in at Susquanny Home Supply to see Colin. Anna was at art class and Tim at band practice, where he whaled the stuffing out of a snare drum and had more fun goofing off with his skater buddies than he actually learned about rhythm. But that was okay. When you were ten, there was nothing wrong with having fun.

Anna, however, was a problem of a darker stripe. She was not having fun. She stayed in her room much more now, and the phone rang less often. Even though she insisted she was fine, Laurie's instincts told her differently.

Colin looked up from what appeared to be a contract of some kind. "What? Counseling?"

Laurie made sure the door was closed and dropped a kiss on his temple. Then she sat in the guest chair on the other side of his desk.

"Something's definitely wrong. She talks to me, but it's not the same. Whenever we get anywhere near the subject of Randi Peizer, she slides around it and fades away. She only comes back when I change the subject."

"Then I suggest you don't talk about Randi Peizer."

That was Colin. So intent on giving a solution that he missed the point completely.

"We have to. It's clear that the whole subject upsets her. Talking about it will help her work through it."

He pushed the contract into the middle of his blotter and sat back in the chair. "You can't force a teenager to talk. Besides, she's always spent all kinds of time in her room drawing and not talking, and it's never bugged you before."

"That was before I found this."

Laurie pulled a sheet of paper out of her tote bag and handed it to him. He tilted the chair back and studied it. "It's a flying girl. So?"

The drawing was one of Anna's manga people, with their big eyes and perky noses and attenuated bodies. Laurie couldn't see the fascination in all these fantasy creatures, but she couldn't argue with the fact that Anna had a gift for drawing them. Thus, the art classes.

"Colin, she's not flying. She's falling."

His gaze dropped back to the picture. "Is this supposed to be Randi?" The girl, sketched hastily with a fine-point felt pen, wore blacked-in hip-hugger pants, a concho belt, and a corset top that cinched up the front with blacked-in ribbons. Her hair flew away from her temples in the updraft, and to Laurie, her eyes were hollow with sadness. But if she said that out loud, Colin would just tell her she was dramatizing things.

"I think so."

"Lor, it's psychological. If Anna has this girl on her mind, then it's natural she would express her feelings through her pictures."

"If she's drawing pictures of falling girls, she's upset enough that she should talk to someone who can help her. She needs to learn to work through it, and I'm afraid that's beyond both of us."

He handed back the picture and she folded it into her tote. "I understand that. What I don't understand is why it's affecting her like this. A girl she barely knows died one night a mile from her house. Most people would just remember Randi with love or friendship and then move on."

"Anna isn't moving on. That's the whole point."

"She can talk to us when she's ready. And she will—you know that. She always has."

"She's never been fourteen before. Things are different now."

If Laurie had had someone to talk to when she'd lost Sharon, maybe she wouldn't have carried that burden for so long. Maybe she would have understood it better and learned to celebrate the years she'd had with her friend instead of mourning the empty years ahead. But there had been no one. Her mother wasn't the kind to plumb her own emotional depths, much less those of her daughter. Mom's cure for distress was community work, so Laurie had learned to throw herself into theater and social events and fund-raisers—activities where there was always too much to do, crowds of people—and plenty to keep her mind off herself and her problems.

"How are they different?" Colin asked. He flipped a pen between his fingers, turning it over and over.

"She's growing up. She wants a little more freedom to make

her own decisions, but I'm not sure she has the emotional tools to do that successfully yet."

"One minute crying over something, the next minute as scatterbrained as can be," he agreed. "But we could give her a little more responsibility."

"She says I force her into doing things she doesn't want to do," Laurie blurted. "I didn't know she didn't want to sing in the choir. A year later she gets around to telling me."

"Did you ask her how she felt about it before she joined?"

"Of course. She sounded positive, so I drove her to tryouts and went over her audition pieces with her. And now I find out she never wanted to do it."

"Maybe she was trying to please you."

"I'd rather she was honest. Like now. I just sense that there's something going on in that head of hers that she won't share. That's why I think counseling is a good idea."

"I'd rather keep it in the family, Laurie."

"We're not psychologists. We don't have the skills."

"We're her parents. We love her," Colin pointed out. "Isn't that enough?"

She shook her head. "I don't think so."

"Well, I do. I'm not going to have my daughter spilling her guts to some stranger."

"It doesn't have to be a stranger. What about my cousin Gregg? He could talk to her."

"Is that what this is about? You want to give that guy some business? He still lives with your aunt, for Pete's sake."

What was wrong with that? Did he want this kept in the family or not? "It's not about giving him business. He has a nice practice all on his own, and you know perfectly well he's looking after Auntie Dawn because she's got MS." She took a breath. "Gregg is part of the family. He's qualified. Call him."

"I'll think about it."

"Or I will." She stood, and he looked up at her.

"We'll decide together, Laurie. After I've done some research and we've made sure your cousin is the best solution for Anna. Don't go flying off half-cocked and do this without me."

There were days when Colin's pragmatic approach to life was a blessing. And then there were days when it was a roadblock.

If he didn't move soon, she'd make the call herself and ask for forgiveness later.

She kissed him good-bye and headed to the school to pick up Tim. At the elementary school, several other mothers were parked in the lot, some driving BMWs or Volvo wagons and some in minivans like hers. So much for her old dream of owning a 1966 Mustang ragtop. At this rate, she wouldn't get one until the kids were grown up and gone and she was too old to remember how to drive a stick shift. However, the minivan was comfortable and practical—and she wouldn't last two minutes on the open road in a convertible in November.

Vanessa Platt leaned on the hood of her mother's Camry and didn't move as Laurie pulled in beside her. Vanessa was the worship team's lead soloist, and as far as Laurie was concerned, was such a great performer she should be studying music and going off to New York to become famous. Instead, she'd graduated from high school two years ago and still hung around Glendale, bringing people to tears with her singing voice on Sundays and serving them chicken-fried steak at the Split Rail Diner the rest of the time.

She must've come to the school today on kid duty. Her eleven-year-old brother, KeShawn, was also a talented musician, though you'd never know it the way he sat at the back of the orchestra and made rude noises with his trumpet.

Laurie rolled her window down. "Hey, Vanessa."

The girl smiled and pulled her puffy pink jacket a little tighter around her. "Hey, Mrs. Hale. You doin' okay?"

She nodded. "How come you're standing out there freezing?"

"I couldn't sit still. Went for a walk around the track." Her gaze jittered away and Laurie's antennae went up. She'd known the Platts since Vanessa was in lacy petticoats and white Mary Janes, singing her very first solo at the age of six. If the girl couldn't look her in the eye, something was amiss.

She patted the seat next to her. "Come on. It's nice and warm in here. If you catch a cold they'll make me sing, and nobody wants that."

Vanessa laughed and went around the front of the car. When she settled into the passenger seat, the cold breathed off her jacket. "Whew." She rubbed her hands. "Colder than I thought."

"Thanksgiving will be here in no time, and then Christmas, and there might be enough snow to go tobogganing. Tim can't wait. I, on the other hand, could wait a long time."

"I know what you mean." Silence fell, and Laurie turned up the heater. "Mrs. Hale?"

"Yes, honey?"

"Can I tell you something?"

"Of course. Anything." Laurie prepared herself to give some sensible career advice, or maybe a word in season about the undergraduate music program at the university.

"You found that girl's body, right?"

Laurie's train of thought derailed. Her gaze swung from

the muddy playing field to the girl sitting next to her. "Randi? Yes."

Vanessa's eyebrows knit together in a worried frown. "I don't want to tell my mom this, but I thought maybe you'd know what to do."

"Do about what, sweetie?"

"Mama was workin' that night, and she asked me to pick her up when she got off shift at eleven." Dorinda Platt was a nurse at the county hospital. "So I was, like, drivin' around, you know? Waiting for it to be time."

"Sure."

"So I'm heading for the Stop-N-Go to get a fake latte out of their machine, and I have to drive over the bridge."

"And?"

"And I see all these kids. Which is no big deal, you know, because I used to hang out there myself back in the day. But then I see Kelci, and that's a different thing, 'cause you know Mama is gonna have a fit if she finds out Kelci was out that late on a school night. So I do a U-turn in the Stop-N-Go parking lot to go get her. I'm thinkin' I just have time to take her home before I have to pick Mama up."

"So this is ten thirty or so?"

"Twenty after. I looked at the clock."

"Okay."

"So I'm turning around in the parking lot and I see something goin' on—like a catfight broke out. You know how that parking lot butts into the park grass there, and if you're standing on the lawn you can look up and see what's on the bridge?"

"Yes."

"And the next thing I see is your Anna runnin' up the park path like her tail's on fire, headin' for the bridge."

Laurie opened her mouth, but nothing came out.

"Those girls on the bridge are yellin' and she's yellin' and I can hear it right through the car windows, and the next thing you know, somebody pushes someone else real hard and over she goes."

"Who? Who pushes?"

"I don't know, but this girl does a cartwheel off the bridge and I'm thinkin', man, that's gonna be one cold landing, and Anna runs under the bridge and I don't see what happens after that, because Kelci sees me and I get her in the car and we go home. We just made it, too, 'cause I picked Mama up at eleven sharp and she never knew a thing."

"What—"

But Vanessa wasn't finished. "So then Friday I'm at the restaurant and somebody leaves their paper and there's this thing about you finding that girl in the river. And I thought, it can't be the same girl, 'cause I never saw it clear, you know. It was just a shape with arms and legs going over. I thought she'd just swim to shore and no harm done except maybe she'd catch a cold." She glanced sideways at Laurie. "You think it was the same girl?"

Anna wasn't out that night. Anna wasn't involved. Vanessa had seen someone else.

She had to say something sensible. "I'm pretty sure it was."

"You think Kelci will get in trouble if I go to the police?"

And have them find out that maybe Anna had been there after all? And that she'd run down under the bridge after Randi had fallen? Making her maybe the last person to see Randi alive? The last person to see someone alive was always a prime suspect, wasn't she? Nobody ever assumed that person was simply trying to help.

No, no, no. Anna had been in her room. Everyone knew that. So it didn't matter if Vanessa went to the police or not. She had evidence, and it could be important. The pushing part was important. Someone else had done that. Not Anna.

"Mrs. Hale?"

Laurie blinked and behind Vanessa's slouched form, she saw that the kids were pouring out of the elementary school and scattering to the various cars. Tim and KeShawn were horsing around and bumping each other off the sidewalk, completely careless of the black instrument cases dangling from their fingers.

"Will Kelci get in trouble?"

Laurie prodded her brain into coherent thought. "Not unless she was the one doing the pushing."

"No, it wasn't her. I'm sure of that."

"Did you see who it was?" she asked again.

Vanessa shook her head. The boys were twenty feet away now. "It was pretty chaotic. Somebody tall, I think."

"I think you should talk to Nick. He's a good guy."

"Yeah, I know. He comes into the restaurant all the time. Reuben sandwich, extra fries."

"But, Vanessa, Anna wasn't—"

Tim jerked open the door, fell into the backseat, and slammed it in KeShawn's face, giggling like an escapee from the local asylum. "Mom! KeShawn's spitting on me!"

Vanessa opened the door and looked over her shoulder at Laurie. "What?"

The words froze in Laurie's throat. Anna hadn't been there. It didn't matter what Vanessa said to Nick, facts were facts. "Nothing. I think you should talk to him soon."

"I will. Maybe even tonight."

Vanessa closed the door, and Laurie glanced back to make sure Tim was buckled in. Then she backed out of the parking space and took off down the county road as if the entire police force were after her.

"What are you trying to do, Ma, try out for the Indy 500?"

Laurie glanced at the speedometer. "Good grief." She lifted her foot from the pedal and the minivan slowed by about thirty miles an hour.

"Good thing Nick isn't around," her son informed her. "He'd have got you for that."

With an effort, she relaxed her grip on the wheel and tried to slow her heart rate, too. "Thanks, sweetie. I needed the reminder."

"I shouldn't have said anything." Tim's eyes crinkled with mischief behind his shaggy skater-boy hair. "I want to see Nick give you a ticket."

"Just remember, what goes around comes around. When you get your license, Nick won't cut you any breaks just because you're family."

Her mouth said mom things while her mind galloped down the road like a frightened horse, trying to outrun its shadow.

Not Anna. Not Anna. She was at home in bed. Everything is all right. Vanessa couldn't see clearly. Couldn't see who pushed, couldn't see who fell, couldn't see who was running under the bridge.

We're okay. We're okay.

"Mom, you're going to miss the turn."

Instinctively she spun the wheel and made the right turn to the high school with no signal and just inches to spare. Behind her, someone honked in irritation and drove through with a rev of his engine.

Get a grip.

They pulled into the parking lot at a sedate ten miles per hour and merged into the line where the kids congregated while they waited for buses and parents. Anna waved good-bye to Kelci Platt and Rose Silverstein and climbed into the front seat.

Kelci was there that night.

Laurie resisted the urge to collar the girl and ask her whether it was true Anna had been there, too. But that was ridiculous. Vanessa had simply seen another teenager with shoulder-length dark hair and made a mistake.

But the problem with mistakes was that once you took them to the police, they weren't treated as mistakes anymore. They were treated as legitimate possibilities until proven otherwise.

Laurie unbuckled her seat belt and tossed it to the side. "Stay here." Both kids looked mystified as she got out of the minivan and crossed the sidewalk to where Kelci waited, presumably for Vanessa.

"Kelci, can I talk to you for a second?"

The girl looked uncomfortable, as if being seen talking to somebody's mother was a social faux pas on the same level as walking down the hall with toilet paper stuck to your shoe.

"Um, sure."

"I hear you were on the bridge last Wednesday night."

Something behind Kelci's chocolate-brown eyes flickered closed, like the shutter on a camera. "Where'd you hear that?"

"It doesn't matter. What you do is your mom's business, not mine. But I need to know something."

"I don't want to talk about that night, Mrs. Hale." Kelci slid one step sideways, as if she were getting ready to duck and run. "Here comes my ride."

"I just need you to tell me if Anna was there too."

A silky black eyebrow rose as Kelci glanced from Anna in the backseat of the minivan, looking mortified, to Laurie. "Why don't you ask her?"

"I already have. I want to hear it from you."

"Naw, she wasn't there."

Your sister says different. But Laurie bit back the words. If Vanessa was going to the police, the fewer people who knew she'd been talking to the older girl, the better. Besides, this was exactly what Laurie wanted to hear. She should be glad.

"Thanks, sweetie. I appreciate your being candid with me."

"No problem, Mrs. Hale." *Time for you to go back on your meds, Mrs. Hale,* her tone said. As soon as Vanessa pulled up in the Camry, Kelci hopped into the car and locked the door.

When she got back in the van, Anna leaned sideways against the restraint of her seat belt, watching Vanessa pull away. "What's up, Mom? What were you asking Kelci?"

Laurie put the van into reverse and didn't answer until they were on the road. "I was just doing a little fact-checking, that's all."

"About what?"

Laurie had nothing to hide. Anna would call Kelci as soon as she got home, anyway. "I just heard some confusing stories about what happened on the bridge the other night. I asked Kelci what happened and she told me. No biggie."

"You asked her what happened? Why, was she there?"

Laurie glanced at her daughter in the rearview mirror. "I think you know she was."

"Why do you say that? I wasn't there. How should I know?"

"I assume you guys talk."

Anna snorted. "Not about this."

"Why not?"

But Anna didn't answer. Laurie glanced at her and saw that she was staring through the front window, her face as rigid as bone.

"Mom, don't go home this way."

"We go home this way every day. What's the matter?"

"Don't. Not anymore. Go through downtown, okay?"

They were approaching the bridge, with one traffic light to go. "Anna, don't be silly. That's two or three extra miles. Why would I want to do that?"

"Mom, I'm asking you. Please don't go over the bridge. I just can't."

"Why?" The light turned green.

"Mom!" Anna's cry was the sound of a baby bird, shrieking in terror as the predator pounces.

For the second time that afternoon, Laurie spun the wheel and made a right turn, which took them down the road behind the Stop-N-Go and along the river to the next bridge in the middle of town.

"Anna Catherine Hale, stop it. There is no reason for you to be scared of that bridge. Yes, a tragedy happened there. But nothing is going to happen to you."

Silence. Laurie glanced to her right as they drove past the shops and businesses of downtown Glendale. Anna's slender body shook as she tried to hold in the sobs. Tears streaked her cheeks.

"Did you hear me, sweetie? Are you all right?"

But Anna buried her face in the sleeve of her coat and didn't answer.

"Anna, please. It's just a bridge. There are no ghosts there. Nothing to be afraid of."

"That's what y—you think."

"What does that mean?"

Silence, except for a sniffle.

"Anna, what's going on here that I don't know about?"

But Anna turned her face away to look out the window, and no amount of cajoling or threatening would make her explain what she meant.

Chapter Eight

Cammie picked up Tanya and brought her to Bible study the next morning, and Laurie ticked off another item on her mental "Taking Care of Tanya" list. It had enough items on it to cover the rest of the week. After that, they'd regroup and see if Tanya still needed them as much.

Normally, Laurie would have loved being needed like this. She'd always considered it a form of creativity to try to make life better for other people. But lately the needs of other people were becoming a burden and a distraction—all she wanted to do was focus on the needs of her daughter.

Was that a bad thing? That was normal, wasn't it—to want to dig down and find what was hurting your child so you could remove the thorn from her flesh and help her heal? Laurie had come to Bible study this morning hoping to find just that kind of help. Not just in a spiritual sense, either, but in a very practical, natural sense.

Janice Edgar held the key.

After the study of their psalm ("Maybe we can skip ahead to something joyful, for Tanya's sake," Maggie had suggested), Laurie cornered Janice in the hallway while they waited for Debbie to come out of the old house's only bathroom.

With her toe, Laurie tucked a patchwork door dog against the door as she spoke. "I meant to call you after we talked on Tuesday, but things have been a little crazy."

Janice smiled. Was this the politician's wife smile, Laurie wondered, or a real one? She couldn't tell.

"I know what you mean. It was my night to be with Tanya last night, so I wouldn't have been home anyway. I was glad for the chance to get to know her a little better."

Laurie tried to imagine Janice, perfectly groomed and wearing tasteful slacks that would probably scream if they ever saw a speck of lint or pet fur, getting chummy with Tanya in her awful little apartment.

"I wanted to talk with you about the night Randi was killed."

Janice stared at her. "Why?"

"I need to get some facts straight. Do you have any plans for lunch?"

"Well, no, but I should—"

"Great!" The bathroom door opened and Debbie came out. "How about going to the Split Rail? Can I meet you there?"

"Well, okay, but—"

Laurie slipped into the bathroom and closed the door, and when she came out, Janice's car was gone. It took five minutes to drive over to the Split Rail, an old-fashioned diner with aluminum trim, a flashing red neon sign, and a miniature jukebox at each table. It was homey and welcoming and lent itself to long conversations—perfect for her purposes. She found Janice at a table by the big center window (who had to move when the mayor's wife asked for it?) and slid in opposite her.

Janice ordered a Cobb salad and Laurie chose a Monte Cristo sandwich, ordering coleslaw on the side at the last minute instead of fries. When the waitress left, Janice looked her in the eye.

"All right. Spill it. What is it you want to know?"

There was no use in playing dumb. That wasn't Laurie's style. "I'm scared stiff that Anna is involved somehow in what happened on the bridge," she blurted. "I want you to tell me it's ridiculous and that of course she wasn't there."

Janice sipped her hot tea and regarded Laurie over the rim of the cup. "I wish I could make you feel better, but I'm in exactly the same boat. The only problem is, I know for certain Kyle was there."

Laurie tried to keep her jaw from dropping. "How?"

Janice put her cup down, and a little of the liquid slopped over the side into the saucer. "Because half a dozen kids were only too happy to tell the sheriff's office that the mayor's son was up on that bridge. I hate that our family is in the spotlight all the time, no matter what we do. If he'd been the son of just about anyone else, no one would have even seen him, much less cared."

"Oh." Their food arrived, and Laurie gathered her wits while she poked at her coleslaw. How could she put this delicately? "Did you know he was out that night?"

Janice made a sound that Laurie was sure was not part of the etiquette manual for mayors' wives. "Of course not. Like a total idiot, I told the sheriff's deputies that my darling boy was tucked up in bed and couldn't possibly have been involved. Only to have my ignorance and lousy mothering skills exposed for everyone to see when the real story came out." Another glance shot across the table like a laser. "You have no idea how difficult my life is right now. Going over to Tanya's last night was a huge relief. She didn't ask ridiculous questions, and her phone didn't ring once."

Laurie bit into her sandwich to avoid saying something really stupid, such as, "No one calls Tanya except for us, do they?"

When she could speak, she said, "I hope this doesn't sound ridiculous, then, but did Kyle happen to mention whether Anna was there?"

"He says not, but I've since heard from at least two sources that she was."

Auto reflex kicked in. "She was at home, in bed."

Janice's lashes lifted. "Famous last words. Do you believe that?"

"Of course. I was there. We watched TV together and then she went up to her room."

"She could have gone out after that."

"You've been to our house. The living room has a direct view of the front door. And the back door squeaks, so we'd have heard it if she'd gone out that way."

Janice dropped her gaze and bit into a cherry tomato. "There are more ways of getting out of a house than through its doors, I've discovered."

"What, are you suggesting she could go out a window?" She and Colin hadn't raised a cat burglar, for Pete's sake. And they hadn't raised a girl who would deceive her parents by sneaking out late at night, either. "Why on earth would she do that?"

Janice nibbled a spinach leaf before she answered. "I think Kyle has a girlfriend."

It took her a second to catch up. "Anna did not sneak out to see a boy. And even if she did, why would she be on the bridge?"

The other woman shrugged. "Who knows why teenagers do the things they do? But Kyle's room is on the ground floor. Getting out is obviously so simple that both his parents and his sister have been blissfully unaware of it all this time."

"All what time? How long do you think this has been going on?"

She shrugged. "A couple of months, maybe. Not because I've been hearing strange sounds at night, but because he's been so dozy in the mornings. And distracted. And irritable."

"Anna is all those things, too. I read in a magazine at work about how much sleep teenagers need, and how few of them actually get it. Anyway, she doesn't have a boyfriend. She's just that way because she's fourteen."

"That you know of."

Laurie shook her head. "She doesn't. I know where she is practically every minute. And when I don't, I call her cell and find out."

"Mm."

Laurie didn't like the sound of that noncommittal little noise. "I trust her." She hoped she sounded as positive as she'd once felt. But ever since last Wednesday, doubt had been nibbling at the edges of her confidence. She could deal with nibbles. It was the big bites of uncertainty she was afraid of.

"I trusted Kyle, too. Now it's more difficult. Every time he opens his mouth, I'm looking for corroborating evidence."

"You sound like Nick."

"I'm more familiar with him than I ever want to be." She glanced up. "No offense."

"None taken."

"But I have to tell you, Laurie—he says that at least two of the kids who were there that night are insisting Anna was in that crowd."

Laurie shook her head. "Of course they'd say that, for the same reason they say Kyle was there. Anna is a bigger target. She's a Hale. There are people in this town who would love to see us discredited over something like this."

"But in the case of Kyle, they're right. He admitted everything to us while Nick was at the house. And if these kids were right about him, they could be right about Anna. You just don't know it yet."

Laurie shook her head. "Nope."

"I wish I had the luxury of certainty." Janice finished her salad and glanced up for the waitress.

Laurie still had half a sandwich. She looked down at her plate, at the crisp, hot batter and melted cheese. The thought of taking one more bite made her feel sick, and she pushed her plate away.

All the way home, she fought with herself. She needed to trust her daughter. Sure, Anna was going through a rough patch, and she struggled with all the things teenagers struggle with— being cool versus making her parents happy and getting good grades, learning that fine line between independence and disobedience, finding her own style without offending her mother's sense of modesty.

But despite all this, she was fundamentally a good kid. And good kids didn't sneak out of bedroom windows late at night.

Laurie managed to hang on to her confidence as she pulled into the garage and shut off the minivan's engine. When she stepped into the house, the familiar smell—a mixture of furniture polish, laundry, and firewood—was like a balm. It was the smell of normalcy, of a happy family without—*thank you, Lord*—major problems.

She hung up her coat and toed off her shoes by the door, then padded upstairs and into the master bedroom, stopping by the bed. What had she come up here for? There were a zillion things to do downstairs, like looking through the mail, doing the laundry, cleaning up the breakfast dishes, picking up the living room.

The silence breathed, suggesting she act while she had the house to herself. *Go look at the window. Just to see.*

No, she couldn't do that. That was as good as saying she didn't trust Anna's word.

Yes, she could. She needed to make sure that Anna was where she said she'd been, and that she couldn't have been on the bridge or under it or anywhere near it. She needed to close any loopholes for the gossips in this town.

She marched down the hall, her stocking feet quiet on the runner that covered the hardwood. Anna's door was closed, as usual, but she pushed it open and walked straight over to the window.

The sash didn't stick at all, which was the first thing she noticed.

The second thing she noticed was the fact that Anna's window looked out on the roof over the garage. The distance between the sill and the roof was just two or three feet. So swinging your legs out and stepping onto the shingles would be easy.

Okay, but getting down off the roof is the hard part. The impossible part, I would say.

Just to be sure, she headed downstairs again, grabbed her coat, and jammed her feet into her shoes. She went through the garage and out the side door onto the lawn.

"No way."

Talking to yourself was a sign of impending dementia. But maybe she was talking to Janice. Or Anna. Or God.

On one side of the garage door stood the clematis trellis—and it was made of wrought iron. No flimsy wood pickets for Colin. He'd brought the trellis home from the store last fall when she'd talked about training a clematis vine over the door. When Colin installed something, he did it right. A platoon of marines could go up and down that trellis, and it wouldn't even quiver.

Closer inspection of the base of the trellis revealed a deep footprint in earth that had thawed and then frozen again. A footprint that Laurie would bet was a size five. She took a couple of steps backward and traced the escape route out the window, over the roof, and down the trellis. Thirty seconds, tops. And in sneakers a person could be both fast and quiet.

The cold seeped through her feet and hands, washing down into the collar of her coat, sinking through her skin and into her heart. It wasn't possible that Anna could have lied to them all. It wasn't possible that she had raised a daughter who was so good at deceit.

And it really wasn't possible that Vanessa was right, that Anna really had been among those kids on the bridge. That Anna could have stood by and done nothing while someone pushed Randi Peizer to her death.

Hot tears of denial and grief welled into Laurie's eyes. Their Anna was no coward. Vanessa had said she was off in the trees, too far away to save Randi from going over. But what about before that? Couldn't she have come to Randi's defense somehow? Could she have stepped up to defuse a situation that was clearly getting out of control?

What kind of a child had she raised? She and Colin had taught the kids that you put others before yourself, that you show people the love of God in your life. Had they failed where Anna was concerned?

No, she couldn't believe that. She knew her daughter. Anna would never have let Randi get herself into such danger if she could help it. The softhearted, loving girl she and Colin had raised wouldn't lie and deceive and put her family in jeopardy like this.

And yet . . . Laurie looked down at that footprint, frozen into the earth. Waiting for someone to notice its silent contradiction of everything she wanted to believe.

Nick informed the dispatcher over the radio that he would be out of service for the next hour and pulled into the parking lot of the Split Rail. He came here because the service was fast—his only requirement in a restaurant.

He always sat at the same booth by the window, with his back to the wall that backed onto the men's room, near the cashier. As a result, he always had the same waitress, a girl named Vanessa who never seemed to wear her hair the same way twice. Tonight she'd put it into cornrows and wrapped all the little braids into a ponytail with a scarf.

"Hey, Vanessa. I'll have the usual."

He didn't bother to look at the menu. She didn't bother to write down his order. But instead of pouring his coffee and sashaying back to the kitchen the way she usually did, she hesitated at his elbow.

"Can I help you?"

She was frowning, as though she didn't want to say something, yet felt compelled to. He'd interviewed many a witness with the same look.

"Yeah." She glanced in the direction of the cashier, who doubled as hostess and manager. "I get my break in twenty minutes. Can I talk to you then?"

"Sure. I'll eat slowly."

She made sure he did. His Reuben took about ten minutes longer to arrive than usual, but when she brought it, Vanessa also carried two slices of blueberry pie.

"You going to eat both of those?" He never ordered dessert. There wasn't time. But it sure looked good.

"No. One's for you." She pushed it across to him. "It's on me."

"So." When she hadn't said anything after three bites of pie, he spoke up. "What's going on?"

"Mrs. Hale says you're investigating how that girl died. The one she found in the river."

"That's right."

"If I tell you something, will you get me and my family in trouble?" Her gaze was an uneasy cross between distrust and pleading. "Mrs. Hale said I should come to you, but it don't mean nothing to me. I can go either way."

"Have you or a member of your family done something they want to hide?" he asked gently.

She shook her head, and the scarf slid off her ponytail and onto the seat beside her. She didn't notice. "But I saw something, and Mrs. Hale said you should know. I want your word you won't get anybody in trouble."

"If someone did do something wrong, it's my job to see they pay for it," he said, "but if no one did anything, it should be okay. What did you see?"

In a low voice that hurried like a current rushing with winter rain, she told him what she'd seen at twenty past ten last Wednesday night. Halfway through, he pushed his unfinished sandwich to one side, pulled his notebook out of his pocket, and began to take notes in his peculiar shorthand.

"You distinctly saw someone push her over the rail?"

She nodded. "It was dark, but from the parking lot of the Stop-N-Go you can see the bridge."

"But you couldn't see who it was."

"No. Just that she was tall."

"She? You think it was a girl?"

Vanessa frowned and poked at the crust of her pie. "I had the impression it was a girl. The way she pushed. It wasn't how guys do it, like they're poking at you to bug you or make you respond. This was a 'Get away from me' push. Or maybe 'You're not good enough to get near me.' Like that. And over she went."

Which fit the evidence exactly.

"Did you see her hit anything on the way down?"

"No. The streetlights don't shine under there. Well, unless you mean the water. There was this big splash, and then Anna Hale went running past my car like a bat out of you-know-where."

"Anna?" *Never mind, just go with it.* "Running from where to where?"

"She was on the grass, you know, where it slopes down to the water. She came out of the trees and ran under the bridge, and after that I didn't see what happened."

The Reuben turned over in his stomach. "Anna Hale. You're sure."

She gave him one of those "I'm not stupid, Stupid" looks. "I've known Anna Hale since she was a bitty baby. I babysat her. I know what that girl looks like. I know how she looks when she runs the hundred-yard dash, the way her arms go, like this." She demonstrated. "It was her running under the bridge."

"Do you think she meant to help the girl who fell?"

Vanessa shrugged. "Don't know. I pulled out and got my sister and we beat it home before I had to go pick up Mama."

He put his notebook down and picked up the second half of his sandwich. "I appreciate you coming to talk to me, Vanessa. You've been a huge help."

"Are you going to get Kelci in trouble for being there?"

"No," he said around a bite that had lost its flavor. "But I wouldn't mind talking to her again. If she was close enough to see who did the pushing, I'd be real interested in knowing who it was."

"You already talked to her."

"Yes, but she omitted a couple of important facts." As had everyone on his mental list.

"Mama probably won't be too happy about you coming back. She about blew a gasket the last time. Kelci got grounded just for giving the police more work."

"Kelci has nothing to worry about as long as she tells me the truth. I'll come by after school tomorrow, okay?"

"Mama will be at work. She ain't gonna like you being there without her there too."

"Then how about I meet the two of you here tomorrow in the parking lot? Your mama won't mind so much if you're here. I only have a couple of questions, but I don't want Kelci catching any heat from her classmates about it."

She was starting to look a little cornered.

"Vanessa, this is important. If Kelci knows who pushed that girl, then she needs to come forward and tell me. We have to do something about it."

"You think that girl meant to kill the other girl?"

"The victim's name was Randi. Randi Peizer. And I can't answer that right now. But I hope Kelci and her friends can help."

But before he talked to Kelci, he was going to have a little talk with Anna Hale. Kyle Edgar and one or two of the others had been very firm that she hadn't been there that night. Vanessa had been equally firm that she had. Someone was lying, and he could no longer afford to make stupid assumptions about whose word weighed more. Kyle, the mayor's son? Vanessa, the waitress? He didn't care anymore.

The only thing he cared about was Randi, and finding out the truth. Because her mother's eyes haunted him. If he could do anything to dispel the darkness he saw there, he would.

For the sake of justice.

The sweetness of the blueberry pie was only a memory by the time he pulled up outside Colin and Laurie's house in the older part of Glendale. Someday he'd have a house like this, with pointed gables and stonework as solid as the love inside. He wasn't an envious kind of guy, but you'd have to be a saint not to want something like this for yourself. Of course, on a deputy sheriff's salary, either it would take twenty years to get there, or he'd have to get in the habit of buying lottery tickets.

Tim answered the door, and his face broke into a huge grin. "Nick!" He craned to look around him, then pushed past. "Did you bring the cop car? Can I work the siren?"

Nick grabbed the kid's sweatshirt just in time. "Not tonight, buddy. Rumor has it there's a noise bylaw around here, and if you turned it on I'd have to arrest you."

"Aw, come on, Nick. Just once. I'll just make it go *whoop* and turn it off."

"Nope. Sorry. Your folks home?"

"Yeah. Mom!" he hollered in the direction of the living room as Nick stepped inside. "Nick's here."

For just a split second, he saw the same terror in Laurie's eyes that he'd seen in the eyes of the mayor's wife the other night. The expression of a woman about to get bad news, and determined to do everything she could to stave it off.

"Nick, what a surprise," she said, and gave him a hug, the same as she always did. She was the closest thing he had to a sister, and he always associated the scent of vanilla and clean laundry with her. Her shoulders were stiff, though, and her hug a little looser, less committed, than usual.

"Hey, Lor." He braced himself to say what had to be said. "Is Anna around?"

The rosy color faded out of her cheeks. "Anna? You already talked to her. She didn't know anything. Besides, she's doing her homework."

"I know. But something has come up, and I just need to ask her about it."

They stood in the warm entry hall. He waited for her to invite him into the living room, the way she had the other night, but she didn't. Instead, she swallowed and took a deep breath.

"I talked to Vanessa Platt this afternoon," she said.

Uh-huh. The neurons in his brain lined up and fired. "Did you tell her to talk to me?"

"Yes. Was that a mistake?"

"No. You did the right thing. Look, Lor, don't panic about this. And don't look like that, you're killing me." He took her hand, which was icy cold.

"Look like what?" Colin came out of the living room, where the TV laughed at its own joke, and now the three of them stood in an uneasy triangle the way strangers did at a cocktail party. Not like family at all.

Colin took one look at his wife's face and turned toward Nick. "What's going on?"

Just jump on in. "I talked to Vanessa Platt tonight at the Split Rail. She says she saw Anna near the bridge when Randi Peizer went into the water. And that Anna ran under the bridge right afterward."

"Anna was asleep in—" Colin began.

"I just need to confirm that. Because even though you believe she was at home and asleep, at least two people place her at the bridge at the time of Randi's death. With this new information, she could be one of the last people to see Randi alive. I need to find out what she did or saw under that bridge."

"What do you mean, *did?*" Laurie's tone was sharp with fear. "What are you saying?"

"Nothing more than that. Did she see Randi alive, did she try to pull her out, did she—"

"She wasn't even there," Laurie hissed. "Come on. We'll go ask her."

She turned on the ball of her foot and marched up the stairs. "Anna?" With Colin on his heels, Nick followed her up in time to see her push Anna's bedroom door open. She leaned in, flipped on the light, and paused. "She must be in the bathroom." It was at the end of the hall, and even Nick could see that the door stood open on an empty room. "Tim, is she in there with you?" she called against his bedroom door.

"No girls allowed!" came the muffled reply.

"Mothers are always allowed." Laurie did a quick visual check over her son's protests, then closed the door and went back into Anna's room. "Anna!"

Silence.

Nick realized Colin was no longer behind him. In a moment he reappeared at the bottom of the stairs. "She's not down here."

"Did you check in the laundry room?"

"Why would she be in there?"

"If the perfect outfit isn't perfectly clean, she has a meltdown. She knows how to work the washing machine. She's probably ironing something." Laurie clattered down the stairs. "Anna?"

But she wasn't in the laundry room. Or in the garage, the attic, or the backyard.

Nick, Laurie, and Colin met up back in the entryway. Now his cousin wasn't just pale. Her face was blanched to the color of old linen sheets.

"Houston, we have a problem," somebody on the television said, and the laugh track cackled mindlessly, over and over.

Chapter Nine

Laurie sat in the dark in the reading chair in Anna's bedroom. She'd wrapped a blanket around herself, not because the room was cold, but because her body wouldn't quit shaking. Little tremors started in her gut and tiptoed out to her fingers and toes. Big tremors shook her shoulders like a sob . . . but no tears would come.

Not yet.

The cell phone in her right hand had become slick with perspiration. Colin and Nick had both taken their cars and divided up Glendale in an organized search, but Tim couldn't be left on his own in the house, so she'd stayed behind. She felt like an assassin, waiting in the dark for her target to show up.

The noise in her head filled the silence as scenarios of what might be happening even as she sat there flickered on the screen of her imagination. Anna walking the darkened streets of Glendale. Anna being followed by a dark shape, with no one around to help.

No, even in her imagination, she had to be honest.

What she really saw was Anna running under that bridge. Randi, falling, falling . . . Anna in court, testifying about how she tried to save her and couldn't. Or didn't try. What had happened under there? Had she been the last person to see Randi alive, or not? Was Nick going to have to arrest his own cousin? Did they put fourteen-year-olds in jail?

She would not cry. She would not let those horrible doubts she'd had earlier, as she'd stood and gazed at that frozen footprint, attack her. She would not sit here and dissolve into a gibbering wreck.

When Anna climbed back in that window, she'd find her mother cool, calm, and immovable—because no reason in the world would justify behavior like this. No explanation would be good enough. And no punishment harsh enough. Maybe Laurie could threaten her with being sent away to some kind of boot camp. They had those, didn't they? Maybe then she'd—

In the silence, the thrum of the trellis against the wall was more a vibration under her feet than an actual sound. No wonder the whole family had been clueless. Anna moved as quietly as a stalking cat.

How was it possible she had raised a girl with skills like that?

A shadow moved in front of the glass, and then the window slid up and her daughter's slender form slipped through and dropped soundlessly to the hardwood.

Laurie pressed a button on the cell phone. The twitter of the little unit dialing out stopped Anna dead in the middle of the floor.

When Colin answered, his voice tight with anxiety, Laurie said quietly, "She's home. Let Nick know, okay?"

"Thank you, Father," he breathed. "See you in a few minutes."

Laurie disconnected, then reached over and switched on the lamp on the nightstand.

Anna's eyes widened and her breath came in pants as she recovered from her fright. Well, Laurie could tell her a thing or two about being frightened. She'd learned whole chapters from *that* textbook tonight.

Without a word, Anna took off her ski jacket and her shoes, and unwound her scarf from around her neck. So she was going to play it cool, was she? Laurie allowed her a few more seconds to speak, but she stayed as stubbornly silent as she had been all along.

The time for silence was over. "I'm waiting," Laurie said at last.

"For what?"

"Don't play stupid with me. I am in no mood. Sit down and spill it."

She sat. "I just went for a walk."

"Most people go out the front door. Maybe they even say, 'Hey, Mom, I'm going for a walk.' Maybe they care enough about their parents' feelings to let them know when they're going out. Do you know your dad and Nick have been driving around for an hour looking for you?"

"Sorry."

"Not good enough. Tell me why you feel you need to deceive us and sneak out of the house."

"I was scared."

Laurie stared at her. "Of what?"

Anna twisted the fringed end of the scarf between her fingers. "Of Nick."

It took Laurie a second to confirm that she really had heard what she thought she'd heard. "You're scared of your cousin? Can I ask why?"

"Not Nick my cousin. Nick the cop."

"Anna, he's been a cop your whole life. And now you're suddenly scared of him? He loves you to pieces. You have nothing to be afraid of."

"Yes, I do."

Okay, she was going to do this the hard way, one word at a time. "Why?"

"He keeps coming over. One of these times he's going to arrest me. So when I heard him come in, I went for a walk until I thought he'd be gone."

Laurie tried to tamp down the whirlwind of fear and guilt and speculation tearing her up inside. "Well, when he comes back with your dad you'll see he's not going to arrest you, not now and not anytime soon. You haven't broken any laws other than lying to a police officer. It's rules you've broken, and you can bet your dad and I will have something to say about that."

"He's coming back?" That bottomless look returned to her eyes, that look that said she was about to abandon all hope. "Tonight?"

"Who, Nick? Yes, of course. He wants to make sure you're okay."

"That's not what he came over for in the first place, though, is it? He wanted to talk to me, didn't he?"

"He had a couple more questions, but—"

"No." She looked around wildly, and Laurie got out of the chair and went to sit on the windowsill, just in case she got any ideas.

"Anna, what is going on? You have to tell me what's wrong."

"I don't want to talk to him." Her daughter toed off her shoes and, fully clothed, burrowed under her quilt. "He'll make me go to jail."

"Of course he won't." Laurie sat on the edge of the bed and tried to hug her daughter's folded-up body. "He talked to some people who said they saw you by the bridge that night, and he wants the straight story. You may as well come clean. I know tonight's not the first time you've snuck out on us. Did you go out that night, too?"

"No."

Disappointment crashed through Laurie's chest at this new lie. Why did she persist in doing it? Was it some kind of mental break brought on by trauma?

Most serious of all, how were they going to get her to stop lying and convince her it was safe to tell the truth?

"Anna. We know you did. Give it to me straight, okay?"

"It was an accident."

A cold shadow moved across Laurie's heart, and fresh panic fluttered under her breastbone. "What was?"

"We weren't even supposed to go to the stupid bridge. I'm never going there again. Ever."

Wait a minute. "We? Who?" *Kelci? Kate? Rose?*

Mumble.

"What was that? I didn't hear you."

"Me and my boyfriend."

The mental tumblers spun in Laurie's brain and clicked into place. "You're sneaking out to see Kyle Edgar."

Anna threw back the covers and pushed herself upright. "You said I couldn't date until I was fifteen."

"Obviously with good reason," Laurie said with an admirable impression of calm.

"But we never get to see each other except at school, and hardly ever there because Rose is always hanging all over him, but he doesn't care about her. She's always with Kate, and Kate's going out with Brendan, and Brendan and Kyle are tight, and—"

"And you're left out. So you see each other at night. Anna, did it ever occur to you that you could just invite him over here like a normal person? And do homework and sit around and watch TV?"

She looked at her a little doubtfully. "You'd let him do that?"

"Why on earth not?" Did she think Colin was going to stand on the doorstep with a rifle and use Kyle for target practice? "That's not a date. That's having your friend over."

"But . . . you and his mom hate each other."

Laurie's mouth dropped open. "What?"

"That's what Brendan said his mom told him. She said that you thought Mrs. Edgar was a social climber, and you were all bent out of shape because at fund-raisers and stuff, the TV people wanted to talk to her when you were in the back doing all the work."

"Oh, for heaven's sake. Brendan O'Day needs to button his lip. Kyle's mom and I are in the same Bible study group. We had lunch together just today."

Had it only been today? It felt like it had happened in another life. Before the doubts set in, chewing at her and jeopardizing her ability to trust her own child. Before the guilt followed like sticky tar on her conscience, darkening her perceptions and spoiling what she believed in.

"But put all that aside for a second. I want you to back up and tell me what you meant when you said it was an accident."

The animation drained out of Anna's face. "I meant we met them by accident. Kate and them. Kyle and I were just walking on the river path, and we bumped into them by the store."

Was that really what she'd meant? "And then?"

"And then we sort of got sucked into their group. It makes me so mad. Like they don't spend all their time at school doing that."

Laurie took a breath to tell her to quit stalling, when she heard the front door open.

"Laurie?" Colin called. "Anna, are you okay?"

She pulled the quilt away and tugged on Anna's hand. "Come on. You should tell your story to Nick."

Once again that strange, bottomless look was back. "Do I have to?"

"He just needs information, that's all. It'll be okay."

But even as she spoke, she wondered if the words were really true.

Anna's resistance was as heavy as an anchor dragging the ocean floor as she followed Laurie down the stairs and into the living room. Whatever she might have expected from her dad, it wasn't being pulled into his arms for a breath-squeezing hug.

"Please, baby, don't ever do that again. You scared ten years off me."

"I'm sorry, Daddy," she said against his chest.

Was Laurie the only one who noticed the absence of what should have come next: "I'll never do it again"? Is this what she had to look forward to? Weighing and testing every single word Anna said from now until who knew when?

Anna curled into the corner of the couch farthest from everyone, and pulled one of the cushions into her lap.

"So, Anna," Nick began in his gentlest tone. "I take it that we've established you were at the bridge on the night Randi Peizer died. Right?"

"Right," she said in a small voice. "I was afraid."

There was that word again. Laurie frowned. Afraid of what? Of the consequences of lying? Of Nick arresting her? Or was there something else?

"Never be afraid to tell the truth," Nick said gently. "Especially not to me." When she didn't reply, he went on. "I understand that you were in the park by the Stop-N-Go when she actually fell. Did you see who pushed her?"

"Nobody pushed her."

"Are you sure about that? Because the evidence the coroner's investigator found suggests otherwise."

"I don't know. I didn't see."

"What were you doing on the lawn?" Laurie wanted to know. If everyone else was up on the bridge, what was Anna doing off by herself?

"I was with Kyle. Talking. Under the trees."

"Kate Parsons said you were talking to Randi there. You and another girl. Who was that?"

Anna shrugged. "She's making that up. I was with Kyle. We were walking on the river path, and when Kate and the others came we all went to the Stop-N-Go to get a soda. Then Kyle and I took off. They all went up on the bridge and we stayed on the grass."

"Talking. By yourselves."

"Yes." She looked at Nick a little defiantly, as if daring him to contradict her.

"So while you were down on the grass, something happened up on the bridge. Can you tell me about that?"

"There was a big splash."

"And then what?"

Anna frowned. "I don't know."

"Let me help you out," Nick said. "According to my information, you came running down the grass at top speed and went under the bridge. What did you do under there?"

"No, I didn't." She looked honestly confused.

"I have a witness who says you did. Could you see Randi in the water?"

Anna shook her head, as if to dislodge something in her ear. "I didn't."

"Anna, sweetie, this is no time to play dumb," Colin said. "It's important to Nick's investigation that you just tell him the truth."

"I am telling the truth." She looked from her father to her cousin. "I don't remember being under the bridge at all."

"You must remember," Laurie said. "Come on. Think."

Her daughter's lower lip began to tremble. "I don't know. Randi came up to us at the Stop-N-Go and tried to be all nice like she was a member of the group—which she wasn't—and Kate said, 'Sure, how about you buy me a latte and we can talk,' and they all walked up on the bridge. Kyle and me, well, we wanted to be alone so we walked down under the trees, and then after a while I heard somebody scream and there was a splash, and after that I was so scared I ran away and came home."

"Anna—"

"I'm not playing dumb, Mom." Tears filled her eyes. "You have to believe me."

Laurie looked into her husband's eyes, where the distress and confusion probably mirrored her own.

"Anna," Nick said very gently. "I have a witness who says you ran under that bridge, not away from it. She saw you. Now please think carefully and tell me again what happened."

The tears trickled down Anna's cheeks. "You want to take me to jail," she accused him. "You want me to say I did something bad."

"That's not true. I just need to have all the facts on the table, and the reason you went under there is very important."

"I didn't!" Anna's voice began to escalate. "I didn't!" Tears streaked her cheeks and she grabbed another cushion, clutching it the way she'd held Laurie when she was a small child.

She's not reaching out for me now. The loss of yet another piece of Anna's childhood, of her innocence, slid under Laurie's heart like a blade between the ribs.

Colin rubbed a hand over his face. "Nick, maybe you should come back tomorrow." He glanced at the clock. "Anna's not in any shape for more questions, and she has to get up and go to school."

For the first time in Laurie's memory, Nick's face, which was usually lit with sardonic humor, looked lined and pale. "Okay. I'll come back. Maybe you can emphasize to her how important this is. Nobody's accusing her of anything. I just need her help in establishing where everyone was and the order of events."

Colin nodded and moved to take Anna in his arms. But instead of going to him as she had just a few minutes ago, Anna turned her body into the corner of the couch and curled tightly around the pillows.

Laurie saw the moment when the hurt struck him, too.

As she saw Nick to the door, Colin slid his arms under his daughter's body and carried her upstairs in the direction of her room. When he came down again, his steps were as slow as if he still carried the burden. He sank onto the couch with a sigh.

"I told her she was grounded," he said. "No cell phone, no privileges. Like that's going to help the situation. Still, we have to do something."

"Counseling," Laurie said.

"It's not counseling she needs, Laurie. It's assurance that she isn't in danger. I don't know where she gets the idea that Nick's going to arrest her."

"Guilt?"

The awful word popped out of Laurie's darkest fears like a bat out of a cave.

Colin lifted his head, his forehead furrowed. "What?"

"You have to admit that only the guilty are afraid of the law."

After a moment, Colin said, "Please tell me you don't really think Anna had anything to do with that girl's death."

"Of course not. But for heaven's sake, Colin, can we really trust anything she says? She lied about sneaking out at night and lied about having a boyfriend. How do we know she isn't lying right now? Vanessa Platt saw her run under that bridge."

"And you choose to believe Vanessa Platt over our own daughter? Laurie, think about what you're saying."

Elbows on knees, Laurie ran both hands through her hair. "I know. It was dark. Vanessa could have been wrong."

"How could you even think she was right?"

"I don't know. I don't know. All I see is that crowd tormenting Randi, and my girl off in the trees with her boyfriend."

"What—are you saying she should have gone up there and done something?"

Laurie lifted her gaze to her husband's face. "Wouldn't you? Haven't we taught her to help where she's needed? To be strong and do the right thing? Maybe she could have helped that poor girl, Colin."

"And maybe the mob mentality would have taken over and they'd have pushed her in, too." His tone turned harsh. "Get a grip, Laurie. The last thing we need is to blame her for what she didn't do, instead of trying to get her to say what she did do."

"I'm not blaming her. I'm torturing myself, trying to figure out why all the things we taught her aren't working."

Colin stood up abruptly. "Well, while you're torturing yourself, spare some time to figure out what we're going to do about this before Nick comes back."

To: Manga15@csm.net
From: kedgar254@hotmail.com

U OK? Heard 5-o on scanner.

To: kedgar254@hotmail.com
From: Manga15@csm.net

Nick was here again. I was so scared. He says someone saw me run under the bridge. I told them I didn't but they don't believe me. What if he comes back? Mom caught me coming in and now I'm grounded forever. No cell, no nothing. She said you could come over for dinner and stuff but that's down the drain now I guess. She doesn't hate your mom. Brendan is full of it. I need you.

Me

To: Manga15@csm.net
From: kedgar254@hotmail.com

Don't tell. You can't tell or you know what will happen. Say you have amnesia.

(((hug))).

How long is forever?

KE

Chapter Ten

*N*ick *had a* lot to be thankful for. He owned his own home, even if its single bedroom and pocket-size kitchen made his brothers roll their eyes. The fact was, it sat on an acre of trees and rhododendrons, and he'd have lived in a chicken coop without complaint as long as he had the land. He had good health and a job he loved on most days. And best of all, he had the occasional day off when the only thing on the agenda was puttering around the house, enjoying the slow process of renovation.

He had looked forward to today—had even gone to Susquanny Home Supply and bought a bathroom sink and vanity to replace the ancient unit that some previous owner had installed in the forties. He'd planned on sleeping in and then spending the rest of the day happily ripping things apart and putting them back together, with maybe a pizza afterward when the guys on day shift got off work.

Instead, he'd awakened at 6:00 a.m. with a brain as clear as a summer day, and couldn't go back to sleep. The sound of Anna's sobs echoed in his head, like a punishment for making her cry. So he'd cut through his two neighbors' backyards and slid down the grade to the river trail. Might as well get his two miles in and try to outrun the bad feelings of last night. It was cold enough to require a jacket and a knitted cap, and his breaths came in regular puffs of white condensation as he warmed up and his pace evened out.

The bridge loomed in the distance, black against a swollen gray sky that promised snow, and he forced himself not to think about it. He'd spent all his mental energy on it for days, and he needed a break. He thanked his lucky stars that the department could afford two detectives. Gil could cover today's shift and today's schedule of yet more interviews.

The river took a bend to the right, and he dragged his focus off the bridge just in time to avoid a sky-blue shape kneeling in the middle of the trail.

"Oops!" He dodged left, and she—it was a woman—keeled over, landing smack on her rear in the frosty leaves.

Oh, man. Recognition came with a shock. "Sorry, Ms. Peizer. I didn't even see you. Here, let me help you."

She brushed away his apologies and his hands and climbed to her feet. "Serves me right for blocking the path." She twisted out of the way of his attempts at help. "Honest, it's okay. No harm done."

He finally got the message and gave her a little space. "How are you?"

"I'm okay." A brown beech leaf, reduced by time to nothing more than veins, stuck to her palm and she brushed it away. "Better than the last time you saw me." Up at his childhood hideaway, when he'd told her what Forrest Christopher and Lisa Nguyen had found.

"I promise I have no bad news today."

"No good news, either, I suppose, or I would have heard." Her gaze took him in, and he found himself wishing his sweats dated from a little later than his days at the police academy, and that he'd picked a T-shirt without a grease stain down the front.

"Afraid not. Our other detective, Gil, works the case when

I have a day off. Like today. Even with a late night, I woke up at the usual time and couldn't go back to sleep, so here I am."

She nodded. "I know what you mean. Hot date?"

Was she just making conversation, or did she intend to be that personal? "No. Work. I can't remember the last time I had a hot date. Maybe last summer, when the temps hit a hundred and four. Remember that?"

As a change of subject it was clumsy, but she went along with it. "I wasn't here then, but I understand it can get pretty warm. I like it, though. In Ohio sometimes you can go for weeks without seeing the sun. Because of the ground fog, you know?"

Why were they talking about the weather? Then again, maybe it was better to talk about that than personal subjects he'd just as soon avoid.

"So, what are you doing out here? Early morning runner, like me?"

"Oh, no." She huffed a laugh. "Exercise makes me break out in hives. No, I was just . . ." Her voice trailed away as she looked out over the river. "I was, um . . . You'll think I'm dumb."

"Not likely." That was the last adjective he'd apply to this woman.

"I was just . . . looking. For anything of Randi's that might have washed up. You know. In the last week."

"Didn't the coroner give you all her things on Friday? It was all in the property closet, as far as I know."

"Oh, no. I mean, yes, he did. It was all nice and neat in a plastic bag. I just thought maybe she might have lost something here where I could see it."

"Well, if they didn't find anything on the sandbar with her, it's not very likely. The current moves pretty fast. Something like a scarf would get carried away, and a bracelet would just go to the bottom."

Her shoulders drooped a little, and he felt like a crumb for puncturing her hopes. "But what do I know? If you feel like company, I'll walk a little ways with you. I could use the cooldown."

For the second time in the few days he'd known her, that tiny, seedlike dimple flashed at the corner of her mouth and disappeared just as quickly. "Okay. At least I won't have to worry about getting mugged."

"Only if you have doughnuts on you."

He had hoped she might laugh, but she didn't. Instead, her gaze fell to the riverbank once more, searching.

In a quarter mile of meandering along the banks of the Susquanny, they found no trace of anything belonging to Randi. They found a sneaker with no laces, a couple of beer bottles, and a broken rack of ancient whitetail antlers, green with algae. They found they had a common love of summer over winter, of the Pittsburgh Penguins over the Columbus Blue Jackets ("I'm a sucker for the underdog," she confessed), and of prime rib over any other cut of the cow ("Not that I can afford it very often," he said, "I'd rather save the bucks to buy a sink").

Which led to a discussion of home renovations, which led to today's project, which led to him opening his mouth before his brain could stop him and inviting her over for a cup of coffee.

And then it was too late to unsay the words. He had no business getting social with the relative of a homicide victim. Granted, she wasn't a suspect, but at the same time he knew that contact any deeper than the business level was unethical until the case was officially closed.

He knew that. He knew it, and still he found himself helping her up the bank and through his two neighbors' laurel hedges and into his own backyard.

"Oh, how beautiful," she breathed. "Is all this really yours?"

From here, you couldn't see the road. You could almost pretend you were way out in the country, when in fact there were tract homes just across the street and then the backs of the downtown Glendale shops just beyond that.

"All point-nine-eight acres of it."

"You are so lucky," she said on a sigh. "The closest I get to having green things around me is tomato plants in pots on the balcony. And most of the time they die because I'm always at work."

"You're doing better than I am. I figured I'd go with what was already here and growing without my help."

"Black thumb?" she asked.

"I don't know. I've never tried to grow anything, even as a kid."

They were almost to the back door. "Try a little pot of herbs for your kitchen window, to start," she suggested. "Something you use in cooking, like basil or parsley."

"Something *you* might use in cooking." He held the door for her, and she stepped into the kitchen. "I don't think ketchup and mustard grow in pots." He'd make a pot of coffee, since he'd suggested it, and then he'd hustle her out of here and back to her own life, where they'd communicate with each other over a barrier of paperwork and protocol.

"Mustard does. But then you have the problem of grinding up the seeds and all that before you can put it on your burger."

He had to smile at the image. "Are you up for the twenty-five-cent tour?" When she nodded, he went on, "Through here is the living room, and the bathroom where the vanity will go is off the front hall."

"I want to see it all. I love other people's houses. They say so much about them."

Now, there was a scary thought. "What does this house say? That I need improving from top to bottom?"

She paused in the doorway of his bathroom and gazed at him over her shoulder. Her eyes weren't blue, as he'd thought before. They were the clear green of jade or of a lake at the foot of a glacier.

"There isn't a thing about you that needs improving, Deputy."

The woman had a knack for saying the most flirtatious things in the most serious way. It could really confuse a man who wasn't operating as a professional.

"If you're standing in my bathroom, the least you can do is call me by my name. Remember? Nick."

Everyone called him that, even the drunks he rolled into the tank. Protocol would not be broken if he asked her to do what all the folks in Glendale did, would it?

"I'll try to remember." She turned to look into the tiny room, and he noticed that the tips of her ears had turned red. "So, tell me what you plan to do. Is everything in here staying where it is, or are you going to switch it around?"

With room logistics, he could be both polite and safe. As they stood in the hall sipping their coffee, he pointed out the changes he planned to make, and then he let slip that the sink and vanity were still out in the truck.

"Can I see?" But when he took her outside, there was nothing to see other than a cardboard container and plastic wrap. "You're going to need a hand getting them into the house," she pointed out. "Why not do it now?"

"Not a chance," he told her. "Come back inside where it's warmer. One of my brothers said he'd come over and give me a hand later."

"I'm stronger than I look." She tugged on the box containing the sink, and it slid down the tailgate. Catching it on one thigh, she hefted it and staggered toward the front door.

"Hey!" Where had all his resolutions gone? Why wasn't he putting his foot down? "Tanya, seriously. You don't need to do this."

But her face looked set and determined, and her gaze fixed on the box as she put it down in the hall as if it were the most important thing she had to get right today.

Maybe it was.

She looked up. "Let me help you. You've been so nice to me and I want to. I—I need to do just one useful, active thing."

He couldn't let her. Not because he was afraid she'd sue him if she dropped his bathroom fixtures on her foot, but because the only people who had ever been in his house were friends and relatives. If she stayed for more than a cup of coffee, he might start feeling as though she were a friend. And he couldn't afford that right now.

"You did that," he told her gently. "Thanks for bringing in the sink."

"Let's go get the vanity."

She wove around him and marched back out to the truck, where, strong as she might be physically, the vanity defeated her.

"Tanya, no."

"Don't argue. Here, get that end and I'll push."

He jumped for it before it tilted off the tailgate onto the

ground, and after that he didn't have much choice but to lug it into the house with her.

"There." She dusted off her hands. "What color did you pick?"

"It doesn't matter. Look, this has to stop."

"What does?"

"You and me being here. Being social."

She stared at him. "Why did you invite me in if you didn't want to be social?"

Now it felt as though the tips of his own ears were burning. Why indeed? "I shouldn't have," he said slowly, searching for words that wouldn't wound. "I should have thought before I spoke. Technically, it's not ethical for me to socialize with a family member directly involved in a case I'm investigating."

"You're not investigating me, are you? I don't see the problem."

How was he going to explain this? "But it could affect how I handle the case. For instance, I might miss something because I was trying too hard to get things wrapped up so I could give you a better report."

"Is that very likely? It seems to me you'd be trying hard regardless, wouldn't you?"

"I know, but—"

She stopped him with a raised hand. "I don't care about ethics. Do you want to know the truth? Just for one day . . . one measly day . . . I wanted to get out of that apartment so I didn't have to listen to the silence, okay? For one day I wanted to think about something other than the fact that I couldn't sleep again last night, and I had to get up to her not being there, and the whole reason I don't have her anymore is because I was a lousy mother and fell asleep. Can you understand that?"

The torrent of her despair and rage threatened to bowl him over, and he had no lifeline to throw. "Tanya, your falling asleep had nothing to do with this crime. There was nothing you could have done to prevent it."

"You say that. But I know different. I know I could have done something."

"Listen. Listen to me." He grabbed her by the shoulders and felt their fragility, the tension in every muscle. "By the time you cashed out and got home, it was already over. Do you hear me? Over. You did not contribute to her death. Someone else is responsible. You can't keep beating yourself up about it."

Under his fingers, her shoulders slumped as the fire went out of her, and he released her.

"I could have done something," she whispered. "I could have changed it."

"So could I," he said roughly. "I could have driven a different route that night. I could have started patrol on the east side of town instead of the west. But thinking like that doesn't buy us anything. It doesn't change what happened. All we can do with what we're dealt is our best."

So what if he contravened the professional standards of conduct. Right now he cared about putting some life back into those eyes, even if it was short-lived. A man could do only what he could do.

"Come on. Help me get the plastic off this vanity."

"What about socializing with family members?" Her tone was dull.

"If you don't tell, I won't."

He found a knife and a pair of scissors, and she ripped into the plastic wrap and paper around the vanity as though she had a personal grudge against them. They built up a head of steam destroying all the packaging, and then lit into the old vanity, breaking it into pieces with a hammer and a crowbar so they could get it out the door. Then they started on the flooring and consequently discovered what shape the plumbing was in.

"Write me a list of all the fittings you need, and I'll go to Susquanny Home Supply," she panted. "I have a fifteen percent employee discount."

"I'll go with you."

"No, you won't. If people see you shopping with me, it'll be all over town by dinnertime that we're dating, and that won't reflect well on your ethics. I'll go alone."

By four o'clock that afternoon he'd somehow managed to spend an entire day with her without guilt, and they'd installed the new sink and vanity together.

"I'll tell you one thing," he said as he turned on the sparkling new faucet and watched water come out of it as pretty as you please, "you are one handy woman."

She snorted with that complete lack of self-consciousness that he was beginning to understand sprang from a refreshing lack of concern about what anybody thought of her. "You forget that I've been on my own for more than twelve years, living in apartments in various stages of disrepair from bad to worse. After Randi's dad left, I swore I wasn't going to depend on anybody. I got a book from the library that told me how to stop the toilet from running, and it felt so good to actually do something real that I just kept on learning." She opened the vanity door and looked at the new plumbing underneath the counter. "I don't have any real power tools, though. That thing with the faucet kit would've stumped me. For a while."

"All I have to do now is replace the flooring."

"Please don't pick some horrible linoleum with black checker board squares on it. People buy it because it looks retro, but I hate the stuff. We had it in our house growing up."

From her tone, bad memories were connected to it all the way around. After their rocky start, they'd had such a good day that he didn't want to spoil it by getting nosy and asking for details.

"How about this, then. You pick the lino, and that will guarantee I don't make a hash of it."

She got to her feet and brushed off the thighs of her jeans. "Serious?"

"Cop's honor. That way, I get fifteen percent off."

Her smile was still elusive, but at least the slump of defeat had gone from her shoulders, and she was moving briskly and with a sense of purpose.

"I like an honest man. Well, you take the measurements, and I'll get it tomorrow when I go to work. You can pay me back when I bring it over."

"Why not have them deliver it? Save yourself the trouble."

She flushed, and the satisfaction faded out of her face. What? What had he said?

"Sorry," she mumbled, looking around for something as if it were vitally important. "It would only be a little piece. I thought it would fit in my car. Of course I—"

Five seconds too late, he got it. "Tanya, I didn't mean—"

"No, no, that's okay. I've used up way too much of your time. Now, where is my—"

"Used up? Whoa. Hold it right there." He realized she was trying to find her jacket, which in his experience meant she was about to take off on him, hurt feelings and all, if he didn't do something fast. "What I meant was, you've done so much for me, with your discount card and everything. I didn't want to put you out any more than I have."

"It wouldn't be putting me out," she mumbled, but at least she'd stopped eyeballing the entryway, where they'd tossed their jackets over the stair railing.

In for a penny, in for a pound. "It's after four. Can I interest you in a can of beans?"

"Oh, no, I couldn't—"

"You're right, I couldn't either. How about pizza? In a real restaurant?"

Her face changed, turned bleak. "Randi loved pizza. We had it so often that I'm probably never going to eat it again. Now that she's . . . Now."

"I can't imagine."

"It's not easy. Especially mornings. I'm not scaring up home-work, lunch, clean clothes, forms that need signing, all the chaos we were used to. And the funny part is that I miss it. That's why the quiet around the apartment makes me cry."

It was always quiet around his place, too. Sometimes it bugged him; sometimes he liked it. But the quiet here wasn't the result of a tragedy. It was because he chose to keep it that way.

"I bet it does."

"I mean, I know she's with God, but I'm never going to get over missing her. And then I wonder if maybe God doesn't like that. Like I'm criticizing his will."

Oh, boy. How did they get here from pizza? And how could they get back—in a hurry?

"I'm sure that if there is a God, he understands grief, Tanya."

"If there is a God? You don't believe there is?" Those green eyes were wide and concerned, and for the first time he regretted that she was a truthful woman who probably wouldn't be put off by the smoke screen he usually set off for his cousins.

He began to pick up the tools on the bathroom floor. "I've seen too much of what people do to each other to believe that any all-powerful God is in charge."

"What people do is different from what God does." She moved in the direction of the kitchen, talking over her shoulder. "You forget that people can choose their own actions. God gives them that gift."

"I wouldn't call child abuse a gift." A handful of screws in his palm, he followed her down the hall.

"It isn't, of course, and you know that's not what I meant. He gives us the ability to choose our course. Some people choose . . . poorly." Did she know she was quoting from a movie that happened to be one of his favorites? One that, oddly enough, was all about faith—and the quest for truth and family instead of fortune and glory.

She stood in front of the open refrigerator, looking over his meager stock.

"Okay, so mostly I eat at the Split Rail," he said in his own defense. Food—or even the lack of it—was a good subject to talk about. He wanted to get away from the topic of God as fast as possible.

"A very eclectic selection here," she said. "I take it you're not serving Thanksgiving dinner next week?"

"Uh, no. There are a dozen women in my family, and every one of them invites me for either Thanksgiving or Christmas."

"Lucky you." Her voice sounded so wistful that something inside him twisted.

"No family around here?"

She shook her head. "It would have been Randi and me. If we

still lived in Ohio, we might have gone to Daryl's—to Randi's father's people on their farm. But we haven't lived there for a long time. And I couldn't afford the gas to get there right now, anyway."

He couldn't imagine not living in Glendale and tripping over relatives every time he turned around. Sometimes they drove him nuts with their matchmaking and sly grins around the dinner table as yet another unexpected female dinner guest dropped over—one who was Christian and conveniently single. But under the bickering and teasing and crowded family events was a bedrock of love so deep he depended on it without even thinking about it.

Leaving Tanya grieving and alone on Thanksgiving seemed like a crime. But what else could he do? He'd been ignoring protocol all day while he pretended that he was helping her escape her dismal present. Instead, all he was doing was enjoying himself and closing his eyes to reality.

A memory flashed through his mind of his brothers, ages thirteen and fifteen, taking the train into Pittsburgh without permission one Saturday night so they could see Pearl Jam. "Better to ask forgiveness than permission," they'd told him when they swore him to secrecy. They'd caught big, big trouble when they snuck in at one in the morning, and so had he for not coming clean about it. But while they were all grounded together, his brothers had been jubilant. They'd seen the concert, and that had been worth it.

When it came to women, he knew his fellow officers would turn a blind eye. His lieutenant might not, but the worst he could do was put a memo in Nick's file. Big deal.

A memo . . . stacked against a holiday that might keep the

ghosts of regret and grief at bay for an hour. It seemed to him to be a pretty even trade.

"Why don't you come with me?" he asked before he could change his mind.

"Where?" She paused in the middle of pulling a block of cheddar out of the plastic bin on the fridge's second shelf.

"To dinner on Thanksgiving, wherever I wind up. Probably Laurie's. She always makes sure she gets her dibs in by the first of the month."

Tanya added two potatoes and a package of bacon to the cheese, and stepped around him to put it all on the counter. "I couldn't barge in on a family dinner."

"You wouldn't be barging in. Everyone's welcome there— usually we have twelve or thirteen people. The kids invite a friend, and there's always a stray somewhere that Colin brings home from the store."

One corner of her mouth lifted in wry acknowledgment. "That would be me. The stray of the week."

"Tanya."

"What?" She didn't look up. Instead, she began hunting through his kitchen drawers until she found another knife, and then through the cupboards until she located a plate.

"Stop running yourself down. I'd be happy to have you come with me. Laurie will understand. And maybe it'll make my sisters-in-law back off for five minutes."

"Why, are they trying to get you married off?"

"They are, they have been, they always will be, world without end, amen. Unless you do me a favor and help me out."

"A defensive play."

He opened his mouth to agree with her and realized what she'd said just in time. "You're doing it again. Stop it. I'm not using you to keep their good intentions in the defensive zone. I'm asking you because you're a decent person, and I think you'd enjoy it."

She blushed, the color starting in her cheeks and washing all the way out to her hairline. Maybe she wasn't used to people being as honest as she was. Maybe it was easier to dish out than to take. Whatever. He was glad he'd said it, anyway.

"Let me think about it, okay? Do you have a cheese grater?"

He found it—one of his mom's old ones—in a drawer and handed it to her. "What exactly are you doing?"

She began to shred the potato into a neat pyramid on the plate. "I'm making potato pancakes. I'll put them with bacon and melted cheese—unless you're on a low-fat diet."

"Uh, no. Potato pancakes?" He couldn't think of anyone who whipped up potato pancakes at the drop of a hat. "I can't let you make supper when I've been making you work all day."

"You worked, too. Do you have an egg?"

He did. For a miracle. "Here."

"What about applesauce?"

"Tanya, nobody has applesauce unless they need it for something specific."

"I do." She glanced up from the frying pan, where four shreddy-looking pancakes were already frying. "Little jars of it, for Randi's lunches." She swallowed, then went on gamely. "You spoon it on the pancakes. My grandma used to make them for me when I was little. It's a German thing, and she was from German stock. A great lady, my grandma was. I named Randi after her—Miranda—much to Daryl's disgust. He wanted her named after his mother, who couldn't stand me."

Whoa. Stick with what was safe. Food. "Sorry, no applesauce. Just a couple of apples I keep around for a snack."

"Cut them up small, and we'll microwave them and mash them."

He'd never mashed an apple in his life, but since he'd bought this house, winging it had become a habit. No applesauce? Nuke an apple and mash it up. Simple.

Fifteen minutes later they sat down to their improvised supper. And it smelled so good and looked so tasty he said nothing when she bowed her head and said grace out loud without even asking if he minded.

The woman had helped him install a vanity and then made them supper. If she wanted to talk to someone who wasn't there, it was none of his business.

All the same, he waited until she finished before he dug into his food.

Chapter Eleven

To: kedgar254
From: JohnnysGrrl

R u threatening me, Mayor Boy?

I know something u dont know and if u tell it goes to the papers.

What will daddy say then?

Want to know what it is?

Laurie left work promptly at three and drove straight over to the mayor's house, which lay outside town on a couple of acres of perfectly landscaped trees and shrubs that would flower in the spring.

Laurie had made a comment at Bible group during one of Janice's rare absences about the army of gardeners it probably took to keep Janice's yard looking the way it did. She'd been informed that Janice and one landscape design student from the university did it all. After that, she learned to keep her mouth shut and think twice before making snarky assumptions disguised as compliments.

That was one nice thing, she reflected as she turned into the driveway. She did put her foot in her mouth, but generally only once on any given subject. The Lord was endlessly patient.

The big item on today's list was Kyle Edgar, who should be arriving on the bus at any moment. Anna was under strict instructions to go to Susquanny Building Supply and stay in her dad's office until five o'clock, and then ride home with him. Tim, at least for now, could be trusted to come home on his own.

The bell played the first four notes of Big Ben's peal when she pressed it, and a moment later, Janice swung open the door.

"Laurie!"

She couldn't blame Janice for being surprised. She'd been here once for a church fund-raising event, and once to hear a visiting gospel singer put on a house concert sponsored by Glendale Bible Fellowship. Other than that, she saw Janice at Bible study and on the news and that was it.

"Can I talk to you?" Laurie asked. "About our kids?"

"Of course. Come on in." She closed the door and Laurie shrugged out of her coat, trying not to be impressed and envious. Her house didn't have solid-looking wainscoting like this, or floor-to-ceiling windows. It didn't have beautiful flower arrangements, either, or a music room with an antique Steinway and a Persian carpet on the floor.

I love my house. It's our refuge. Quit coveting.

"I was just making a snack for Kyle when he gets home from practice," Janice said. "Come on and let's eat it all instead."

The snack turned out to be carrot cake from a boutique bakery whose sweets were more than Laurie could ever afford. The first bite was bliss.

"So what's happened to bring you all the way out here?" Janice asked, licking a quarter inch of cream cheese frosting off her fork. "You said it was about our kids. And something to do with . . . that night?"

"You could say so. You told me at lunch yesterday that the kids were pointing fingers at Kyle, saying he was there, and you found out he was?"

"Yes."

"Well, guess what. Someone else pointed a finger, and I found out Anna was, too."

"Oh, dear."

"You were right. About the bedroom window as an escape route. She goes over the roof and down a wrought-iron trellis next to the garage."

Janice put her fork down and sighed. "I'm sorry to hear it, Laurie. I really am."

"I also found out who Kyle's girlfriend is."

"Anna told you? Who is it?"

Laurie had to laugh at the irony of it all, and how completely their kids had flimflammed them. "Her. *Anna.*"

Janice stared, then blinked, then picked up her fork and put it down again. The tiny clink sounded like an alarm bell in the silence of the glossy kitchen.

"Our kids are sneaking out to see each other?"

"You'd think they'd just invite themselves over for dinner, wouldn't you? Or come over to watch TV or study like normal people."

"Does Anna think I'm some kind of evil witch or something?"

Poor Janice. She looked ready to cry at the thought that a fourteen-year-old would make her boyfriend bike a mile into town in the middle of the night, just to avoid running into his mother.

"According to Brendan O'Day, who got it from Nancy, it's because I think you're a social climber."

Janice choked on her cake and fumbled for the mug of tea next to her plate. "A what?"

"Apparently I'm upset because you get all the TV coverage when I'm in the back room at community events, doing all the work."

Janice clapped both hands over her mouth, but a sound suspiciously like a giggle escaped. Laurie had never thought she'd see the day when quiet, elegant Janice Edgar would laugh out loud with her mouth full.

"Do they have any idea?" Janice gasped at last, grabbing the mug for another gulp of tea. "Do they have a single clue how hard it is for me to speak in public? That I have to carry breath mints in case I throw up in the ladies' room before a speech?"

She did? Laurie had never had stage fright in her life, but she could imagine it. Just take the kind of fear she'd been living with over the last few days, water it down a little, and focus it into a pinpoint of time. Maybe it would be like that.

"Of course not. They're just petty, jealous people with tiny souls who can't do anything themselves, so they talk about the people who *do* do things."

"No one knows better than I do what you contribute to this town, Laurie—how much organizing and cooking and legwork go on behind the scenes. If they knew how hard it is to be Barrett's wife when all I want to do is stay home and grub around in the garden, they'd sing a different tune." Janice shook her head and took another sip of tea. "I'm having a terrible time getting this plan for the women's shelter off the ground. Maybe I should ask Nancy O'Day to be on the fund-raising committee."

"If you promised her a TV crew, she'd be your slave for life."

"No, thanks. But she has a gift for getting under people's

skin. That could come in handy if I set her on some of the cor-porations who've promised funding and not come through." She sighed. "But you didn't come over here to talk about my civic projects. We have a mutual problem."

Did she mean their two kids sneaking out to see each other, or the bigger problem of why their stories didn't jibe about what went on at the bridge?

"I wondered if Kyle has said anything to the police about Anna being at the bridge that night. Nick knows she was, but they're going to want a statement from a witness."

Janice lifted her head, like a greyhound sniffing the wind. "Here he is now. Why don't we ask him?"

Laurie hadn't heard a thing. Janice must have good hear-ing—or else she was so attuned to Kyle's whereabouts lately that it had become almost another sense.

Kyle Edgar came into the kitchen in sweat-drenched soccer togs, muddy to the knees and, from the look in his eye as he zeroed in on the cake, starving hungry.

"Hey, you." Janice kissed one damp temple as he swiped the last piece of cake without bothering with a plate.

"Hey, Mom." He did a double take as he realized there was more to this room than his mom and food. "Oh. Mrs. Hale. Hi." He looked from one woman to the other, and Laurie could prac-tically see his neurons rearranging themselves into defensive po-sition with this new information.

Moms have been talking. What do they know?

Laurie took a sip of tea while she arranged the words in a way that might encourage him to be straight with her. "I was just asking your mom about what you might have seen that night at the bridge, now that we know Anna was there, too. Maybe you can help me out with some details, okay?" She glanced at his long legs and filthy clothes. "Or maybe you'd rather take a shower first?"

"Uh—"

"It's okay, Kyle," Janice said. "Mrs. Hale and I need to help each other through this the way you and Anna are probably standing by each other. We need to get all the details out in the open so we can move on to happier things, like inviting Anna over once in a while. After your grounding is finished."

The wariness faded from his eyes and mouth. Under the mud and the adolescent angles of his face was the potential of a fine-looking young man who would hopefully learn from this experience and maybe even make the kind of date Laurie would approve of once Anna turned fifteen.

"I'll be back in ten," he said, and they heard the thump of his feet on the stairs as he took them two at a time.

"He's a nice kid," Laurie commented. "You've done a good job with him."

"Clearly not, if he thinks it's okay to lie to get what he wants." Janice put her mug down and sighed. "Other than bars on the windows, I'm having a hard time coming up with a punishment I can actually enforce."

"Look at it this way. If Anna's out of commission—and once Colin takes that trellis down, she will be—he's got no reason to sneak out."

Janice brightened. "True. Now if we can just get them to grow a spine so they can talk to each other at school, they won't feel so oppressed."

With a snort, Laurie said, "Don't hold your breath. I've discovered that Anna's just not the kind to walk up to the A-list girls and tell them to back away from her boyfriend."

Janice would have replied, but Kyle jogged back into the

kitchen. Laurie wondered if he'd actually gotten wet—but he must have, because he was clean and changed. "Any more of that cake?"

"Afraid not. I ate your second piece," Laurie said without much remorse.

"That's okay." He snagged an apple out of the bowl on the counter and inhaled it in a couple of bites.

"So, about Anna," Janice said over the crunching.

Laurie spoke up. "From what we can gather, there was a commotion on the bridge and somebody pushed Randi over the rail, whether accidentally or on purpose, we don't know. All we know is that you and Anna were under the trees talking, and when she heard the splash, Anna ran under the bridge. But she says she doesn't remember anything after that. We're hoping you can fill us in."

Kyle shrugged and reached for another apple. "I don't know. I didn't go under there."

So much for protecting the girl you wanted to date from possible danger. "Why not?"

He bit into the second apple and chewed, thinking. "Mrs. Hale, if you'd have been there, you'd have seen a bunch of girls screaming and crying up on that bridge, having a mass breakdown. Anna's got a brain, and compared to her, these girls were totally losing it. If anybody needed someone with a level head, it was them, not her."

Laurie said nothing. *So you let my daughter go into the dark under that bridge by herself, where for all you knew there was a homeless serial killer living in a cardboard box, to try to see if Randi was still alive? You chose instead to help a bunch of girls who were perfectly safe?*

Never mind. Focus. "Then what? Who was the one who did the pushing?"

"I don't know. I didn't see it, and I couldn't get any of them to make any sense. At least I got them off the bridge, and when a couple of the guys from the team showed up at the Stop-N-Go, I asked them to make sure they got home."

Janice glanced at Laurie. "The entire ninth grade, apparently, is out on the streets at night. Maybe it's not just you and I who are clueless."

"Not everybody," Kyle said a little defensively. "Just a few of us. The point is, the guys took the girls home, and then I went back down to see if I could find Anna."

"And did you?" his mother asked.

"Yeah. She was standing there in that mud where the grass breaks and goes into the water."

"Standing in the mud?" Laurie repeated incredulously. "In November?"

"I think she was in shock. She was just standing there, looking at the water, like she thought Randi was going to swim up to her."

"She never surfaced?" his mother asked.

"Not while we were there. So I kind of shook her arm and she came out of it and I walked her home. Then I rode back here."

"That's it?" Janice asked. He nodded. "And you didn't see who pushed Randi over? This is really important, Kyle."

"I didn't, Mom, honest. Up until we heard the splash, Anna and I were talking and not paying attention."

"That can't be right," Laurie said. "This thing about her standing in the water. I'd have noticed muddy socks in the laundry, or damp shoes the next day."

Here was a way out, and Laurie latched on to it fiercely. She could not bear to live like this—examining every sentence that came out of Anna's mouth, looking, as Janice had said yesterday, for corroborating evidence before she accepted even the simplest words as truth.

If it wasn't Anna telling these lies, then she was going to make sure everyone knew about it. How long could her relationship with Anna survive otherwise? Once trust was lost, it would be a long, hard road back, like reeling in a boat that had already left the dock. It might take years—teenage years that would be difficult enough if their relationship was loving and steady. Laurie couldn't face those years if they were going to become a steadily widening chasm of rejection and distrust and guilt. She knew perfectly well what waited on the other side: Anna going off on her own to find people who accepted her. Maybe she'd attach herself to another family. Or worse, to friends who would lead her away from God and into drugs, alcohol, and unwanted pregnancy.

Oh, Lord. Deep inside, her heart cried like a child to heaven. *Please don't let that happen. Please help me find a way to get through this.*

"I surprise myself with the things I don't notice." Janice's lips twisted wryly. "She could have rinsed her socks out, or stashed the shoes in the closet until they dried."

"But Anna says she ran *away* from the bridge, not under it."

"She went under it," Kyle said. "The river path goes under there and keeps going on the other side."

"But Kyle, no one but you has said anything about her standing in the water. And there's no proof she did."

"What are you saying, Laurie?" Janice's eyes had narrowed slightly. "Are you saying Kyle isn't telling the truth?"

Laurie pushed at her plate, then picked it up and carried it to the sink. Both Janice and Kyle stayed at the table, watching her.

She needed to walk circumspectly here. Both these people could do Anna a lot of damage if they chose.

And wasn't that a horrible way to think about a woman in her own Bible study group, whom she'd prayed with countless times?

"No, of course not," she said carefully. "I'm just a little uncertain about what it means if Kyle is the only one saying this."

"I was the only one there," he pointed out. "The others had already left."

"But Anna says she didn't go under the bridge, and I choose to believe her."

Kyle shrugged. "That's up to you. I just know what I saw. And it's no big deal. There wasn't anything under there anyway."

"Then why bring it up, Kyle?" Laurie wanted to know. "Why tell anyone about it? Did you tell Deputy Tremore?"

"I said she ran under the bridge. I didn't say anything about her standing in the water."

"Good. Because without another witness, it's your word against hers. And I know whose word I want to believe."

"Laurie, you're sounding a little combative. I'm not sure I like you using that tone with my son." Janice's voice was very quiet.

Laurie felt as though her breath was backing up in her lungs, as though she couldn't breathe deeply enough to get more oxygen. Was this what a panic attack felt like?

"I feel combative," she said. *Breathe in. Out. Calm down.* "I feel angry and scared, and I don't know who to believe."

"You can believe Kyle."

"No, I can't."

"I'm telling you how it was, Mrs. Hale."

"Are you?" Laurie looked him in the eye. "Or are you just saying whatever will take the pressure off you? You're the mayor's son, right? Whatever you do reflects on your dad, so it's natural you'd want to protect him. Even at someone else's expense."

"Laurie, I think you've said enough." Janice's voice had lost its calmness and taken on an edge. "Kyle, please go do your homework."

"No kidding," Kyle said under his breath and left, keeping to the far side of the room as though he expected Laurie to lunge at him if he got too close.

Janice's face was white as she stood, gripping the back of the chair. "That was uncalled for. I think you owe Kyle and me an apology."

Fear kept Laurie's spine straight. "Maybe. But I'm going to wait on that until I find out who's telling the truth."

"In which case, I think you should leave now."

"Fine." Laurie grabbed her handbag and walked to the front door, where Janice handed her her coat. But when Laurie tried to take it, she hung on.

"I'm sorry you feel you can't believe my son, Laurie. But you have to believe me when I say I'm having a difficult time with this, too. The word of one kid against another." She released the coat, and Laurie shrugged it on without a reply. "I don't want it standing between us at Bible study."

Laurie opened the door and looked over her shoulder at the woman she'd almost begun to like. "That would be up to you," she said and closed the door behind her.

Less than a mile down the road, Laurie pulled the van over to the grassy shoulder and bent over, her forehead against the top of the wheel. She gripped it with both hands as though it were a life preserver while a wave of fear and pain and uncertainty washed through her body.

She'd told herself she couldn't, and yet she'd gone and alienated Janice anyway. But how could she have said anything else? Her only priority was Anna. It just didn't seem possible that nobody knew who had pushed Randi over. And when you'd dispensed with the impossible, all that was left was the improbable . . . or the not so improbable, which was that someone was lying.

The evidence pointed both ways. Maybe she'd been unjust to Kyle. But she was already feeling so guilty and frightened about Anna that she had no emotion left over for him.

When her cell phone twittered, it took two rings just to gulp the pain out of her throat, and another to see that it was Nick.

Maybe he had something concrete to tell her. "Hi." The word came out in a raspy whisper, and she tried again. "Hi, Nick."

"You don't sound so good."

"I'm not feeling so good." She didn't explain. "What's up?"

"Not much. Gil just called. It's my day off, so he's been grilling teenagers all day."

Hope expanded in her chest, and she found she could take a breath. "And?"

"I can't tell you the details, but suffice to say that we're back at square one."

She slumped in the driver's seat. "Nobody knows who pushed Randi over? Nick, that's impossible. All those girls on that bridge have to know."

"You know it and I know it, but getting someone to say it is a whole different ball of worms."

"Wax."

"I dunno. It feels pretty wormy to me. Everybody wriggling out of the way as fast as they can. Everybody telling a different story, pointing fingers here and there. Nobody's story matches up where it should. I swear, if there's a collective unconscious, maybe there's a collective amnesia, too."

She didn't want to hear about the fingers pointing at one another. "Or a collective lie."

"We're going to have to bring a couple of them down to the station and lean on them. Maybe that will shake a fact or two loose. But that's not why I called."

"It's not?" Laurie couldn't imagine any other reason for Nick to be talking with her right now. "What's going on?"

"I was calling about Thanksgiving."

She hadn't given a single thought to it, and it was six days away. "Nick, please don't tell me they've scheduled you to work on Thursday. I was really counting on all of us being a family. Anna needs to see you as her cousin again, not as a cop."

"No, no, it's not that. I have enough seniority now so that the rookies have to work major holidays. Gil and I are working this in tandem so neither of us gets too burned out."

She exhaled. "That's good. You've missed enough Christmases and Fourth of July weekends."

"I was wondering if I could bring a guest."

A guest? A woman? At any other time she would have been keenly interested, but now it just seemed as though a guest who wasn't family, who couldn't understand their troubles, was an intrusion she couldn't face.

But neither could she turn this person away. Hospitality was a gift extended from one Christian to another—or in this case, from one Christian to whoever came to the door. "Of course you can. We're putting another leaf in the table anyway. Mind me asking who it is?"

"Tanya."

Tanya? She only knew one Tanya. And it couldn't be that one. "Who?"

"Tanya Peizer. You know."

Laurie's jaw hung open for a second. "You're seeing . . . Tanya? Is that . . . legal?"

"Well, she's not my cousin or anything. And I'm not exactly 'seeing' her."

Oh, my, if he was getting defensive, then there were emotions involved. And if there were emotions involved, which hadn't happened in years with this guy, then maybe he was getting serious.

But . . . *Tanya*?

"No, of course not. I only meant—with the case and everything. Isn't it like fraternizing with a witness?"

"If I were dating one of the ninth graders, Laurie, *that* would be fraternizing with a witness. Tanya is the victim's mother. And yeah, maybe it isn't a hundred percent ethical, but at this point I'm not too concerned. It just doesn't sit right to leave her alone in her apartment when it's in our power to do something."

"I know, I know." Laurie tried to make her tone soothing and welcoming and happy for him, even though she was so surprised she hardly knew what she felt. "Of course she can come. She's in my Bible study group, you know. I—I was just surprised. That she could get the day off, you know."

"Isn't Susquanny Home Supply closed that day?"

"Well, yes. But she works more than one job."

"The school's closed, too, so they won't need the shuttle drivers."

He knew what jobs she worked, and on what days. That meant this wasn't just a pity invite. It meant they'd actually talked.

And what's it to you, anyway? You've been as bad as his sisters-in-law about wanting to get him married off.

Yes, but not now. And not to—

She stopped herself before the thought even formed. She had nothing against Tanya. Nick was right. The poor woman deserved sympathy and comfort and everything a Christian sister could give her. And that included Thanksgiving dinner. Hadn't she thought just a few days ago that Tanya's dinner would probably be a turkey burger and not much else? If the Hales and Tremores could make even one moment of her first holiday without Randi easier, then their work would have been done.

"I'm looking forward to seeing both of you, then," she said. "We'll probably eat around two o'clock. Come early."

"Thanks, Lor." The defensiveness was gone, and if he was back to using her childhood nickname, then all was well. "I know she'll appreciate the welcome. And so do I."

When he hung up, she could tell he was smiling. After a second, she closed the phone and dropped it into her purse. She started the van and pulled out onto the highway.

Nick was a big boy. He wasn't the type to be taken in by a needy woman, or a good-looking one, or one who was looking for a daddy to take care of her. Nick was smart and well-balanced, and it was absolutely none of her business who he invited to dinner on a holiday that was meant for family.

Her business was to make sure Tanya had a plateful of food and as much sisterly support as she could manage.

Under the circumstances.

When she pulled the van into the garage, she saw Colin through the window, busy wrestling the trellis off the wall. She called up to Anna and Tim, and when they both answered, she told them, "Homemade pizza for supper. Half an hour." From behind his door, Tim cheered. Behind Anna's door there was nothing but silence.

Laurie went down the stairs and pulled out frozen pizza crust and tomato sauce and cheese. Then she saw the light blinking on the answering machine.

"You have one new voice message," the digital voice told her.

"Laurie, this is Janice. Look, I'm really upset about the way we left things this afternoon. Can you call me, please?"

Click. Beep.

Your son can endanger my daughter.

Vanessa's story about seeing Anna running through the dark could be discounted. At that time of night she could have made a mistake. But Kyle's story could be dangerous. If it came to light that Randi had surfaced . . . or that she was alive when she did . . . and Anna was there . . . Laurie shuddered. Innocent people went to prison all the time. A net of circumstances closed around them, and there wasn't a single thing their frantic family could do about it.

Whether Janice could have been a friend or not, Laurie had to distance herself from Janice, and Anna from Kyle. She had no choice.

She reached over and pressed the Delete button. The machine blinked and the digital recording came on.

"Your mailbox is empty."

Chapter Twelve

To: Manga15
From: JohnnysGrrl

5-o is all confused. No one to arrest.

Keep it tight girlfriend and maybe u wont be the next one.

Hows little bro anyway? He been on any bridges lately?

To: JohnnysGrrl
From: Manga15

Leave me and him alone. Im not saying anything.

I hope u die.

To: Manga15
From: JohnnysGrrl

We all die stupid. Some of us go sooner than others thats all.

Way sooner.

On Sunday, Laurie got her family organized and out the door only ten minutes late. It took all of that extra ten minutes to convince Anna that "total lockdown" did not include church.

In fact, her whole attitude toward being grounded was a little off. Instead of complaints and tears and drama in order to wring just one night out or one concession out of Laurie and Colin, she seemed almost happy to stay in her room. She didn't even complain about not being allowed to watch TV, and if nothing else, that was strange.

But at least Laurie knew where she was every minute. If her cub was safely in the den, then she was in no danger of prowling animals out there in the dark.

Or at least gossiping classmates.

Meanwhile, over the issue of church, Laurie won a Pyrrhic victory. Anna came with them, but she pulled on her sloppiest pants and shirt and ran a brush the absolute minimal number of times through her hair.

At one end of their pew, Rose Silverstein and her mother were already seated. As the Hales, led by Colin, filed in, Mrs. Silverstein and Rose got up and moved a couple of rows back. Laurie ignored them and tried to concentrate on the beauty of the hymns, but even as she lifted her hands in praise, her thoughts whirled like a dust storm on the prairie.

She needed to talk to Colin again about getting Anna into counseling. It just was not normal that a girl who ordinarily took an hour in the bathroom to get her hair and makeup perfect would be seen in public like this—especially if there was a chance that Kyle Edgar would be here, too.

Laurie looked around. There he was, sitting with his mother and the O'Days. She wondered if Janice had done that on purpose, in order to talk to Nancy after the service about the women's shelter project.

Janice looked up, but Laurie didn't meet her gaze. Instead, she glanced behind her. Tanya was at the back, alone except for

Cammie and Debbie with her family. No Nick. Laurie didn't know whether to feel relieved about that or not.

Of course she'd be delighted and praise God without ceasing if Nick became a believer. His family had been encouraging him for years, but maybe it would take someone outside the family to wake him up. She just wasn't quite prepared for it to be Tanya. Because what did she have to keep her in Glendale? Two jobs of a kind that she could pick up anywhere? If Tanya thought she could make Nick fall for her and then up and leave him when the next big idea hit, she had another think coming. Nick was an honorable guy. Any woman should be proud to be his choice. And he didn't deserve to have his heart broken by a woman who didn't plan to stick around for the long term.

As the hymns ended and they sat for the opening prayer, Laurie reflected that she was doing it again: overdramatizing. Here she had the whole relationship mapped out, right to the big breakup when, to her knowledge, Nick had become acquainted with poor Tanya only long enough to invite her to a family supper so she didn't have to spend the holiday alone.

No big deal. Probably nothing would come of it, especially if he was concerned about the ethics of seeing her. Laurie had bigger fish to fry, like what was going to become of Anna if the case didn't break soon.

Counseling was the first step. Which meant another talk with Colin.

Cale Dayton's sermon was on the subject of being busy with the right things—so appropriate for her frame of mind this morning. She really needed to stop the dust storm in her head and concentrate on the message God had for her heart. So she tried, and by the end of the sermon had managed to find a little peace and maybe even some direction for the coming week. Cale would know a good Christian counselor. Anna could go to the one at school, but that person might not see things from a Christian point of view. They were literally talking life and death here, and Anna, once persuaded to talk, was likely to open up along those lines.

After the final hymn, everyone was so busy chatting with one another that it was difficult to get a word in edgewise. With Thanksgiving falling on their usual Thursday, she needed to find Maggie and ask if it would be okay to have Bible study on Tuesday that week instead.

"Cammie, have you seen Maggie?" she finally asked when she'd migrated with the crowd to the back of the church and still not managed to locate her. "I'm hoping she can reschedule Bible study to Tuesday."

Cammie turned from whatever she had been saying to Debbie and Tanya, and Laurie smiled at them both. Their smiles were quick and preoccupied, and Debbie took Tanya's arm to hustle her out the door. Probably a good thing, since it was obvious large crowds disturbed her. How did Tanya manage to drive a university shuttle, with all its distractions?

"I think I saw her heading out to her car with the kids," Cammie said. "She's probably gone by now. Try calling a bit later."

"What do you think? Tuesday sound all right?"

"Wednesday's better for me. Debbie, too."

"But I have to work Wednesday. Wait, what about Friday? I have that off."

"We have family coming for the long weekend."

"It'll have to be Tuesday, then, if Maggie is free. Can you rearrange things?"

"Laurie, I know you're our study leader, and of course we

always take your workdays into consideration, but really, this week Wednesday would be better for Debbie and me."

Laurie blinked at her. "Okay. I guess."

"Don't look like that. It's not personal. Well, maybe it is, a little."

"What do you mean?" How could changing their study day be personal? What was she missing?

Cammie pulled her aside into the anteroom where the extra chairs were stored. "We kind of hoped we wouldn't have to have this conversation—"

"We?"

"But don't you think we should be putting Tanya first, under the circumstances?"

Had she not had enough sleep last night? Why couldn't she follow whatever Cammie was trying to say? "What circumstances?"

Cammie hunched a little under her winter coat. "You know. With Anna being under suspicion and everything."

Laurie stared at her. She'd known Cammie Petersen since third grade and would have banked money on her friendship. Through the years they'd spent in Bible study together, they had come to know each other's struggles, strengths, and weaknesses as women and as parents. She never would have expected words like this out of Cammie's mouth.

"Anna is not under suspicion."

"Well, maybe not officially. But don't you see how awkward it would be? It's Tanya's first week back in study group since Randi's funeral. How do you think she's going to feel if the mother of someone who was there that night on the bridge is the one leading the study?"

Laurie's lips felt cold. Stiff. "I hope she would feel loved and included."

Cammie shook her head. "Be realistic, Laurie. It's going to hurt her. You know it is. Everything hurts her right now. It's just for a little while, until the police find out who really did it."

"That could take weeks."

"If it does, it does. But in the meantime, we have to do what we can for her, don't we? Look, why don't I check with Tanya, and you call Janice and Mary Lou. I'll fit in with whatever the majority decides, but Debbie and I really feel strongly about this."

"Cammie, this doesn't make sense. She's invited to our place for Thanksgiving."

"Yes, but is she coming?"

Laurie opened her mouth to say, "Of course," but Cammie spoke first.

"All of us have invited her, and of course you would, too. But do you really think she'd come to your house instead of Maggie's or mine, and look at Anna across the table?"

This is ridiculous. "We'll have to see, won't we? Have a good holiday, Cammie."

Laurie walked out the door. She felt as though a bomb had gone off, leaving her shell-shocked.

How was it possible that people could take these rumors and speculations so seriously? It was one thing to gossip and talk behind people's backs. It was quite another thing to act on rumors in the name of brotherly love. Hadn't she proved she cared as much about Tanya as any of them? Who had organized the funeral supper? Who had put together the rotation of women who had been keeping Tanya company for the last week and a half? Did none of that count?

Out in the parking lot she saw Janice talking intently with Nancy O'Day, their heads close together. This was not going to be easy, but it had to be done. She had to let Janice know about the proposed change in their meeting day. Why did it have to be Nancy O'Day, of all people, who was close enough to hear what would probably be a very uncomfortable conversation?

Hanging back near the rear fender of Nancy's silver Mercedes, she waited as Janice laid out a convincing argument for the women's shelter. Nancy nodded her head in agreement, but Laurie noticed she didn't commit herself one way or another— probably to have the satisfaction of keeping the mayor's wife on the string while she withheld a decision she'd probably already made.

Some people were so petty.

At length Janice turned and noticed Laurie standing there. A fact that Nancy, who had been facing in her direction, had not brought to her attention.

Petty.

"Laurie! How are you?" Janice held out a hand and Laurie squeezed it. Even on a morning that promised freezing rain and sleet, Janice looked like she'd just stepped out of a fashion magazine in her camel overcoat with arabesques of black soutache braid at collar and cuffs. A black tapestry tam sat on her blonde hair. The whole effect was stylish and jaunty, but her eyes spoiled the pretty picture. They were filled with pain, even as she made small talk.

"I'm fine. You look wonderful."

"One of the council members invited us to lunch. I'm afraid it's a cover for a funding pitch, but because Barrett said yes, I have to go, too."

"Nice to see you, Nancy," Laurie said politely.

"I'm a bit surprised to see you, though," the other woman said.

"I'm here every week." Unlike some people, who showed up in their Mercedes maybe once every two months.

"No, I mean considering the new developments in the case."

"Case?" As if she didn't know what case. Two could play games as well as one.

"Maybe you've been asked not to talk about it, seeing as you're so closely involved."

"That depends."

"You're probably right. If I had a daughter—and I'm always so glad I had boys—I'd be keeping it quiet, too, to protect her."

"Keeping what quiet, Nancy?" Janice said, saving Laurie from giving Nancy the satisfaction.

Nancy leaned in a little. "Well, I can say this to you two, can't I? I can't tell you how many people I've heard it from, even right here at church."

"Heard what?" Janice's voice merely held polite interest, as if it didn't matter to her whether Nancy passed on her gossip or not.

"Why, about Anna being the last one to see Randi alive. I've been dying to ask you. Oh, Laurie, please tell me it's not true she's being investigated as a possible suspect?"

From her tone, Nancy was eager to hear that Anna had not only done the pushing but dashed down to the water to hold Randi's head under, too.

Was everyone talking about this? Was everyone judging Anna and finding her guilty whether they had the facts or not?

"I don't think anyone is being singled out for investigation." Her lips felt stiff again, as though she'd just had a shot of novocaine. "The sheriff's office is asking everyone the same questions."

"But it is true that Anna saw Randi last?"

"We don't know."

"Oh, of course. She was alone under there, wasn't she?"

"Where are you getting your facts, Nancy?" Janice asked. The perfect politician's wife. Never take sides. She behaved as if the conversation in her kitchen had never happened.

"Oh, all over. Everyone's talking."

"You should really tell them to leave it in the hands of the sheriff's office," Janice said. "Talking in the parking lot after church isn't going to solve this crime, is it?"

"I just thought you'd like to know what everyone is saying. I know I'd hate it if people were talking behind my back about something Brendan did. Not that he'd ever be in a position like this, but you know what I mean."

"Anna isn't in 'a position like this,'" Laurie informed her in as calm a tone as she could manage. "And we'd all be better off concentrating on finding out who really pushed Randi off the bridge, not on passing on our guesses as if they were facts."

Nancy eyed her with that glassy china-doll smile that was part of the reason Laurie disliked dolls of any kind. Totally fake, a smile like that gave no clue as to what the person was thinking. "I'm not so sure anyone did push her off. I think the kids were just goofing around and it was an accident."

"Not according to the forensic evidence," Laurie said.

"Oh, the forensic evidence." Nancy enunciated each syllable as if it were in a foreign language. "Goodness, you sound so official. But then, I suppose you have an inside track on the investigation, don't you?"

"Only what I read in the papers, like anyone else. Nick is too much of a professional to blab details, even to the family."

"Of course," Nancy said with a smile that told everyone in

the vicinity she didn't believe a word of it. "Well, I have to hustle. We have a crowd for lunch. Janice, I'll be in touch about"—she glanced at Laurie—"that matter we were discussing."

With a waggle of her leather-gloved fingers, she slid into the driver's seat of her Mercedes and rolled out of the parking lot.

After a moment, Laurie said, "You're going ahead with asking her to be on your committee?"

"She has skills, and I need them." Janice's tone was still mayor's-wife polite. "You should see her with men. One smile, and they can't get their checkbooks out fast enough. It never works when I try it."

Here was a perfect opportunity to mention Janice's voice mail, apologize in her turn, and move on. But the words jammed in Laurie's throat. It seemed as though everyone was talking, and all the fingers pointed at Anna. No one was saying nasty things about Janice's son. Laurie's instinct was to pull back, to retrench, and above all, to confide in no one.

She may as well say what she needed to say, collect her family, and head home. "We need to move Bible study this week because of the holiday. Are you free Tuesday?"

Slowly, her face averted, Janice pulled her datebook out of her Coach handbag. "Let me check. Yes, eleven on Tuesday is open. At Maggie's?"

"I need to check with her. Debbie and Cammie say they can't make Tuesday, so keep Wednesday free, too, just in case."

"Call my cell when it's set up." She hesitated for a second, as if she were going to bring up what Laurie wanted to avoid. Laurie backed up a step and Janice's shoulders fell. "I've got to run. Bye." She hurried off to her car, a discreet beige Volvo S60 with the same stylish lines as she possessed herself, and Laurie turned away with a sigh.

She'd done the wrong thing. Her instincts may have told her to retrench, but her heart told her that Janice could be a friend, an ally where she really needed one. And now she'd not only failed to return a call that had probably been heartfelt and difficult to make, she'd just rebuffed her a second time.

Janice probably wouldn't allow a third.

After lunch, she finally managed to get through to Maggie, who had obviously taken the kids somewhere to eat after church.

"Hey," she said as cheerfully as she could. "I'm calling about rescheduling Bible study this week. I don't think any of us will be able to come on Thanksgiving Day."

"Way ahead of you." At least Maggie sounded completely normal. "Everyone's coming Wednesday, same Bat-time, same Bat-channel. Debbie's going to lead."

Laurie's shoulders drooped. "Maggie, do you agree with this idea Debbie has about it being better for Tanya if I'm not there?"

"I wouldn't say I agree with it, exactly," Maggie said slowly, "but I can see where it might be helpful. Just for a short time. Until they . . . clear up the case. I can imagine how I would feel."

"It would be nice if someone imagined how I feel." Did she sound like a whiner? She hoped not. But Maggie was her neighbor and her friend. They'd shared coffee and babysitting duty and a hundred details of daily life. Surely she could say these things to her. "I heard the most awful rumors just today in church. If there were ever a time that I needed you all, myself, it's right now."

"But Laurie, there's a huge difference between needing your friends because of rumors, and needing them because you've lost your daughter in a horrible way. You're strong. Tanya isn't."

If that wasn't a slap in the face, she didn't know what was. That was the solution, according to her friends. She needed to quit feeling sorry for herself and take a look at someone who had real problems.

"Okay." There was nothing else to say, was there? Even if she told them Tanya was coming to Thanksgiving dinner and these excuses were silly, their plans were already made. Without her.

"Have a blessed time." She hung up.

She did look like a whiner. Because of course no one knew about Anna's sneaking out, or that her story didn't match those of the other witnesses. No one knew how deep the fear ran inside Laurie that maybe the others were right and Anna was hiding something dreadful. Guilt stabbed her anew for even harboring the thought.

Somehow she and Colin had to find a way to make Anna talk. That strange look in her eyes told Laurie that there was something more going on than a girl sneaking out to meet her boyfriend and getting caught. When she looked into those wide blue eyes, she didn't see what a mother usually expected. She didn't see honesty or love. She saw fear.

And that deepened her own. Deep, black wells of fear that she wouldn't allow Cammie and Debbie and the rest of them to see. Because none of their kids were in danger. Only Janice could share this with her, and Laurie had just gone and alienated her.

Okay. Enough feeling sorry for herself. She needed to find Colin and have another talk about getting Anna into counseling. No girl of Anna's age—or any age—should know fear like this. She had to do something, and soon.

On Sunday afternoons Colin's escape from the headaches of the store was to close himself in the little room he called his study. In his ancient recliner that he'd bought when he was single, he'd read the Pittsburgh papers and eventually wind up with the sports section tented over his chest as he snored.

He'd gotten only as far as the entertainment section when she slipped inside and leaned over him from behind, looping her arms around his neck.

"Any expensive concerts we should see?"

"Not a one." He folded the section and tossed it in the pile on the floor next to his chair. "What's up? Bible study all straightened out?"

With Colin, sometimes it was best to stick with the facts rather than the truth. "It's a bit weird this week. Most of the girls can only do Wednesday, so I'll skip it. Short weeks are always crazy at school, anyway." She came around the chair to sit on the floor and lean her head against his knee. "I wish everything would just go back to normal."

"Define *normal*."

She waved her hands as if to encompass them, the house, the town. "Anything is better than the way we're living right now. Everybody's talking about Randi. And about Anna being the last one to see her. People seem to be getting the wrong idea."

"We don't know Anna was the last one to see her."

"Nobody cares about that. They're all happily gossiping and insinuating she had something to do with Randi's death. Didn't you hear them at church?"

He snorted. "That's ridiculous. And no, no one said anything to me."

"Well, they did to me. More than once. It's probably sheer agony for Anna at school. We really need to get her into counseling, so we can help her deal with all of this in a more effective way than hiding under the covers."

"Already done."

Now it was her turn to swivel her head and stare. "What?"

"After our talk the other night, I called your cousin Gregg. Teenagers aren't his specialty, but he says he has a few clients in that age range. I'm not sure he's completely qualified for this situation, but at least he'd keep it in the family."

"You could have told me about it sooner, Colin. I've been worrying for days about how to convince you it was the right thing to do. Talk about a waste of mental energy."

He leaned down and squeezed her shoulders. "I'm sorry, Lor. You know me. I like to get all the ducks in a row before I say anything, in case it doesn't work out."

"We're supposed to be a team," she protested. "If you'd done it when I first brought it up, maybe we'd be days closer to making things better for her."

He pulled back and snapped open the next section of the paper. "Excuse me for not jumping when you said so. I wanted to check around first and make sure Gregg was a viable choice."

"Of course he's viable. He's known her since she was born."

"That has nothing to do with his professional qualifications, Laurie. I see the guy at family events and he doesn't counsel people there. If he's going to talk to Anna, I wanted to make sure he checked out. I'd do the same for any counselor we were considering."

Did it have to take days? Couldn't he have made some phone calls and come to his conclusions sooner than this? But if she asked that, they'd have an argument. She didn't think she could stand one more person withdrawing from her and looking at her over their shoulder as though she were the bad person.

That morally corrupt woman who had raised a morally corrupt daughter.

Was that what Cammie and Debbie were really thinking under all this nice talk about considering Tanya's feelings? Were they laying some of the blame for Randi's death on her?

No, she couldn't think that way. She needed to focus on the positive, on the fact that Colin now agreed that counseling with Gregg was a good solution for Anna. Instead of berating him for taking so long, she should bite her tongue, be a good wife, and thank him for what he had done.

"I know you would," she said. "Thanks for standing with me on this."

"Somebody has to stand with someone around here."

What was that tone in his voice? "What do you mean? You're the only person standing with me at the moment."

"And who's standing with me?"

"I am, of course."

He put the paper down. "Are you? You treat me like the enemy, Laurie. I've put up with it for days, but it's wearing a little thin. You expect me to side with you on every single thing, but when are you going to start supporting me and my decisions?"

Enemy? Colin? How could he say such a thing? And why would he need someone to side with him, anyway? His men's group wasn't abandoning him.

"I don't understand."

"Well, let me lay it out for you. You're not the only one whose top priority is Anna. Her welfare is my concern, too, and when you snipe at me for doing what I think is right, it hurts. You need to ease up and realize that you have a family, not an armed camp."

She couldn't seem to get enough air into her lungs. *Breathe. Slow and steady. That's it.*

"All I can think about is my family," she finally got out around the lump in her throat.

"When was the last time you talked to Tim about what's going on?"

"I hope to heaven he doesn't know."

"Don't be naive. Of course he knows. It's all over the elementary school. These teenagers have little brothers and sisters, and they feel just as involved as anyone."

"Have you been talking to him?"

"Of course. Someone has to. You might want to back off on organizing Tanya's and Nick's and who knows whose lives and pay some attention to the one you have here at home."

Well, that wasn't going to be a problem, since she'd been cut out of Tanya's life by people who thought they knew better.

But isn't organizing people what you do?

In the back of her brain, the question niggled at her. Did she really think she knew better than everybody else how their lives should be run? That was the essence of what Colin had just told her, wasn't it? Did people translate her love for helping and organizing into the kind of behavior she hated—the know-it-all who bossed others around?

Surely not.

She didn't want to think about that right now. Since Colin wanted her to concentrate on her family, she'd do it. The rest could take care of itself once her family was safe.

"You're right," she said. "I will. Meantime, I'll call Gregg tomorrow and get Anna set up with him ASAP."

ASAP turned out to be Tuesday morning at ten thirty, which was the only half hour that Gregg had open in a short week, even for his cousin.

"It's the holiday season," he said in his psychiatrist voice, which was not the one he used at Super Bowl parties and birthdays. There must be someone waiting in his office. "This and Valentine's Day are my busiest times of the year."

Which did not bode well for the mental health of Glendale. Still, getting Anna some help was number one on Laurie's list, and if she had to pull her out of school to get it, then that's what she'd do.

As she drove across the university campus on the way home Monday afternoon, a shuttle passed her. A glance at the driver told her it wasn't Tanya . . . not that it would have made any difference outside of a honk and a wave. Maybe it was just that she was still feeling a little strange about Tanya and the others in the study group. Did Tanya know what they'd done? Was there any hope for a friendship between herself and Tanya? Did Tanya think Anna had played a part in Randi's death?

And how could she bring it up gracefully on Thursday without giving Tanya more pain?

Her cell phone rang, and she welcomed the interruption to such a gloomy train of thought.

"Mrs. Hale, this is Tracey Tillman, the attendance secretary at Lincoln High."

"Hi, Tracey." Uh-oh. What now? Was she calling to tell her that the gossip about Anna had reached epic proportions and they were recommending switching schools? "What can I do for you?"

"I wonder if you're aware of the situation with Anna, Mrs. Hale."

"I am, and as a matter of fact, we've arranged for counseling for her. Her first appointment is tomorrow."

There was a pause. "That wasn't quite the situation I meant, though I'm sure they're related. In fact, I'm positive they are."

"What . . . situation?" Laurie gave up on trying to drive, talk, and speculate at the same time. One-handed, she wheeled the minivan into the commuter lot at the bottom of the hill and parked.

"Anna cut her last two classes today," the woman said bluntly. "I thought you'd like to know so that you can talk with her about it. Her grades have begun to slide, too, which under the circumstances is very understandable. I'm glad you've arranged additional counseling for her, to stop the situation before it gets out of control."

Cutting classes? Slipping grades? Laurie's blood seemed to chill in her veins with shock and apprehension. "Is there a reason nobody called me about this before?" she asked.

"Is her behavior at home normal?" Ms. Tillman inquired.

"Would you answer my question, please?"

"It's school policy to notify parents that a student was absent from class at the end of the day. I just got everything compiled, so this is the soonest I could call about that. As to the other, her math teacher says her grade on the last weekly quiz was a D. The one she missed today, of course, netted her an F."

"Anna has never had a D or an F in her life!"

"Well, she has now. And she's not alone. Two of the other girls in her class are seeing the grief team because of similar problems."

"Grief team?"

"I can't say more due to confidentiality issues, Mrs. Hale, but if it's any consolation, this is normal. We just have to be as aware and supportive as we can."

"You can count on that. You say Anna has been seeing the grief team on her own?"

"Yes. Three times this week, according to my records, because one of the sessions overlapped a class."

She fought back a comment that would probably get a kid detention. "Thank you for telling me. Nobody else has."

"Again, we try to respect the confidentiality of the students as much as possible. If there's anything any of the faculty can do at this end, please let us know."

Laurie disconnected with a stab of her thumb. Cutting class. Slipping grades. Grief team! If they had gotten Anna into outside counseling right away, maybe this wouldn't be happening. If Colin hadn't been so unfair about poor Gregg, maybe Anna would be finding her balance right now.

Ooh, she was going to give Colin an earful. What did he know about girls and their troubles, anyway?

Then, as she turned on the ignition in the van, she realized what she was doing. *I get bad news and what do I do? I blame Colin—I treat him like the enemy, just as he said.*

Did she do this all the time, or just when her stress levels were off the charts? How long had he been tolerating this ugliness in her character without saying a word? The fact was, they were in a crucible right now, and the layers of illusion she had about herself were boiling away.

If she'd been asked about this last month, she'd have cheerfully expected to find gold at her core. But at the moment all she could find was lead.

By the time she got home and put soup and sandwiches together for dinner, she had sobered enough to tell Colin about this latest bombshell calmly. No more attacks if she could help it.

"A D and an F!" he exclaimed in the same tone she'd used herself. "Our Anna?"

"The result of cutting classes. That was the other news I got this afternoon. She skipped the last two periods today, and I bet if I called Janice Edgar, I'd find that Kyle did the same."

"He probably isn't getting D's, though."

"What is that supposed to mean?"

"I just mean that math isn't Anna's best subject to start with."

"That does not excuse D's."

"Of course not. I just meant that Kyle could probably skip a few classes and still get A's and B's on his papers. He's a pretty bright kid, from all accounts."

"This conversation is not about Kyle!"

"Laurie, I understand you're upset, but there's no need to shout."

So much for her good resolutions. When had she developed this temper? Controlling it was like trying to hold down a demon with a garbage-can lid.

But she had to control it, for the sake of her family. "I'm sorry," she said as calmly as she could. "But it's clear that the grief team at the school is not helping Anna. Asking Gregg for help was the right thing to do. I just wish we'd done it sooner." She crossed a carpet that had almost become a battlefield and burrowed into his arms. After a moment, the stiffness went out of them and he held her the way she needed to be held.

"I wish they'd find the kid who did the pushing," she murmured into his chest. "It's putting me on edge, hearing everybody talk about our daughter like she's the one who did it."

"I know. I do, too. Though nobody has had the guts to say anything to me."

With a flash, she remembered the Silversteins getting up and moving to a different pew on Sunday. "Whether they do or not, they'll get their reward," she said grimly. "And I hope I'm there to see it."

"In the meantime, what are we going to do about our girl?"

"I'm going to go talk with her right now. Cutting classes has to stop, first of all."

"But if it's a symptom of something bigger, it may not. Go easy on her, Lor."

She gave him the kind of "gimme a break" look that Anna and Tim turned on her at least once a day. How could she go easy on cutting classes and failing tests? But all she said was, "I will."

Laurie climbed the stairs to Anna's room and tapped softly on the door. "Sweetie?"

"Come in."

Anna was propped up against her pillows, drawing.

"Can I see?"

She turned the pad toward her, and for once it wasn't a picture of a fairy or even of a falling girl. It was Kyle, drawn with all the loving detail of a girl with a heavy crush.

"That's beautiful, sweetie. It really looks like him. You're so talented."

Anna didn't reply. Instead, she began filling in the shadows, giving Kyle's face relief.

"I got a call from Ms. Tillman today," Laurie began as she sat on the edge of the bed. "The attendance secretary. She says you cut your last two classes."

No reply. The only sound was the whisper and *skritch* of the pencil on paper.

"Mind telling me why?"

"I dunno."

"Was it to be with Kyle?"

Anna shrugged and looked at the drawing with a critical eye. "Do you think I should detail his hair or leave it?"

"I think you should put that down and answer me."

With a put-upon sigh, Anna laid the drawing on the coverlet beside her. "It's not a big deal, Mom."

"Cutting class is a huge deal. If you're doing it with Kyle, it's even huger."

"I'm not."

"You're not doing it to see him?"

"No. He likes math. The big geek."

"You can't pass your quizzes unless you're in class. Rumor has it you got a D on the last one. This has to stop here, Anna. You have to get it together, and Dad and I want to help."

Anna's lower lip set in a line that Laurie recognized all too well. She'd seen it in her own mirror a time or two.

"Don't give me that look. Tell me the real reason you skipped and let's get this solved."

To Laurie's surprise, the mutinous lip didn't have a temper tantrum to follow. Instead, it softened and Anna's eyes welled with tears.

"Mom, you can't solve everything."

"Why not? If the math problems are too hard, Daddy can work with you on them. If you can't see the board, we can get you glasses. There's always something you can do besides skipping out and not being responsible. You're not some kind of slacker chick. You're a Hale, and Hales lead by example."

"Not always," Anna mumbled.

"Even if they don't, they do the right thing. We're Christians, Anna. We don't lie about where we are and deceive our parents and teachers."

"Maybe I don't want to be a Christian."

The breath went out of Laurie's lungs. "Don't say that." A hot blur of tears filled her own eyes. "Why would you ever think such a thing?"

"What's it buying me, Mom? I go to school and people look at me sideways and throw stuff at me in the cafeteria and talk, talk, talk all the time. I go to church, and the same people are there. The only person who doesn't look at me like I'm some kind of criminal is Kyle, and you won't let me see him."

Guilt. Oh, Lord, help me out from under this burden of guilt. Especially since I'm one of those people who actually wondered if she could have done . . . something . . . that night.

No. She could no longer afford to think that way. The guilt would grow and grow. Was that what was making her so angry? Was she lashing out at people so she wouldn't lash out at herself for thinking such things about Anna?

She had to trust her daughter. She had to. Otherwise, their family would splinter and fall apart.

"People are idiots, and as soon as Nick and the police solve this case, everyone will know it." There, she could almost convince herself. "In the meantime, let's stick to the point. You can't cut class. I don't want to get any more phone calls from Ms. Tillman. If you do—"

"What?" Anna sounded so weary. "I'm already on total lockdown."

Good point. "Daddy and I can be endlessly inventive. Think about the inches of muck on the floor of the lumber shed at the store. Somebody has to clean it."

"Um, like the janitors?"

"Um, like they have better things to do in the showroom and the garden center. Believe me, you're on a Hawaiian vacation right now compared to what we can come up with if I hear from the school again."

"Mom, give me a break. You just don't understand."

Laurie wondered if every teenager was issued this line at

birth, and it blossomed in their DNA when they hit an age with double digits.

"You'd be surprised what I understand. I've been in love, too, you know."

"It's got nothing to do with that."

"What does it have to do with?"

But Anna just shook her head. Laurie decided to take the plunge. "Ms. Tillman also told me you've been seeing the grief team."

Anna lifted her head with a jerk, and glared at her. "That's supposed to be private!"

"Oh, your conversations are. Don't panic. But Daddy and I think you need to talk to someone else. On a—a steadier basis. Tomorrow morning we're going to see your cousin Gregg."

"I have school."

Now you worry about it. "I know. I'll call and tell the attendance secretary so you won't get in trouble."

"Why do I have to go see Gregg? I'm already talking to J—a guy on the grief team. He's nice."

"Because Gregg's a professional. He'll know what to do to help you work through this."

"Nobody knows."

Oh, the egocentrism of youth. "Anna, he's probably seen kids in your situation before."

"I doubt it."

"Come on. Just talk to him. You've got nothing to lose, and maybe it will help."

"Mom, how many times do I have to say this? Nothing's going to help. If I want to talk to someone, I'll talk to the grief team. Not you, not Gregg. He'll probably blab everything I say to everyone in the family anyway."

Do not lose it. This is too important. Stand firm. "He can't. Your conversations will be completely confidential. I'll pick you up tomorrow at 10:15."

"I won't be there. That's English, and I like it."

"Remember the lumber room."

But Anna didn't answer. Instead, she picked up the drawing pad, tore off the sketch of Kyle, and ripped it straight down the middle.

She wasn't going to get anywhere tonight. Laurie got off the bed and paused by the door in time to see Anna toss the pieces of paper on the floor to join the dirty laundry, homework, miscellaneous books, CDs, and other flotsam of the teenage life.

"We'll talk about this again in the morning."

She had to settle for having the last word. She certainly hadn't gotten any other satisfaction out of this little talk.

Chapter Thirteen

To: KelciP

From: JohnnysGrrl

Getting pretty friendly with Poser2 huh?

Careful what u talk about.

Can u swim?

*N*ick had had enough of teenagers to last him for the rest of his life. If he believed in reincarnation, he'd have said he'd done some horrible crime in a previous life to deserve this.

It was Monday night, and in interview room A he had Kate Parsons, with one of the female dispatchers silently serving as matron. In room B sat Rose Silverstein, with Gil and one of the second-shift clerks. And in the waiting room he had two sets of parents, both screaming lawsuits and demanding that their daughters be released immediately. He was thankful he had the seniority to avoid working the front desk. The poor rookie out there looked as though he was seriously considering a career change.

He closed the door of room A and sat opposite Kate, who looked as cool and chic as a model on a magazine cover.

"Can I have a soda?" she asked as soon as his rear was planted in the chair.

Without a word, the matron got up and fetched a paper cup

of water from the cooler. When she put it down in front of her, Kate wrinkled her nose and said, "That's not soda."

"And this isn't the Marriott." From next door Nick heard a muffled sound that could be someone crying, and Kate shifted in her chair.

"Who's that? Is that Rose? I saw her, you know, when you brought me in here. What are you doing to her? Is she all right?"

"She's fine, Kate. She's sitting there until we're done."

"But she sounds like she's crying!"

"She's probably a little nervous. Look, the sooner we get this over with, the sooner you all can go. So let's focus."

"But—"

"Now, we've talked a couple of times at your house about what happened that night on the bridge. What I need you to do right now is try to remember exactly what happened from the time Randi came over to your group to the time she went over the rail. Can you do that?"

"I already told you. Don't you have it recorded?"

"No. But we are being videotaped now."

"Yeah? Where's the camera?"

He pointed up at the corner of the room, and Kate smiled and waved at it. With a sigh, he said, "So, for posterity, how about you tell me again what happened?"

The girl moved her chair six inches to the right and turned sideways. What was she doing? Making sure the camera caught her best angle?

"Well, like I told you, we were all hanging out at the Stop-N-Go."

"Who do you mean by 'all'?"

"Me, Rose, Kelci, and Michelle Gibson. Then the boys joined us—Kyle, Brendan, and some friend of Brendan's whose name I forget. We all walked up on the bridge and then Poser came and we started goofing off."

"For the record, Poser is . . . ?"

"You know. Randi. Sorry, that's not very respectful of the dead, is it?"

He wondered why she bothered, when she clearly hadn't respected the girl when she was living. "And then?"

"Then Kyle saw Anna Hale down on the grass, so he went down to talk to her, which totally made Rose mad because she has such a major crush on him." She glanced at the camera. "Oops. I wasn't supposed to say that. It's a secret."

"The tape is confidential, Kate."

"So anyways, we started goofing off and shoving around and the next thing I knew, Randi was hanging all over Brendan like she wanted to be his girlfriend, so Rose got in her face—she's my best friend, you know, so she was totally defending me—and Randi leaned back to get away from her, and the next thing I know, there was a big splash. I always thought the rail was higher there. You know, to stop people from doing that."

"Can you back up a little? Are you saying that Rose Silverstein pushed her?" Now they were getting somewhere. Maybe— screaming parents aside—this had been the right tactic.

"I don't know if I'd say that, exactly," Kate hedged. "All I know is she got into Randi's face and they shoved back and forth. I must have looked away for a second because then Randi was just . . . gone."

"What did you see after that?"

"I don't remember. We all started screaming and running around."

"Did you call for help?"

"Somebody must have, because Kelci Platt's big sister showed up just then and she got in the car and they took off."

"Did anyone go down to try to get Randi out of the water?"

"I don't know. It was dark. And I was pretty upset."

He wondered about that. "And it never occurred to you to go get help? Or call 911?"

Her eyebrows rose. "Well, sure. That's what we were doing— running around trying to think what to do."

Were they? Because the only person who had actually done anything concrete was Anna Hale, if Vanessa's story about her running under the bridge was to be believed, and even still he hadn't been able to find out exactly what had happened after that. It bugged him that none of these kids had done the logical thing and called for help. Was it out of guilt? Or ignorance? Deliberate malice? Or worse—apathy?

"Anything else you'd like to add?"

"No, but if this tape goes on *America's Most Wanted*, they need to remember that my real name is Kathryn. That's R-Y-N. Kate is just what my friends call me."

Nick resisted the urge to remind her that this was the homicide of a classmate, not a reality show. "We'll try to remember that, Kate. Thank you for coming in."

He deposited the girl in the loving arms of her parents, who were still shouting recriminations and threats. After instructing the sergeant to hold them until Rose's interview was complete, he went to check on Gil's progress. Instead of joining them in interview room B and possibly interrupting a vital train of thought, though, he walked down the hall to the video closet. The tech indicated a chair and he sank into it, watching Gil's technique with the petite brunette in the expensive leather jacket.

"So you're saying Randi had a crush on Brendan, who was Kate's boyfriend?"

"Yes, which was totally not mutual. He couldn't stand her. So when she showed up and started talking to him, Kate got upset and got in her face."

"What was everyone else doing at this point?"

"I was talking to Kyle because we have this thing going, and I don't know what Kelci and Michelle were doing. I was busy, if you know what I mean."

"So Brendan and Kate were with Randi?"

"We were all kind of in this big group. So anyway, Kate gets in her face, and I go to help her, 'cause she's my best friend and all, and Kate gives her a shove, and then Brendan does, and then I do. Just little shoves, you know, like this." She flicked her hands as though she were on a volleyball team setting up the ball.

"Then what?" Gil prompted her.

"So Poser is over by the rail and Kate is in her face and I turned to look for Kyle but he was gone."

"Where'd he go?"

"Anna Hale showed up. He feels sorry for her that she's not in our group, see, so he goes to talk to her."

"So he wasn't there."

"No. But meanwhile Kate's getting really mad, and she pops her fingers against Poser"—again the volleyball flick—"and she's up against the rail and so I turn around and suddenly she's not there."

"Who?"

Rose glanced up at Gil through her bangs as though he were a complete idiot. "Poser, of course. Then there was a big splash and all you-know-what broke loose."

"What did you do?"

"I just started crying. And nobody carries tissues so I had to go over to the Stop-N-Go and buy some. I missed a lot of what happened then."

"So, to recap, you saw Kate push Randi over the rail?"

"It was her popping her in the chest, so yeah, she could have done it."

Great. So much for being best friends. And so much for my bright idea about getting the real story.

"What happened while you were at the Stop-N-Go?" Gil went on.

"Nothing. I got my tissues and went back up on the bridge, but by then mostly everyone was gone. Some sophomore guys walked me and another girl home. They were on the soccer team, I think, if you want to talk to them."

"Where was Kate?"

She shrugged. "I guess she went home. Brendan probably went with her. They live on the same street."

"What about Anna Hale?"

But on the tape, Rose just looked blank. Gil wound up the interview and when the room had emptied, Nick met him in the hall as he escorted Rose back to her mother.

"Get that?"

"Yep. Same story, different bad guy. Same bunch of stone-walling they've been doing all along."

"Why, who did Kate say was the bad guy?"

"Rose."

Gil cursed and then put on his solemn cop face as they stepped into the waiting area.

"Thank you for coming down tonight, folks," he said. "We appreciate your willingness to help us find the person responsible for this."

After more shouting and threatening with at least three different flavors of lawsuit, the parents got themselves mobilized in the direction of the door. Just as her father put his arm around her to guide her outside, Kate turned.

Her perfect oval face was white. "Wait," she said.

"Kate, come on. We're going home," her father said.

"No. No. This isn't right. Deputy, I—I have something I need to say."

"Not without Jack O'Day here to advise you, you don't," her father snapped.

"Daddy, no, this is important."

"Go ahead, Kate," Nick said. "That is, if your dad says it's okay."

She pulled away from him and he rolled his eyes. "Fine. Whatever."

"I didn't quite tell you everything back there."

"No? How about you tell me now?"

The desk sergeant leaned on his elbows in his glassed-in window, and even Rose's mother stopped in the doorway to listen.

"After—after Randi went in, we all kind of fell apart and went running around 'cause we didn't know what to do."

"Yes, you said that."

"Well, what I didn't say was that for a few seconds I was by myself, over on the other side of the road, where you can kind of look down on the park."

Where Kyle had told him he'd found Anna Hale. "Yes?"

"And I saw—I saw Anna there."

"Where?"

"In the water. With—with Randi."

"What?"

Pandemonium broke out. If this had been a movie, Nick

would have fired his service weapon into the air to get everyone to quiet down. It took at least half a minute before he could even hear Kate speak.

"Kate, this is serious. Slow down and try to remember exactly. Didn't you say it was dark and you couldn't see anything?"

Tears streaked her cheeks. "Yes, I did. I didn't want her to get in trouble, honest. But I can't keep this to myself anymore. It's eating me up."

"She's right," her mother said. "She can't sleep, doesn't eat properly—she's a mess over this."

"Tell me what you saw," Nick repeated. He was not in the mood for a sympathy ploy right now.

"She was in the water, and Randi was kind of floating, and Anna reached out and touched her, and she just kind of . . . sank."

"Was she alive?" Gil put in. "Could you tell if she was conscious?"

"No," the girl said. "I told you, it was dark."

"When you say 'touched her,' what do you mean?" Nick tried to keep the urgency out of his tone, but it wasn't easy.

"She—she put her hand out, kind of over Randi's face, and went like this." The heel of her hand dipped, as though she were pushing an imaginary canoe away from shore. "And then Randi just went under."

The sobs she'd been trying to hold back burst out of her, and her parents put protective arms around her and hustled her out the door.

Nick looked from Gil to the desk sergeant to the overhead camera, which had recorded everything. He'd heard the same rumors as everyone else, but he'd dismissed them as insubstantial since no one had actually been able to confirm them.

Anna. His heart squeezed with anguish.

Had he ever once thought that she might be involved as deeply as this? Had he ever been willing to consider that rumors are sometimes rooted in fact? Had he let love blind him to the truth?

Had love blinded them all? He thought of Laurie, as staunch as any soldier in her belief in her daughter. What would she do when she heard?

Family aside, what was he going to do? The pressure to make an arrest had reached the boiling point. The switchboard fielded twenty or thirty calls a day, from people who thought they had leads to people demanding a recall of the sheriff because he hadn't found the guilty party yet. Once the word got out—and he had no doubt at all that it would be all over town by break-fast—the department was going to have to act decisively, one way or the other.

The department, of course, meaning him.

Anna.

Without another word, he went back to his desk and called up the file on the system. He did his duty and wrote up the report, then put in a requisition to have the lobby security tape logged into the exhibit room as evidence.

Anna.

These girls pointed fingers at one another so easily. It was easy to be skeptical and dismiss them, but somewhere in all this videotape lay the truth. And now that Kate's accusation had been made in public, he was bound to perform due diligence and investigate her claim as carefully as all the other leads and hints he'd followed up on.

Whether he believed it or not.

～

On Tuesday morning, Laurie had just pulled into the garage after dropping off Tim (still half asleep—he was not a morning person) and Anna (sulky and adamant that she wasn't going to miss English to talk to a cousin she saw at least once a month anyway), when her cell phone rang. She threw the gear shift into park and shut the engine off, then pressed the answer button.

"Lor, it's me."

She smiled at the sound of her husband's voice, which had lost that frightening, closed-off tone and sounded more like the best friend she'd depended on for more than half her life. "Nice timing. I just got home." Looping one hand through the straps of her purse, she slid out of the van, slammed the door shut, and walked into the kitchen. "What's up?"

"Have you seen a paper this morning?" His tone stopped her.

"No. I only read it at school. Why?"

"Anna made the front page."

"How can that be?" Anna was grounded. She wasn't out running around and getting into trouble. Not anymore.

"It says here that two girls were questioned in connection with Miranda Peizer's death, and in a 'dramatic exposé straight out of *America's Most Wanted*,' one of them said that not only was an 'unnamed juvenile' the last person to see the victim alive, she also pushed her head under the water. And we know who they mean. So will everyone else."

Laurie's jaw dropped, and she spluttered through the dam of furious denial that backed up in her throat. In the end all that made it out was, "That's a fabrication and you know it."

"All I know is that Anna doesn't tell it that way. It's more important than ever that she see the counselor today."

"Don't worry. She's going if I have to drag her out of English class by her hair."

"We might have to keep her home a couple of days, Lor, if this is all over the school. Even though they didn't print her name, you know how nasty kids can get."

"What, and make her look like she's guilty? The kids are already nasty, Colin. They're throwing stuff at her in the cafeteria." *Fight or flight.* Adrenaline flooded her system as her body prepared to do battle—even though there was no one in her empty kitchen. "Who is saying all this, anyway? Who are these girls the paper is talking about?"

"It doesn't say here, but the simple process of elimination tells me one of them has to be Kate, or maybe Rose or Kelci."

"I'm going to get to the bottom of this." How dare these criminals-in-training shift the blame onto Anna? It was a fact that one of them had done the pushing. If there had been no pushing, there would have been no death. The evidence supported that, and everyone knew the evidence didn't lie.

Unlike teenage girls who were too afraid to come clean about their own horrific behavior.

"Lor, don't fly off the handle. Leave this to the police."

"Believe me, that's my very next call."

"Lor—"

Laurie could count on the fingers of one hand the number of times she'd hung up on her husband. This made one more. And for a miracle, Nick actually answered the phone at his desk.

"Tremore."

"Nick, it's me."

"Lor, I'm so sorry the paper ran the story before I could call you." Nothing like getting straight to the point. But was it propelled by guilt? Laurie decided she didn't care.

"You have to get them to retract it. If it wasn't already, my little 'unnamed juvenile's' life is going to be sheer hell, starting today."

"I couldn't stop it. There was a reporter there picking up a news briefing, and he happened to be in the waiting room when Kate made her big announcement."

So it had been Kate. Tall, slender Kate Parsons with her unlimited clothing budget and her big brown eyes.

"She's lying through her teeth, Nick. Anna would never do something so horrible. If she really did run under that bridge, she did it to see if she could help. I know that much about my daughter."

"Has she given you any other details at all?"

"Nothing more than what she told you, but think about it for a second." In view of this new twist, he needed to know what she knew. "I talked with Kyle Edgar the other day, and he said he found her standing in the water. But you know that part of the river as well as I do. There's a big drop-off about four feet out. We know where Randi fell, and there's no way Anna could have gotten that close without swimming. She was only wet up to her ankles."

"Laurie, think carefully. What was Anna wearing that night? Do you remember doing her laundry?"

She and Janice had talked about this, before their visit had gotten ugly. "There was nothing. No muddy socks, nothing."

"You don't remember wet pants or a wet shirt?"

"Nick, my daughter isn't going to go swimming in the Susquanny in November, no matter what the provocation. She's the world's original cold-water wimp."

"But she was suffering from severe agitation and trauma. She could have jumped in and not even felt it."

"Nope. Kyle said she was just standing there, up to her ankles in water."

"But we have no way to prove it."

"We have no way to prove what Kate said, either. We need to focus on who did the pushing, not the hysterical stories of fourteen-year-olds who are trying to foist the blame on an innocent girl to save their own skins."

"You don't need to tell me how to do my job, Laurie."

His tone was so cold she blinked, feeling the sting of his rebuke right through the connection. "I—I'm sorry. Of course not. I'm just a little hysterical myself right now. I want to tear apart anyone who points a finger at my little girl."

"That's natural. I know how protective you are. And I want you to know I'm doing everything I can to get to the bottom of this."

She sighed and ran a hand through her hair. "Okay. I'll try to possess my soul in patience while poor Anna is probably having the worst day of her life at school today."

"I think we should cancel Thanksgiving."

For a second her mind went blank. They'd cancel a holiday gathering because of a lot of gossip? "Thanksgiving?"

"Yes. Remember I asked you if Tanya Peizer could come along with me?"

Oh. Of course. "Right. I was thinking of something else. Why would you want to cancel it?"

"In light of this news . . . I think it would be awkward, not to mention a little weird."

What was it Colin had said about armed camps? Everyone seemed determined to put Tanya in one camp and Laurie in the other. And that was reasonable—if you believed that Anna had come within twenty yards of being responsible for Randi's death.

"Nick, Anna is innocent. She did not push Randi under the water, and she did not see her alive once she fell. If you believe that, really believe it, then having Tanya here is not awkward at all. It's simply two families helping each other through a rough time."

Static crackled. He must be on his cell phone.

"Nick? You believe that, right?"

"I don't have the luxury of believing anything other than the evidence," he said slowly.

"And there's no evidence to support what Kate said in the paper. So no, we're not going to cancel Thanksgiving. Dinner is at two o'clock, as usual. And Tanya is very welcome."

"Thanks, Lor. I meant it, you know. I'm doing everything I can to find out the truth."

"The truth shall set us free." She reminded herself of the Bible's promise aloud, and wondered if something that had been recorded two thousand years ago applied to the here and now in Glendale, Pennsylvania.

"Are you quoting the Bible to me, the family heathen?" Nick said. At least the cold note had gone out of his voice, and he was back to being the teasing cousin she loved.

For once, she didn't go along with the joke. "I was just thinking out loud. Hoping that what the Bible says really is true."

"I thought all you Christians believed that. The process of law is based on it," he pointed out.

"Provided you have all the evidence."

"Yeah. The evidence. I have to say, though, that I believe it as a general principle. I couldn't do this job if I didn't think that the truth divides the people doing wrong from those doing the right thing."

"Maybe you're closer to Christianity than you think."

"Don't push it," he warned, and she wondered if he was kidding, or if she'd overstepped the boundaries of his privacy. Maybe she should change the subject.

"You take good care of my daughter, Nick."

He was no dummy. He caught the implication right away. "You can count on me. Look, I've got to go. See you Thursday."

"Will do."

She hung up the phone slowly. Love and truth. She had those on her side.

Surely that was enough?

Enough for Anna, who had to be vindicated. Enough for Tanya, who must lie awake at night wondering who could have done this to her child.

Enough for this town?

That brought her thoughts back to Debbie and Cammie and the women in her study group who were so determined to create those imaginary camps set against one another, all in the name of kindness. If Nick and Tanya came for dinner, she'd show them. Anna was innocent. There was no reason for Tanya not to come. And when Tanya told those women where she'd been for dinner, they'd see how wrong they were to make separations where they shouldn't exist—between sisters in Christ.

She'd been feeling frustrated and guilty because she couldn't act to help her daughter, couldn't do anything to solve this mystery. But there was one thing she could do.

She could cook. And it would mean far more than an ordinary turkey dinner usually meant.

It would be a statement of faith and trust.

Feeling lighter in spirit than she had for days, Laurie pulled a notepad out of her purse and sat down at the counter. She wrote

Pick up turkey at the top of her list before the blinking light of the answering machine caught her attention.

She leaned over and pressed the playback button. Janice's voice said very stiffly, "Hi, Laurie, this is Janice. I'm afraid I can't make Bible study this morning after all. I'll go with the others tomorrow. I apologize for the late notice. Bye."

Armed camps. Trust.

Here was another person she'd pushed away, whom she'd allowed to fall into that opposing camp. She'd said unkind things about Kyle, just the way the people in Glendale were saying unkind things about Anna. What right did she have to say she didn't trust his word? She had no choice but to trust Anna's, or she'd find her family in pieces around her. Janice would feel the same. Families operated on love and trust. So did friendships. How many of those was she going to allow to fall by the wayside over this?

Before she lost her courage, she picked up the phone. Janice answered on the second ring.

"Janice, it's Laurie."

"Oh. Hello." Silence. "Did you get my message?"

"Yes. Both of them. Janice, please let me say that I'm sorry. I shouldn't have said those things I said to Kyle. He and Anna are both telling the truth. It's this town that's spreading lies and mistrust all over the place, and I'm tired of letting it get to me."

Silence.

"Janice?"

"I'm here." Her voice was scratchy. "I'm just . . . surprised."

"About what? You were brave enough to apologize when you hadn't done anything wrong. The least I can do is apologize when I'm the one at fault. I hurt you, and I accused your son of lying, and I'm sorry for it. I hope you'll forgive me."

"Oh, Laurie," Janice said on a sigh. "Of course I forgive you. We're mothers and we're scared, and we tend to lash out at people who threaten our kids."

The tension snarled under Laurie's heart relaxed enough to allow her a deep, cleansing breath. Forgiveness. What a wonderful, freeing thing.

"But that wasn't why I was surprised to hear from you."

It wasn't? "Why, what's up?"

"I shouldn't listen to gossip, that's all there is to it. Sometimes I wonder if I'll ever grow up and be able to make decisions based on something other than 'what will people think?'"

Gossip. Didn't it say in Proverbs that the person who kept a watch over his mouth would keep his life? Maybe she should suggest that passage to Cale Dayton for his next sermon.

"I just got off the phone with Maggie," Janice went on. "This article in the paper has everyone upset and saying things they don't mean."

"I bet they do mean them. Like what?"

"Neither of us needs this burden, Laurie. Trust me."

Trust me. "No point in bearing it by yourself."

"You already have enough to bear. I just don't understand it. We're all supposed to be sisters, supporting each other, not speculating and raising doubts about each other."

Janice might be surprised, but Laurie wasn't. "Ignore them. The important thing is that everything is out in the open between you and me, right?"

"Yes." Janice paused. "I'm praying for you, Laurie."

"Pray for our kids, my friend. They need it most of all."

Chapter Fourteen

At 10:15, Laurie pulled up at one side of the school parking lot, where the kids who weren't bused usually waited for their rides. Anna was nowhere in sight.

She tapped the horn, in case Anna was standing just inside the door talking, but when there was no movement besides the wet flapping of the flag on the flagpole, she turned the engine off and marched inside. Anna's English class met in one of the classrooms behind the library on the first floor. When she peeked in the door's wire-reinforced glass window, she couldn't see Anna anywhere in the classroom. The last thing she wanted to do was interrupt the teacher, so she slipped into the nearest of the girls' bathrooms.

"Anna?"

Silence.

Okay, this was going beyond annoying and becoming downright odd. The counselor's office was on the other side of the library, with its own outside entrance. She walked into the waiting room and knocked on the inner door. "Hello?"

"It's open."

She peered around the door and saw a young man with a soul patch and an earring lounging at the desk. "I thought—is Gail Burke here?"

"No, she had a meeting. I'm Jed. I'm a member of the grief team."

"Hi, Mom."

There, curled up on an orange beanbag chair, was Anna. She wriggled to a sitting position as Laurie exhaled a long breath made up of two parts relief and one part irritation.

"Do you mind telling me why you're not out front?" She needed to keep this short and authoritative. "We're going to be fifteen minutes late because I had to run through the school looking for you."

"Late for what?" Anna looked honestly puzzled.

"Our appointment with your cousin."

Memory dawned. "Oh, yeah."

"Oh, yeah. Let's get moving."

"Why? I'm already talking to a counselor." Anna nodded at Jed. The stud in his eyebrow glinted, as if to punctuate the huge gulf between the counselor Anna had chosen and the one Laurie and Colin had chosen for her.

Talking about what? The latest fashions in body jewelry? "Anna, stop wasting time. Where's your backpack?"

"In my locker. Mom, I'm talking to Jed. I don't need to see anyone else."

"At a hundred and fifty bucks an hour, you most certainly do."

The beanbag chair seemed to puff around her daughter's body as she sank into it, as though unwillingness were as heavy as those lead aprons you put on at the dentist's office.

"Anna, I'm not discussing this. Get up." She moved to the door, but Anna didn't heave a put-upon sigh and get to her feet. Instead, she glanced at Jed, her eyes full of appeal.

"Mrs. Hale, if you don't mind my saying so, Anna and I are making progress."

Laurie didn't reply. Instead, she glanced at her watch.

"I've been talking to him since it happened, Mom."

"So I understand." Laurie flicked a glance at Jed. "What I'd like to know is why I wasn't told."

"Parents aren't told as a general rule." Why was he so comfortable with this? How much experience had he had with skeptical parents? "The kids are free to tell their parents, of course, but we're as bound by confidentiality as any other professional who might see Anna."

"That's ridiculous." *How could Anna see a counselor behind our backs—opening up to a stranger who may or may not know what he's doing?*

"Not really. It's important for Anna to know that anything she says here doesn't leave the room. Otherwise, what's the point?"

"The point is, we could have been working together." She ignored Jed and spoke to Anna. "We could've talked about this stuff at home. So Daddy and I wouldn't have been worrying our heads off about things like you not wanting to ride over the Susquanny Bridge or deciding to beat on your brother for no reason."

"Mom, everybody beats on their brother," Anna pointed out.

"Not in our family, they don't." She took a deep breath and looked at Jed. "So the bottom line here is that you've been counseling my daughter without my permission and leaving me totally in the dark about what's bothering her."

"I've been counseling your daughter and helping her work through some issues," Jed corrected gently.

"That's very vague. How about we get specific?"

"Not without Anna's permission."

"No," Anna said instantly. "You promised."

Jed looked at Laurie and spread his hands, indicating, she supposed, that the matter was out of them.

"I don't know anything about you, Jed. And I don't feel confident that you'll bring her through this." Anna's mental health was far too important to trust to a slacker who poked holes in his head.

"Mrs. Hale, everyone on the grief team is licensed by the state. But aside from that, you can feel comfortable that Anna will do the right thing for herself."

At fourteen? "But—but what if—" What if it all went wrong? What if Anna had some kind of mental breakdown, and the only person who knew the cause or effect was Jed? He could go back to Pittsburgh or wherever he came from at a moment's notice, leaving them to deal with the fallout.

"Anna is making progress," he repeated. "The school's policy is that if a student is in danger in any way—if they threaten harm to themselves, for instance—the parents are to be notified immediately. But I don't think that's going to be a problem."

"I'm glad to hear it." *You'd let me know if my kid was going to commit suicide, but when she screams at bridges and refuses to come out of her room, I'm on my own?*

"Anna's a good kid." He tossed her a grin, and Anna grinned back. She hadn't seen Anna smile since before Randi's death, Laurie thought with a pang. Not one smile. "She has some issues, but we'll get through them. And"—he glanced at his watch—"we have half an hour left, so if you don't mind . . . ?"

He got up and offered his hand. Laurie took it out of habit, not because she was harboring any goodwill toward this man who had just dismissed her as though her opinions and plans didn't matter.

"Fine. I'll see you at home, then."

"Bye, Mom."

And then there was nothing to do but leave. Oh, and call Gregg to inform him they wouldn't be coming after all. And since his office had a twenty-four-hour cancellation policy, family or not, she was stuck paying a hundred and fifty dollars for nothing.

When he got home from work and heard about it, Colin pulled out one of the kitchen stools and stared at her. "You mean you didn't haul her out of there and keep the appointment?"

This was not her fault. They were a team. She would not get angry and take it out on Colin.

"No, I didn't. Apparently she's been seeing the grief counselor since it happened, and he says she's been 'having issues' but they're 'making progress.'" She made quotation marks with her fingers in the air. "If she already has a relationship with this guy and she's talking to him, I don't see what good it will do to bring someone else in."

"But you said he was a slacker type. With piercings! Honestly, Lor, what kind of example is he for Anna? At least with Gregg we know he's a Christian."

She yanked open the fridge and hauled the turkey out. "Oomph." A couple of seconds digging through the cupboard produced her biggest roaster and gave her time to rein in her temper like the runaway horse it was.

"I hardly think his skill as a counselor depends on his faith, Colin." Good grief, now she was defending a stranger. "If you want to talk to Anna and inform her we're taking her elsewhere, so that she has to start all over again with someone new, you can try. But she's so fragile right now I don't think it would be a good idea."

"But you don't even know what he's saying to her. What kind

of methods he's using. What kind of ideas he's putting in her head."

"We wouldn't if she were seeing Gregg, either. Confidentiality."

"But at least I'd know she was in Christian hands. I may not know as much about his qualifications as I'd like, but I do know his faith is sound."

"Colin, this is about what Anna needs, not what we need to know."

"We're her parents! Of course we should know."

"Not according to the school system."

"So, what, you're just going to give up and let her do what she wants instead of what's good for her? This is not boding well for the rest of her teenage years."

Only Colin used expressions like "boding well."

"Talk to her if you want. See how far you get. I have to do something with this bird and then get dinner ready."

"I just want what's best for Anna."

"I know. We both do. But Anna isn't a child anymore, Colin. You can't just tell her what to do. She's fourteen, and she wants to make a few decisions on her own."

"This situation is too important for her to decide on her own. That kid has no clue about what's good for her."

"Mom? Dad?"

Laurie pulled the package of giblets out of the turkey's cavity. Anna stood in the doorway.

"Are you having a fight about me?"

Colin's face lost its intensity as tenderness softened his eyes. "No, sweetie. We're having a discussion about you. Come on in."

Anna sidled into the room. "What are you talking about?"

"I'm concerned that you blew off your cousin Gregg today. Mind telling me why?"

"Oh." Her shoulders straightened a little, as if this wasn't what she'd been expecting. "I told Mom. I'm already talking to Jed and working out some stuff about Randi and what happened. I don't want to talk to anybody else."

"Jed may be a perfectly good counselor, but I want you to talk to Gregg instead."

"Why?"

"Because I feel he's a better choice for you, honey."

"Why? You don't even know Jed. Did Mom say something bad about him?" Her glance flicked from her father to Laurie.

"No, of course not. But Gregg is a Christian, and leaving out the fact that he's family, he's very well qualified. Now, Jed—"

"He's a Christian, too." Anna swiped a box of crackers off the counter and crunched into them. "He goes to Calvary Christian Center."

The biggest church in town, where people like the O'Days went. This, in Laurie's opinion, was no kind of recommendation. But at least it proved he was local. If he'd been from Pittsburgh or some other big place, they might not be able to reach him if Anna needed him.

"You just don't like him because he's cool and you're . . . parents."

"Oh, Anna, don't be silly," Laurie said. "We're concerned about his qualifications."

"Jed is just as qualified as Gregg. He's got a Ph.D. And even if he didn't, I still wouldn't go to Gregg. As soon as I was out of the office, he'd be on the phone, blabbing to Auntie Dawn and Grandma and you guys about what I said."

"Anna, he can't do that." Colin was *this close* to losing his temper, which happened about once a year. Laurie knew it was because getting help for Anna was so important to him, and he just didn't understand why she would refuse his efforts to help her.

"You'd find a way to make him tell, and then what would happen to me?"

"I don't know why you're treating your feelings like some big secret." Colin stood, the thin lines of his face set with anger.

"Do you know what's in the paper, Anna?" Laurie said. "Kate Parsons, that's what, telling the whole world that you held Randi under the water. They can't put your name in the article, of course, but you can bet it won't be a secret for long. I suggest you start sharing with us, I really do."

Anna's color faded, but she kept her mouth firmly shut.

"You're worried about what'll happen to you?" Colin said. "Here's a news flash. You're on lockdown for two more weeks on top of your current sentence, that's what."

That got her. "But Daddy, that's all of Christmas break!"

"What a coincidence. That's the deal. Either you see Gregg as soon as he has an opening, or you're looking at six weeks with the same rules. Straight home from school, no phone, no TV, no friends over. No Christmas dance, and no church activities unless your mother or I are there. Take your pick."

Father and daughter stared each other down while Laurie held her breath.

Finally Anna shrugged. "Oh well. Mrs. Blake always gives a history paper over break. I guess I'll have lots of time to write it."

With that she turned and, head held high, walked out of the kitchen. Colin looked as though he'd like to kick the nearest turkey. "I'm going to take a shower," he said tightly and left the room.

Laurie regarded the roasting pan for a moment. "That went well," she observed. The turkey said nothing. When the phone rang, she jumped about a foot.

"Hello?"

"Laurie, it's Janice again. Janice Edgar?"

"How many Janices do I know?" She forced cheer into her voice. "I'm glad to hear your voice. How are you?"

"I'm fine. I was sitting here cutting up vegetables when God laid it on my heart to call you, so here I am."

Her eyes stung with sudden tears. "His timing is impeccable. I've had a lousy day."

"Can I help?"

"Not unless you can convince Anna it would be better for her to talk to her cousin the psychologist than the twenty-something grief counselor at the school."

"Ah. Well, if it's any comfort, Kyle talked to him, too. Which one was it?"

"His name is Jed."

"Yes. Same one."

"I'm having a hard time trusting my little girl's emotional health to a guy with a stud in his eyebrow."

"Apparently he relates really well to the kids. Gail Burke is on one of my committees, and she says he's gold."

Her spirits lightened a little. "Really? I'm glad I have some good news to give Colin, then." She lowered her voice. "Between you and me, it's turning into a power struggle."

"I bet it is. But as long as she's talking to the grief team, I really believe she'll be in good hands. They didn't have help like this when I was in high school, and goodness knows some of us could have used it."

Their friendship was too new and green for Laurie to jump

in as she might have done and ask for details. "Thanks for the encouragement, Janice. I can't tell you how much I appreciate it."

"Keep your chin up. I need to get back to making dinner before Barrett and Kyle get home. Just remember, God is still in charge. He'll see that everything turns out for good for those who love him."

Laurie said good-bye and hung up the phone. Truth be told, she wasn't as sure about that as she might have been, say, a couple of weeks ago.

Chapter Fifteen

Tanya, Nick saw when he picked her up, had dressed in her best for Thanksgiving dinner at the Hales' house. She wore a navy-blue dress that wrapped across the front and tied with a bow at the waist. On a lot of women this would have been fatally boring, but Tanya's skin seemed even more soft and fragile, and her reddish-blonde hair glowed. Instead of tying her hair up in a bun or scraping it back in a ponytail, she'd allowed it to curl loosely around her face.

It took ten years off her. And the dress didn't hurt, either. Nick had been so busy seeing her as the victim's bereaved parent that he'd completely missed the attractive woman . . . until now.

He opened the door of his truck and helped her into it, noting with interest how slender and shapely her calves looked. Where had his eyes been all this time?

In her daughter's case file, the thinking part of his brain answered. *Right where they should be, until you get this mess straightened out.*

And while he was on that subject . . .

"Are you okay with this?" he asked. "Going to the Hales', I mean."

She looked at him curiously. "I hope you're not having second thoughts after I wrestled my way into panty hose for the first time in two years."

The image produced a quick grin, and then he got serious again. "I just thought that you might have changed your mind after that article in the paper."

"It was a shock." Her skin paled, and her fingers tightened on her handbag in her lap. "But it's not true, of course, what Kate said. That paper should be ashamed for printing stuff like that, even if they didn't name the juvenile in question. Like that helps."

"You know who the juvenile was."

"Oh, sure. Debbie and Maggie got it from Kate's mother, who's been broadcasting it far and wide."

"So we're okay?"

She smiled at him, but it wasn't the kind that meant dimples. It was a sad smile. "As okay as it gets."

That was good enough for him, all things considered.

At Laurie and Colin's, he gave a peremptory knock on the front door and opened it. "Happy Thanksgiving! Two hungry people, incoming."

"Nick." Colin came out of the living room with a hand extended and a cordial smile. "And Tanya. We're so glad you came."

"Thanks for having us," he answered, while Tanya murmured the same. "Where's Laurie? And the kids?"

Colin took Tanya's navy-surplus coat, which didn't go very well with her dress but was evidently the only one she had that would do the job of keeping her warm in late November. "In the kitchen, scarfing appetizers. Better hurry."

The only one doing any scarfing, though, was Tim. Laurie stood in front of a double oven, checking a bubbling pan of sweet potatoes flavored, by the smell of it, with orange and brown sugar.

"My favorite," he said.

She pushed the pan back into the top oven, closed the door, and shook her mitts off her hands and onto the counter. "I know. Along with dressing, brussels sprouts, cranberry salad, and mashed potatoes. You are so predictable." She leaned in and gave him a hug, then turned to Tanya. "Welcome," Laurie said with a smile that didn't quite reach her shadowed eyes. "We're so glad we get to have you to ourselves today."

"Thanks, Laurie." Tanya didn't seem to be aware that there was anything amiss. And there was obviously going to be no further discussion of newspaper articles or anything connected to them. "I don't know what I would have done if Nick hadn't invited me. Gone and had a burger somewhere, I guess." A spasm flickered across her face.

"No burgers here, I'm afraid, much to Tim's relief. He prefers brussels sprouts." Tim stuck his finger in his mouth and mimicked throwing up. "All right, you. Remember the rules. You have to eat one single sprout. As in, two halves."

"Aw, Mommmmm," he whined.

"Cheer up, bud," Nick said. "They'll build your muscles so you can play pond hockey with the big kids." He turned back to Laurie. "Where's Anna? She might not be a big fan of brussels sprouts, but she's like me. She can scent a pan of sweet potatoes in a lead-lined bunker sixty feet underground."

"Up in her room, sulking. She's grounded for two more weeks."

"Through Christmas break?" Tanya asked.

"That's the first thing she said." Laurie pulled a can of whole cranberries and one of cranberry jelly out of the fridge and dumped the contents of both into a cut-glass bowl. "But if she's going to disobey us, her social life will just have to suffer." As she mixed the berries and the jelly together, the clang of the spoon on the glass sounded like a miniature alarm.

"Can I do something for you?" Tanya asked. "Make a salad? Put out pickles and olives?"

"No, I have it handled." Laurie smoothed the top of the pulverized mixture. "You can put this on the table, though. Everything's nearly ready."

Laurie was the most together person Nick knew. Whether she was making spaghetti for her family or organizing a potluck for the entire church, she went at it armed with her lists and an unshakable belief that everyone would support her. The problem was, sometimes that kind of efficiency was formidable, and once in a while, if she was having a bad day, she took an offer of help as an insult, like maybe the person thought she wasn't doing a good enough job.

He hoped this wasn't that kind of day.

Tanya took the cranberry sauce into the dining room with a meekness that, for some reason, caused a little twist of pain in the region of his heart. He consoled himself with the thought that the two women had been in the same Bible study group for months. Tanya knew Laurie well enough to know she wouldn't deliberately set out to hurt her.

Tim leaned into the open fridge. "Hey, Mom, are we having pumpkin pie?"

"Of course. The pies are sitting out in the garage. Don't even think about touching them."

"Where's the whipped cream, then?"

"We have to make it. After dinner."

"But there isn't any cream."

"What?" Laurie checked the fridge herself, and sighed. "I knew I'd forget something. Tim, take a couple of dollars out of my wallet and run to the store, okay?"

"I can do it," Nick offered. "Take me five minutes." The Stop-N-Go was on the other side of the river, but it was still closer than the supermarket, which had probably closed at noon anyway.

"No, Tim can go," Laurie said. "He needs to work off some energy." Tim already had his coat and boots on. "And no stopping, either. Straight there and straight back, or no pie for you."

"Bye, Mom, back next year!" The door slammed behind him and Laurie rolled her eyes.

"You should have sent him after dinner," Colin observed. "If he gets distracted, we could be eating cold turkey."

"If he's more than ten minutes, I'll walk down and fetch him," Nick said. "But I bet he won't be. He's pretty serious about his food."

"KeShawn lives close to where the walking path goes over the river," Colin pointed out. "He's been sucked into the vortex before. Meantime, where's my other offspring? She needs to get down here and say hello like a civilized person."

"Anna!" her mother called. "Time to come down."

There was a mumble from above that didn't sound very promising.

"Anna Catherine Hale, you come down. Now."

No response.

Nick spread his hands. "Was it something I said? Suddenly I'm not her favorite cousin?"

"You're a cop, and everyone thinks she's a suspect," Tanya said, coming back into the kitchen. "She's hiding."

The eight-hundred-pound gorilla that everyone was determined not to talk about landed in the middle of the kitchen with a thud. Silence fell as the three of them looked anywhere but at Tanya.

Laurie was the first to find her voice. "What do you mean?"

"Hiding? That's ridiculous," Nick said. "We're family."

Tanya addressed herself to Laurie. "You know what I mean. I'm just telling the truth. What have I got to lose? It's my daughter who's not here to have turkey and cranberry sauce."

"Anna's *not* responsible for that."

"She was there that night."

"What's that supposed to mean?"

"Lor." Colin put a hand on his wife's arm. "This isn't easy for Tanya."

"Of course it isn't." Laurie shook him off. "But no one seems to be thinking about us. Or about a young girl who is completely innocent. And you haven't answered me, Tanya."

Both women faced off over the marble breakfast bar. "Okay, so I don't believe Anna would have pushed Randi's face under, like people are saying. But she was there. She could have done something to help. I'd give a lot to know why she didn't."

"She was *not* up on that bridge," Laurie hissed, her face white, her skin stretched over her cheekbones. "You should be saying these things to Kate's mother, or Rose's, or Kelci Platt's."

"If she was close enough to run under that bridge and look, she was close enough to go up on it and stop them."

"She couldn't have——" Nick began.

"My daughter is not responsible for your daughter's death." Now dark blood flooded Laurie's cheeks in a rush, and she bit off the consonants one by one.

"Why didn't she stop them, then? Why didn't someone stop them? All it would have taken was one kid to say, 'Wait, this is nuts,' and Randi would still be alive."

Again, Nick tried to intervene. "It might not have been as simple as——"

"And you think my daughter should have been that kid?"

"Well, aren't you the church leader around here? Sophie

Dayton might be the pastor's wife, but everybody knows you really run the show."

"That's not true!"

But Tanya was relentless. Her face was so pale that the freckles stood out on it like measles spots, and her eyes were wide with unshed tears. Nick looked at Colin and tried to signal that maybe he ought to step in and separate them.

"Everyone says so. So what I'd like to know is, why won't she come forward and tell the truth even though it's too late? For that matter, why won't she come down here and look me in the face? Do you know what that says to me?"

Again, silence fell like a rock—the kind of appalled silence that was too hard to break and inflicted injury on every soul it touched.

Into it came a young, frightened voice. "Does anyone know where Tim is?"

Nick turned to see Anna standing in the kitchen doorway. Automatically, he glanced at his watch and part of his mind recorded the fact that Tim had been gone for twenty minutes. Twenty agonizing minutes that he wished had never happened.

"I'll go get him," he volunteered. "Tanya, want to come? I think maybe a break would do us all some good."

"It doesn't sound like Tanya has anything to be thankful for where we're concerned."

"Lor—"

"She's right," Tanya said. "I'll go with Nick, but it's probably better if I don't come back."

"Isn't he here?" Anna said.

"Who?" her father asked, looking from his wife to Tanya as if he couldn't believe two Christian women could speak to each other this way.

"Tim! Isn't he here?"

"For heaven's sakes, Anna, he went to get whipping cream."

"And he's not back yet? Dad, we have to do something."

Nick felt as though he'd stepped into an alternate universe. People were saying the unspeakable. Getting upset about the trivial. No one was reacting the way normal people were supposed to.

He latched on to concrete action. "Fine. Tanya, get your coat. We'll go find Tim and send him home. Then we'll go get some supper somewhere else." *And maybe I'll step back through the looking glass tomorrow and find out I dreamed the whole thing.*

"Fine." Laurie's face, which he hardly ever saw without a smile, was set and expressionless. "Thank you."

Nick hustled Tanya out the door and down the sidewalk. He had three blocks before they came to the walkway over the river and KeShawn Platt's house—and he intended to use every step.

"Mind telling me what that was all about?" he asked.

"I'm not going to apologize."

"I'm not asking you to. I just asked what it was all about. I always thought Laurie was good to you."

"She was. Is. I know she's your cousin and you love Anna. I thought I could handle it. Obviously I made the wrong decision."

Two blocks.

"I hope you meant what you said about Anna not pushing Randi under. I've interviewed a dozen kids at least twice each, and Kate is the only one who brought it up. It still needs to be investigated."

"But the mayor's boy said he saw Anna standing in the water. His mother said so yesterday at Bible study."

"Sure. And the place where Randi went in is a good thirty or forty feet away. The current isn't strong enough to have taken her over to the bank in those few seconds."

"Then why did Kate say what she said?"

One block.

"I'm guessing it's a diversionary tactic. We're bumping up the heat on those three girls, and when you're cornered, your first reaction is to lash out or throw up a distraction. A smoke screen. It's just unfortunate that that reporter happened to be in the waiting room when she did it, and went public with the story before we could prove whether it was true or not."

Tanya sighed, and with the Platt house and the river walk in sight, she slowed her pace. "Anna still could have done something."

"Maybe. Maybe not. But speculating or dwelling on the what-ifs isn't going to get us anywhere. And neither is hurting Laurie and Colin."

"It hurts *me*, Nick."

Inside, he felt himself shift from cop mode to protector mode. Almost before he could think about it, he'd slipped an arm around her shoulders, right there on the sidewalk.

"I can't imagine how much it must hurt. I'm not a parent, so I don't have much room to talk. But Tanya, I swear to you, we're closing in on a resolution. I'm doing everything I can, and Gil, my partner, is working on it today. This case is the department's highest priority."

"I know." She turned so that her next words were muffled in the front of his jacket. "And I'm going to regret saying what I said to Laurie. But there she was in her beautiful house with her perfect kids and her husband, who is my boss, and what do I have? Nothing. No house, no husband, no daughter. Sometimes I think I can face it, and then a day like today happens, and I know I never will."

"You have me," he blurted, then felt like smacking himself on the forehead. He wasn't ready for a relationship. His job was too demanding. And she was a Christian—and he'd already made up his mind that wasn't the path for him.

"Do I?" she asked in a hopeless way that gripped his heart and wrung it like a sponge.

"I'm your friend, Tanya. And even if it wasn't my job to find out what happened, I'd do everything I could to get you an answer."

Her friend. That's all he could be to her right now, because of the investigation, and in the future, because they were just too different.

But despite that, time seemed to stop and his surroundings faded as his consciousness spiraled in on this woman, this moment. He felt the dense wool of her coat under his hands. Smelled the flowery scent of her shampoo. Realized for the first time that the top of her head came exactly to the level of his nose, so she wasn't as small as he'd thought all along.

She tipped her head back and looked him full in the face. He fell headlong into her eyes, those eyes that had seen far more pain and disappointment than he had ever experienced.

Those eyes could make him doubt the wisdom of his decision to avoid her. They could—

"Nick!"

Tim's reedy voice sounded from far away. A couple of seconds drifted past while Nick swam out of the bubble he and Tanya had created. Then sound and movement resumed all around them.

"Hey, Nick!"

Tim, KeShawn, Kate, and Kelci waved at them from the halfway point of the footbridge. Beside him, Tanya sucked in a breath and stiffened. She jammed her hands into her pockets as if she were preventing herself from reaching out for the older girls and shaking the truth out of them.

Or maybe that was just how he felt.

"Hey, bud, you are in deep with your mother. Don't you know what straight there and straight back means?"

Tim laughed and grabbed at the carton of whipping cream, which Kate held just out of his reach.

"Don't be mad at him, Deputy," Kate said as they joined him and Tanya. "We all walked over together, and Kelci took some pictures with her new digital camera." She handed him the cream with a grin over her shoulder at Tim.

Kelci's face was expressionless as she waved a palm-size silver unit at him, one Nick had seen advertised for about five hundred bucks. Where did the daughter of a night-shift nurse get the money for that kind of toy?

"We'll send you copies, Tim," Kelci promised with a glance at Kate. "Bye."

Tim grabbed Nick's and Tanya's hands and pulled them around in the direction of home as the other kids trooped across the Platt yard and into the house. He chattered for three solid blocks, to the point where neither Nick nor Tanya could get a word in edgewise. When they reached Nick's truck, parked in the Hale driveway, they stopped and he handed Tim the cream.

"Take this to your mom, okay? We're going to head off."

The ten-year-old stared at them, confusion darkening his brown eyes. "Aren't you staying for dinner?"

"We were, but Ms. Peizer isn't feeling up to it. Give me a rain check?"

Tim shook his head and looked sorry for him. "Man, you're giving up Mom's pumpkin pie. Are you nuts?"

"Well, sometimes we have to make sacrifices when we put someone else's welfare first. But I'll be getting a double burger with the works at the Split Rail. Think of me when you're working on that brussels sprout."

Tim blew him a raspberry and ran into the house, where Nick could hear Laurie's voice from out in the driveway before the door shut.

As he opened the door of the truck for Tanya, he wondered just how much the Hale family planned on thanking God for a day like today.

Because if he were honest, he'd admit he had more to be thankful for right now than they did. And who was responsible for that? God—in a case of giving with one hand and taking away with the other? Or was it all just a matter of chance and bad timing?

Not the most cheerful outlook. Faith seemed to make incurable optimists out of people—except maybe for Tanya, who appeared to have her feet on the ground.

"Penny for your thoughts," Tanya said as they motored at a law-abiding twenty-five miles per hour to the other side of town.

His smile was a rueful tightening of one corner of his mouth. "I was just thinking that I have a lot more to be thankful for than the Hales do today. And wondering if it is a case of God giving with one hand and taking away with the other."

"I wasn't feeling very thankful this morning," Tanya admitted. "It didn't seem worth it to even get out of bed, and putting on good clothes was almost more than I could handle. But then you drove up and things seemed to get better. For a while." She paused. "Losing it in the kitchen wasn't so good."

"I'm sure Laurie will understand."

"Maybe. I don't know what happened to me. Those words just came up out of nowhere and I couldn't control them."

He hesitated. "Are you talking to anyone? Like a counselor?"

"Where am I going to get the money for that?" She threw him a glance.

"It might not cost money. Maybe through your church? Laurie would know."

"Maybe I'll ask her. Right after I apologize."

"You should talk to someone, Tanya. You're grieving. Nobody expects you to handle this all alone."

"I'm not alone. My Bible study group is always around. Laurie wasn't there yesterday, though."

He thought about Kate and the scene in the police department's lobby, and about Anna's face. "She's got a lot on her mind."

She straightened a little. "Well, now I have you and a burger. I'm thankful for that."

"Lucky for me your expectations are low."

He meant it to be a joke, but she didn't take it that way. "They aren't, you know. Since I met Christ, my expectations have done a one-eighty."

He didn't want to hear about Christ. He didn't want to know about her expectations. Maybe this was a mistake.

"Maybe some of the problems between Randi and me were because my expectations for her weren't high enough."

"Problems?" He hadn't heard her mention those before. All he'd seen was the love and the loss.

"Oh, we had problems, believe me. But I seemed to live down to my parents' expectations. I wonder if I was encouraging Randi to do the same. Maybe if I'd done things differently, she would still be here."

"Tanya, don't go there. It's no good blaming yourself. It won't change anything. We have to live with what's real."

He could see the Split Rail from where they idled at the light. The streets of downtown Glendale were practically empty, and he found a parking spot only half a block away.

"I know," she said. Her gaze was fixed on some view in the landscape in her mind. One that probably didn't include storefronts. Whatever it was, it didn't look good.

"After all," he said, "God made reality, right? That's what we have to deal with. What he made."

She swung to face him. "What are you saying? That my wishing for what might have been is wrong? That Satan is behind it?"

Oh, no. He wouldn't get into a discussion of theology for anything. "I can't say. I'm no authority. But let's concentrate on what we have. We have you. We have me. You have friends who care about you. And we both have a double burger with the works. Right?"

She pulled her coat more closely around her as the wind swept fallen leaves in front of itself down the street. "I suppose that's something to be thankful for. I'll mention that when I say grace over my supper."

Her eyes challenged him.

"You do that," he said, and she smiled, as if she'd won a victory.

Chapter Sixteen

Father in heaven, thank you for this wonderful feast during this season of thanksgiving," Colin said from the head of the table, the huge turkey in front of him. "Thank you that we can gather around this table as a family. Lord, I pray that you would heal the breach between Laurie and Tanya. I pray that you would speak to Nick and bring him to a realization of your love. And most of all, Lord, I pray that you would give Anna the strength and courage to get to the other side of this rough experience. Give Nick the discernment to solve this case, so that this cloud of stress could be lifted from all of us. In Jesus' name, amen."

Laurie murmured an "amen" while Colin got up to carve a turkey that was far too big for only the four of them. She was going to have to pull out all the stops as far as getting creative with leftovers went, or they'd be eating turkey with their ham at Christmas.

Over Tim's chatter and Anna's monosyllabic replies, Tanya's voice rang in her head, saying aloud the dreadful things that had been hiding in her own thoughts. Common sense and Nick had both told her that Randi had gone into the river too far away for Anna to have reached her. But subversive thoughts didn't pay attention to common sense. And neither did small-town gossip.

She forked turkey, dressing, and cranberries into her mouth

at regular intervals. It may as well have been sand for all the enjoyment she got out of the fruits of her labors.

"—and then me and KeShawn and Kelci and Kate came back. We saw Nick and Ms. Peizer in the path, practically kissing."

Laurie tuned her son back in with a jolt. "What?"

"Ewwww!" he added for emphasis around a mouthful of sweet potato casserole.

"Kissing?" Colin asked. "No kidding." He exchanged a glance with Laurie, as though she should have some reaction. But she didn't have much in the way of emotion left. Tim was probably mistaken.

"Practically. Gross."

"Kate?" Anna repeated, a beat off. "Kate Parsons was with you?"

"She was with Kelci. Me and KeShawn let them come to the store with us."

"What did you do there?" Anna persisted. Which was strange, because normally she couldn't care less what a couple of kids did. She and Tim occupied different universes, and most of the time that suited them both just fine.

"I got the whipping cream, duh."

"Tim," his father said in a warning tone.

"What about after that? You were gone for*ever*."

Tim shrugged, clearly more interested in his casserole than in giving his sister a blow-by-blow. "We goofed around. Took some pictures. Kelci says she'll send them to me. You can put 'em on MySpace and tell everyone about how cool I am."

"Tim, listen to me," Anna said, her tone strained. "Don't go anywhere with those two. You get me?"

"You're not the boss of me, banana head."

"Mom," Anna appealed to her mother. "Tell him."

Laurie sighed. Teenage histrionics, maybe, but she could hardly blame Anna. "Tim, your sister is right. Kate is saying nasty things about us, and until this is cleared up, you probably shouldn't hang around with her."

"I wasn't! I was with KeShawn. Those girls just butted in."

"Still—"

"I mean it," Anna broke in. "Kate could—" She stopped.

Tim eyed her. "Could what?"

"Could . . . talk about you," she finished lamely. Then her eyes filled with tears and she pushed away from the table.

"Anna, where are you going?" Laurie put out a hand to stop her. "You've hardly eaten anything."

"Up to my room." Her chest hitched, as though sobs were about to burst the dam of her shaky control.

"Sweetie, I know this is upsetting, but we have to put it aside for a while and think about what we have to be thankful for."

"Yeah? Like what?" Anna's whole body shrieked of defeat and challenge, all at once. "What do I have to be thankful for? The whole school hates me. Nick thinks I'm a murderer, and so does Randi's mom. You guys have your heads buried so far in the sand you can't even see daylight, and you're telling me I should be thankful? Way to go, Mom."

"Anna!" Colin exclaimed.

But she was already pounding up the stairs to her room.

Laurie tried to keep her lip from wobbling, but there was no stopping the tears that flooded her eyes, blurring the sight of her plate and everything around her. She gasped and then just gave in to it, pressing her napkin to her mouth and hunching over like an animal in pain.

Because it did hurt. Everything hurt. It hurt that Anna only spoke the truth. It hurt that Tanya had thrown Laurie's deepest, darkest doubts about Anna's innocence right out into the kitchen to wound them all. And worst of all, it hurt that Anna's pain was probably double hers, and she couldn't do a blessed thing about it except sit here and cry like a two-year-old.

"Mama?" Tim said in a way he hadn't since he'd been small enough to pick up and cuddle. "Don't cry."

Colin got up and put his arms around her. "Lor. Sweetie, please. Tim's getting upset."

Which only made the tears come faster. "I've had enough!" she said with a gasp. "I'm done. I can't take any more."

Oh, Lord, how long?

The Bible said that, didn't it? Wasn't it David who was being hounded on all sides, with everybody in the kingdom giving him grief? The story of her life. Here she was, trying to be strong, getting Anna what she needed, getting Tanya what she needed. She looked after everyone. And everyone on all sides was attacking her for it.

"Who's going to take care of me?" she choked, trying to control the sobs that seemed to have a life of their own.

An expression of complete bewilderment showered Colin's face. "We need to think about the kids, Laurie. Come on, now Tim's starting to cry."

She turned in her chair and gulped back the tears as she gathered Tim into her arms. "It's okay, baby. It's okay. It's not your fault. I'm just upset."

Tim lifted his wet face to look into her eyes. "I'm sorry I was late bringing back the cream."

She kissed him and used her dinner napkin to wipe both of their faces. "No, not about that. I'm upset that Tanya and Nick had to go."

"Nick said she wasn't feeling well," Tim said.

"I guess she wasn't."

"They get to have hamburgers."

"And you get to have pumpkin pie. Why don't you and Daddy go put a movie in, and we'll digest for a little while, okay?"

"Okay."

Colin ruffled his hair affectionately and took him into the family room.

Laurie surveyed the wreck of her Thanksgiving dinner over the massive carcass of the turkey. She scrubbed the napkin over her cheeks one more time, and still she sat while the casserole cooled and the gravy congealed in its white china boat.

Then she took a deep breath and went out to the kitchen. Moving like a robot programmed to elegant efficiency, she began to clear up. First the condiments—including olives that the kids used to love to stick on their fingers like puppets. The cranberry sauce—her favorite, especially on turkey sandwiches later in the week. The potatoes and casserole, the gravy, the vegetables, and finally, the turkey. That took thirty minutes to deal with all by itself, and in the end she used every single Tupperware bowl she owned for its final resting place.

The dishes followed, then the pots, then wiping down the counters. Two hours later, you'd never know a family had sat down to Thanksgiving dinner except for the extra leaf in the dining room table and the lingering scent of roasted meat.

Two days of preparation, twenty minutes of meltdown, two hours of cleanup. Had it been worth it? She wasn't sure.

But in its own way, making order out of chaos was therapeutic. Mindless and sheer drudgery, yes, but therapeutic in that her sadness and anger and despair seemed to have leached away with every brussels sprout that went down the disposal. And she was left feeling empty and resigned and, well, kind of numb.

Numb was good. Numb might get her some sleep tonight, because she sure hadn't had much since the story of Kate's dramatics in Tuesday's paper.

Numb might get her through the talk she had to have with Anna. She couldn't let her poor darling go to sleep believing that Nick thought she was a murderer, or that Laurie was so clueless that she had no idea what Anna was going through.

So, before her comfortable calm wore off, she walked past the living room, where Colin and Tim were watching *Robots*, and climbed the stairs to Anna's room. The door, naturally, was shut, but despite the seriousness of her visit, a house rule was a house rule. She knocked.

Anna, as she might have expected, didn't answer. "Anna, it's Mom. Can I come in?"

No reply. She pushed open the door and flipped on the light.

No Anna.

Oh, no. Not the window again.

A quick check told her that the window was locked from the inside, so Anna hadn't risked extending her punishment into the New Year by running over to Kyle's for comfort. She must be in the bathroom.

Sure enough, a strip of light showed under the bathroom door. "Anna, I want to talk to you."

Silence, except for the sound of running water. "Anna?" she called a little louder.

Well, this was just rude. There was no excuse for the silent treatment—something her grandmother Tremore had dished out with regularity and which Laurie hated and refused to allow.

She pushed open the door and for a moment, her brain couldn't frame what her eyes were telling her.

The medicine cabinet was open.

A bottle of Tylenol lay on its side on the counter. A couple of capsules lay beside it. There were more on the floor.

Next to Anna.

Who was unconscious and barely breathing, with half a dozen capsules still locked in her hand.

"Colin!"

The scream that tore from her throat gave her a flash of pain, as if it had shredded flesh on its way past.

Colin came pounding up the stairs, Tim on his heels, and they both skidded to a halt in the bathroom doorway. One look was all it took.

"Nine one one." Colin did an about-face and dashed into the bedroom, where Laurie could hear him giving details to the emergency operator with grim precision.

"Mom, what's the matter with Anna?" Tim's lip began to wobble again, and from the bathroom floor, she reached up for him.

"She took too many Tylenols and they knocked her out," she managed. *I will not cry again. I will not. I've got to keep it together.*

"We learned about that in Health. People do that to kill themselves."

"Anna did not try to kill herself." She hoped she was lying firmly enough to be convincing. Against Tim's warm body, her heart pounded with such force she wondered that he couldn't feel it. She couldn't get any air into her lungs. "She just made a mistake."

A mistake. *Please, Lord, let it just have been a mistake.*

"They'll be here in a few minutes." Colin appeared in the doorway, his face gray and drawn. Already the siren wailed in the distance, the sound like the keening of a bereaved parent. "Tim, go outside and flag the ambulance down." When Tim bolted out of the room, he asked, "Is she still breathing? Did you give her CPR?"

Laurie put a gentle hand on her daughter's chest. From where she knelt on the linoleum, she could see the slight—dangerously slight—rise and fall.

"She's breathing. Oh, Colin. I'm so sorry."

He knelt, too, folding his height so he could slip one arm around her shoulders and hold Anna's wrist with the other hand while he felt for her pulse. "There's nothing to be sorry for."

"I should have seen it. Jed should have told us. We could have done something before it came to this—before she thought this was the answer."

"Shhhh. It will be okay."

The siren penetrated the very walls of the house, then shut off. In the ringing silence, they could hear Tim's voice downstairs. "My sister took too many Tylenols. She's in the bathroom. Up here."

The EMTs pounded up the stairs, and in less time than Laurie would ever have expected, they had Anna intubated, strapped to a gurney, and loaded into the back of the ambulance.

"I'm going with her." Laurie already had her coat on and her purse over her shoulder.

"I'll take Tim to my mom's and meet you at the hospital."

She nodded and climbed into the back of the ambulance. Then she hung on for dear life—in more ways than one.

Susquanny Medical Center moved like a well-oiled machine, where every part knew exactly what it was supposed to do—every part but the mother of the patient. Finally, a nurse took pity on her fluttering around outside the locked door and led her away to a waiting room, where she sat her down with a cup of something hot that might have been tea or coffee—it was hard to tell—while Anna had her stomach pumped and her electrolyte levels balanced. Laurie had been to the emergency room before, of course—with a boy as curious as Tim, there were bound to be things like the fishhook incident last summer, and the broken leg when he was learning to ride his skateboard. But it wasn't the same as coming in an ambulance, where triage was immediate and you didn't have to wait for two hours while your child suffered.

"Laurie."

She looked up at two voices calling her name. Colin came in from one direction and Dorinda Platt from the other. She stood and gripped her husband's hand as she searched Dorinda's face for a sign of . . . anything good.

"Anna is going to be fine," Dorinda said in response to that look, and Laurie's knees buckled. Fortunately, she hadn't moved far from the vinyl-covered sofa, and she collapsed into it like a marionette with severed strings.

Dorinda sat on one side of her while Colin took the other. "Thankfully, she underestimated the number of capsules it really takes to shut down the human nervous system," she said. "Her stomach has been pumped, and we have her on a drip so she won't become dehydrated. The ER doc is having her admitted for observation overnight, but you should be able to come and get her in the morning."

"Can we see her now?" Colin asked. Laurie couldn't speak.

Her throat was closed with the effort to keep from bawling and waking up everyone within three floors.

"They're not quite finished, but I'll see if you can see her for a few minutes. Then I recommend you head home and try to get some sleep."

That's easy for you to say, Laurie thought.

"We're required to report suicide attempts to the police and to Child Protective Services," Dorinda went on. "I just wanted to prepare you. You'll probably be getting a visit from both agencies after they get the reports."

Laurie's throat cleared with a vengeance. "CPS won't take her away, will they?"

"I can't speak for them, but I can't imagine they would. They'll do a home inspection, though, and the police will be interested in the whys and hows."

"They already know the whys and hows," Laurie said, unable to keep the rasp of bitterness out of her tone. "It's this whole town thinking that she killed Randi Peizer, and no one being able to find out who really did it."

"God will make all things known," Dorinda said softly.

"Yeah, well, I wish he'd done it before Anna got ahold of that bottle of pills."

"Laurie," Colin said.

"Don't *Laurie* me. I can't believe it's God's will to take both Randi and Anna away."

"Seems to me it's not," Dorinda put in. "Your girl is going to be fine. Maybe it was a—"

"If you say *wake-up call*, I'm going to get up and walk out," Laurie warned. "God doesn't use innocent girls' lives as wake-up calls."

"I wasn't going to say that," Dorinda said calmly, and in some distant part of her brain, Laurie wondered if too many hysterical parents had given her the ability to be so unflappable and objective about the things they said. "I was going to say maybe it's part of his plan to flush the guilty party out."

Laurie didn't think much of that theory, either. Speculating about the will of God was a pointless exercise—like an ant trying to figure out why humans didn't want him at their picnic.

Dorinda glanced at the swinging doors to the ER. "They should be finished by now. Come on back."

Anna was in the third bay, behind a set of yellow curtains. Laurie's heart squeezed in distress at the sight of her slender body on the bed with its backdrop of plastic tubing and monitoring instruments and flashing lights. Laurie had no idea what any of the equipment meant, other than it was helping to make her baby better.

Anna's eyes fluttered open when the rings on the curtains clashed as Dorinda pushed them back.

"Hey, sweetie." Colin touched her cheek while Laurie took her hand. "You're going to be okay."

"I'm sorry," Anna whispered.

"It's all right," Laurie said softly. "Everything is going to be fine. You're going to sleep here tonight, and we'll come and get you in the morning."

"Nice way to get out of being grounded for the night." Anna smiled at her father's gentle joke, and her eyelashes slid closed.

Laurie looked at Dorinda, who said, "She's on a mild sedative. She'll probably sleep now. You folks should go home and try to do the same."

"I want to stay here with her," Laurie said. "Who should I talk to?"

Dorinda shook her head. "I'm afraid not, Laurie. Please. The best thing you can do for her is to get some rest."

No matter what Laurie said to convince her, Dorinda wouldn't budge. In the end, Laurie let Colin walk her out of the room and down to the hospital parking lot, where he held the door for her while she buckled herself in.

"Dorinda's right," he said as he pulled out of the lot. "Things will look better in the morning."

Their daughter had attempted suicide. How was ten or twelve hours going to make that look better?

But she managed to put a lock on her lips and simply nod instead of just blurting out every rebellious and angry thought that flickered through her brain. Great. At the advanced age of thirty-eight, it took an appalling week like this one to teach her discretion.

Hardly any traffic moved on the streets, some distant part of her mind observed on the drive home. Everyone was settled into their postcard-perfect lighted houses, the only thing on their minds whether or not to raid the fridge again before bed.

The silence yawned between them like a physical entity, and Laurie couldn't bear it for another second. She was doing it again—using anger and sarcasm to beat away the darkness of fear. But this was not the enemy. This was Colin, her best friend, her partner, her lover. She'd known since the day they'd first kissed that he was an analytical, practical kind of guy. She was an emotional, dramatic kind of woman. Most of the time there was a time and a place for all of these qualities, and they worked pretty well side by side. But lately she'd seen his efforts to be reasonable as attacks on her.

Maybe she was the one who needed counseling.

Colin turned into the driveway and parked with the engine running. "I'll go over to Mom's and get Tim."

She should say something. They needed to talk out the fear and worry so that they could both sleep. But she was so tired it was an effort to lean on the passenger door and open it.

"Okay," was all she said as she left him and stepped into the house.

Chapter Seventeen

It wasn't often their place was empty at night. Laurie moved from room to room, taking off her coat, dropping her purse on the counter, making sure the kitchen light was on for Colin when he got in.

In their bedroom, she undressed and climbed into her flannel pajamas, as though even her skin needed something soft and comforting lying against it. Then she sat on the bed and, with the swiftness of a pouncing cat, the grief ambushed her.

A soft pillow against her stomach was small comfort, but she toppled sideways and curled around it anyway, weeping her sorrow and fear and regret into the dark, feeling the pillow's velvet cover go from fuzzy to damp to slick under her cheek, wishing Colin hadn't gone to his mother's, wishing he was there to hold her. And still she couldn't stop. It was as though every tear, every shriek, every molecule of defiance she'd been bottling up for the last two weeks rolled out of her in a wave, pulling her in, sucking her under in her own maelstrom of emotion.

And the problem with catastrophic waves was that they held you under, churning and somersaulting and out of control, until their energy was spent and you could swim out.

Laurie wasn't sure she'd ever be able to swim again.

It was just too hard. Death had brought this upon them all, but life was just too hard.

Then the proud waters had gone over our soul.

What was that from? Laurie grabbed a tissue from the night stand and blew her nose, hard. Then, hiccuping with the last of her tears, she gazed at the Bible sitting next to the tissue box like a silent reproach.

Then the proud waters had gone over our soul.

She picked it up and found the verses. The psalmist again. That poor guy had really had a hard time.

Then they had swallowed us up quick, when their wrath was kindled against us:
then the waters had overwhelmed us, the stream had gone over our soul:
then the proud waters had gone over our soul.

That was it. The waters were over her head and she couldn't—

The phone rang and jolted her out of her meditation. "Yes?"

"Lor, it's me," Colin said. "Tim has been upset all evening, and he doesn't want to go home. Mom thinks I should stay over with him to see if he'll calm down."

Oh, her poor baby. Her arms ached to hold her son and comfort him, to give him a little of what she needed so badly herself. This family just had to find its way back to balance again. "Okay." Her shoulders drooped. "It's probably better if he has a change of scenery right now anyway. Come by here first thing tomorrow and pick me up so we can go get Anna, okay?"

"Will do. Tim needs to see that Anna is okay, so I'll bring him, too."

"Good choice." She took a deep breath. "I . . . I love you."

In the beat of silence, she heard his throat working, and tears welled again in her eyes. "Love you, too." He cleared his throat. "See you in the morning."

Laurie hung up gently. If they couldn't find comfort in holding each other, she'd have to make do with what she had. She picked up the open Bible and wandered down the hall to Anna's room. The lamp on her study desk was the jointed kind architects used, but Laurie turned on the Tinkerbell lamp on the night stand. They'd lugged it all the way back from Disney World the summer before Anna turned five, and Anna had refused to give it up even when she was long past believing in fairies.

Laurie sat on the bed and tried to find comfort in her daughter's things, in the smell of baby shampoo and cherry lip gloss, in the jumble of clothes in the closet that mapped a girl's journey to finding her own style. "BoHo or Classy?" asked the cover of *Seventeen* from the floor. "Goth or Geek?"

Laurie remembered buying magazines and trying to figure out what kind of body type she had (which clashed with the one she wanted) and then what kinds of clothes could best enhance or hide it while still communicating her style. If she had a style back then. She couldn't remember.

Ping!

The monitor of Anna's computer was in sleep mode, but apparently the machine was still running.

Laurie's body still felt heavy, as though it would be too much effort to get up and turn the thing off. Her tired gaze returned to the floor, and her thoughts to the psalm she had just read.

Maybe that was why Anna had gone into the bathroom and taken down that bottle of pills. The waters had gone over her head, too, and she couldn't see her way to the surface. Was life just simply too much to bear, and she didn't see any other way through except to check out and not try? At fourteen, how many choices can you see from that chaos under the waves?

Randi Peizer had had no choices at all. The water had closed over her head, and she'd never come up again.

The spiritual parallel stopped there. She and Anna could still fight their way to the surface. But how?

The Bible in her lap felt the way it always had, the leather handled to a comfortable limpness, the gilt worn off the pages in the middle. Once, it had been her guide for nearly everything. Now it was an accessory she took to Bible study group, the way she grabbed her handbag and keys. When was the last time she'd read something just for the sheer comfort of hearing God's voice in the words? When was the last time she'd opened it for counsel, or even prayed?

Laurie couldn't remember that, either.

Her life was filled with religion—with Bible study group, with service, with friends all from the same church, with making sure Anna and Tim grew up with Christian principles. But what about under the surface? What was the core holding her together? Was God there, or was it simply an empty space with church activities packed tightly around it?

Oh, Lord, have I replaced you with the church?

Ping!

She glanced at the computer and frowned. Downstairs, Colin's grandpa's mantel clock gave a single chime. Why was the computer pinging at one in the morning?

She'd turn it off in a minute. Meantime, she located the psalm about the waters and read the rest of it:

Blessed be the LORD, who hath not given us as a prey to their teeth.

Our soul is escaped as a bird out of the snare of the fowlers: the
   snare is broken, and we are escaped.
Our help is in the name of the Lord, who made heaven and earth.

Well, there was a happy ending for you—and she could use
one of those right now. Was it really possible that the One who
had made heaven and earth could pay attention to her family's
problems and help them find a solution?

Lord, give those girls on the bridge a shake and order them to tell
the truth.

There you go again, she heard Colin's voice in her mind, *telling*
people what to do. When talking to God, it was probably better to
ask than to tell. But wasn't that what she'd been doing all along?
Effectively telling the Lord that he wasn't doing a very good job
of organizing things, and taking it upon herself to do it? And
what had been the result?

I've lost everything.

Almost. Everything that she'd thought counted, anyway.
She'd lost the trust of Glendale Bible Fellowship, and the
friendship of women she'd known all her life. She'd lost Anna's
trust. She'd probably even lost her relationship with Nick, and
her marriage was battered, if that crack in Colin's voice was
any indication—not to mention the fact that he'd rather stay
at his mom's house than come home and see this through with
her.

Surely there must be something left.

Her gaze tracked down the page:

As the mountains are round about Jerusalem, so the Lord is round
   about his people from henceforth even for ever.

In other words, she had God. When all else failed, he was with her still. But was he?

She could ask and find out.

Tears thickened in her throat again as she bowed her head over the pages that, despite her neglect and hardheadedness, were trying to tell her something.

Lord, are you there? Has it really taken all this to drive me back to you? Am I that stubborn and filled with my own self-importance that I abandoned you and took over the job of steering my own life?

Please help me, Lord. I've got nothing else to work with here. I'm done. I'm at the end of myself. I know you can fill that space inside. Bring me back to you, please, and make me one of your own again. Please, Lord. You're all I've got.

Laurie had never felt so alone, so empty. And yet, wasn't that the perfect condition to be in if you wanted to be filled with the Spirit? Motionless, she waited in the silence of the deserted house, feeling still and quiet for the first time in months. Maybe even years.

That still, small voice. Maybe it needed a place like this to work. Maybe if she would just shut up and listen, God could tell her what she should do. God could open a way once he'd opened her heart. He was good at that. Look at the Red Sea.

Ping!

Oh, for heaven's sake. Laurie cocked an eye at the sleeping monitor. What was with these kids? If Anna was getting instant-message alerts when she was in total lockdown, there was going to be trouble.

Excuse me a minute, Lord.

She pulled out Anna's desk chair and jiggled the mouse so the monitor would light up. When it did, little IM notes littered the desktop.

JohnnysGrrl: Check ur mail yet? Good pix.
B good or b sorry.

What on earth was this? Both her kids' e-mail addresses were sub-accounts of her own. Normally she wouldn't invade their privacy by logging in and reading their mail or their IMs, but life was no longer normal. And what exactly was "B good or b sorry"? With just a few keystrokes, Anna's mailbox came up and she was in. She didn't even need a password.

The first thing she saw was that every e-mail except the last few had been read, which meant Anna had been ignoring the rules. Half of the list was from kedgar254@hotmail.com. No surprise there.

The other messages were from a variety of people with names like "edancer" and "mrsbloom" and "mwah." At the top of the list were three from someone called "JohnnysGrrl." Laurie opened the first one.

Kelci sez ur on lockdown but Kyle sez ur reading mail.
Got a present 4 u.

The next one said:

B good or b sorry, Poser2. As long as Im alright, ur alright. But if u fink, baby bro gets it. Proof coming.

A 140KB image was attached to the most recent message, which said:

See how ez? B good or maybe baby bro wont be smiling.
Maybe he'll hit his head like Poser.

Laurie's fingers felt cold and stiff on the mouse as she scrolled down and looked at the image. There were Tim and KeShawn on either side of Kate Parsons, who had a boy under each arm in a mock headlock. The boys' eyes were crossed and their tongues lolled out as they mugged for the camera.

Kate was smiling . . . and in her eyes was something that chilled Laurie to her core.

Laurie had no idea where they were or when the picture had been taken, but the message was clear. JohnnysGrrl was threatening Anna and using her love for her little brother as leverage to keep her quiet.

Laurie would bet her mortgage she knew who JohnnysGrrl was.

She scrolled through Anna's e-mail, and every message from JohnnysGrrl was a threat. Some were veiled and rambling, some brief and to the point:

Tell ur cuz what happened and baby bro goes swimming.
Just try me.

She had to nail down JohnnysGrrl, or at least find someone who would know. The girl in the picture was Kate, but who had taken it? Was Kate JohnnysGrrl, or was it the person behind the camera?

Ping!

KEdgar254: Babe, u OK? Cell dead?

Laurie grabbed the extension sitting next to the computer and dialed Janice's house. Kyle Edgar answered on the first ring.

"Anna?" he whispered.

"This is Anna's mom."

Silence. "Oh."

The least of her worries was who was grounded and who wasn't. "Never mind that now. Why did you ask if Anna was OK?"

"I heard something weird on Dad's scanner, and I've been trying to get ahold of her all night. Is she there? Can I talk to her?"

"What did you hear?" She wasn't even interested in why the mayor was monitoring the police bands.

"An ambulance got called to her street and I thought —" He cut himself off.

"Thought what?"

"Nothing."

"You thought she'd been hurt?"

"Um, yeah."

"By someone?"

Silence.

"Kyle, I'm sitting in front of her computer. I know someone's been sending her threatening e-mails. There are dozens of them, going back over the last two weeks. And they start on the night Randi Peizer was killed."

Silence.

"Kyle? Answer me."

"I can't."

"You'd better. Someone called JohnnysGrrl wrote all of these. Do you know who that is?"

When he finally replied, it sounded as though every word was being pulled out of him with a pair of tweezers. "I can't tell you, Mrs. Hale. She'll—"

"She said she was going to hurt my little boy. Send him swimming, the way Randi went swimming. That's the hold she had on Anna. What has she got on you?"

"She—" His voice broke, and he took a breath. "She said she'd tell the papers some dirt about my dad."

"That's impossible, Kyle. Your dad is a good man. He doesn't have any dirt. That's why I voted for him."

"She said he had an affair with Randi's mom. That Randi was really his daughter. And if I said what happened, she'd tell the papers like she told them Anna did it."

Bingo. "It's Kate Parsons, isn't it, Kyle? Kate pushed Randi off the bridge, didn't she?"

She could practically feel the misery coming through the phone. "I didn't say that. You guessed."

"Has your dad ever lived in Ohio, Kyle?"

It took him a minute to catch up with the swerve in topic. "No. We moved here from New Mexico when I was a baby."

"Tanya and Randi lived in Ohio before they moved here a few months ago. Randi's dad is a drifter named Daryl, and he was last known to be living in Columbus. The man who donated his chromosomes to Randi was not your dad."

Silence. "You must think I'm pretty stupid."

"No. I think you love your dad a lot. And now I think you'd better go tell your parents the truth about what happened that night."

"But what about Tim? And Anna?"

"Kyle, I don't want to make this worse for you than it already is, but Anna tried to . . . She took too many Tylenols earlier.

That ambulance call was to our house. She's in the hospital—and Kyle," she said when he made a sound halfway between a cry and a moan, "she's going to be fine. They have her there for observation, but they pumped her stomach, and everything will be okay."

Again she heard the sound, only muffled this time, and she realized the mayor's son was crying.

"Sweetie, this is not your fault. It's Kate's fault. And my very next call is to Deputy Tremore. I'm going to tell him everything, and then this whole nightmare will be over."

As she hung up, she spotted the Bible where she'd left it on the bed: *The snare is broken, and we are escaped.*

Chapter Eighteen

Hospitals and police stations never sleep. Nick stood next to Anna's bed and traced the line of the IV drip from the bag hanging on the tree, to the rail of her bed, to the needle taped into the back of her hand—a hand that looked too fragile to support it. Didn't those things come in kid sizes?

He'd heard the call for the ambulance on the scanner in his kitchen after he'd left Tanya at her apartment, and recognized the address at once. No one here was giving out any details, no matter how many times he'd flashed his identification, but he could see all he needed to see from here.

Anna was pale, but breathing.

They were looking after her. That was enough for now.

The pager on his belt vibrated like an agitated bee, and he recognized the Hales' number. He hit autodial on his cell.

"Nick?" Laurie picked up on the first ring, her voice thick with emotion. "Were you asleep?"

"I'm at the hospital, outside Anna's room. What happened?"

"She took a bunch of Tylenol."

"She tried to kill herself?" His voice spiraled into soundlessness. "Why?"

"Kate Parsons has been threatening her. Over e-mail. They call it cyberbullying."

"Why would Kate Parsons be doing that?" But he already knew.

"Because she did it. That night on the bridge. Kate pushed Randi over and then threatened all those kids with harm—to themselves or to people they loved—if they told. She told Anna she'd hurt Tim, and sent her a picture of her and Tim and Ke-Shawn Platt. She's got them in a headlock and her face is downright scary. Don't ask me where or how it was taken, but I'm betting that picture is what finally sent Anna over the edge."

"I know where and how. Earlier today, I mean yesterday, remember, when Tim went to get the whipping cream? The boys were coming back over the bridge with Kate and Kelci Platt. And Kelci had been taking pictures with her brand-new digital camera."

"That was just yesterday?" Laurie sighed. "It feels like last year."

"Who else did she threaten?"

"Kyle Edgar. He says she was going to tell the world that Randi was his dad's illegitimate daughter."

Nick said something that definitely did not fall within the rules of conduct for a peace officer. "And he believed her?"

"They all did. Obviously. Normal kids don't go attempting suicide over something they don't believe."

She had a point. "You have proof of these threats?"

"I'm on Anna's computer printing out all Kate's e-mails and the picture now, plus I'm saving them all to a flash drive to give to you. There's a lot. Two weeks' worth."

"Bless Anna for saving them, then. Most kids would have been so scared they'd delete them just to pretend they made the threat go away."

"You need to come over and get this stuff. And then arrest Kate."

"Laurie."

"You're right. Don't tell you how to do your job. Sorry."

"Don't apologize. We're thinking the same thing. You just have a tendency to say it out loud."

As he climbed into his vehicle and radioed Gil to meet him over at the Parsonses' place, he wondered what had prompted his cousin to go into her daughter's computer and start snooping around. Laurie and Colin had good intentions where their kids' privacy was concerned, but in Nick's opinion, respect for privacy only went so far when you were talking about teenagers. Protecting them from harm sometimes overrode that. Maybe Laurie had come to that conclusion, too.

It took just a few minutes to get to Laurie's house, but she was already at the bottom of the driveway waiting for him with a manila folder in her hand. He made her go inside where it was warm, with instructions to leave this to him, and then spent a few minutes reviewing the printouts of the messages Johnnys-Grrl had sent to Anna.

What he read left him shaking his head and wondering what kind of influences and environment had produced a girl like this. He made sure he had his badge in his pocket and a spare set of cuffs. Then he fired up the truck. It was time to find out.

When he turned onto the street where the Parsonses' comfortable four-bedroom home was located, he saw Gil's vehicle parked out front. Every window of the house was dark except for one in the rear, which was probably the kitchen. It was 3:00 a.m. Someone was either a very early riser, or an insomniac.

He nodded at Gil, who followed him around to the back deck. "This ought to be fun," Gil commented. "Looks like we've been spotted."

Dressed in his bathrobe, Neil Parsons stood in front of the

French doors that led onto the deck. A cup of coffee steamed in his hand.

"Can I help you, gentlemen?"

Like he hadn't spent hours down at the station, swearing at the two of them while he tried to keep his wife and daughter from throwing fits of hysterics. Nick braced himself for a fight. "You keep late hours."

"Early, actually. I'm usually at my desk by five. Even on a long weekend."

"Early lawyer gets the worm, huh?" Gil said.

"Plenty of worms in family law. But you probably didn't come by to discuss my practice, did you?"

"Information has come to light about Kate, Mr. Parsons. Apparently she's been cyberbullying some of the kids in town to keep them quiet about what happened on the bridge. To cover up the fact that she is the one who pushed Miranda Peizer over the rail."

"Ridiculous," Neil said in a voice as cold as a reptile's blood. "You better not ever show your face in this town again if you mention it to anyone."

"We have proof, and it's in writing."

"Whose writing?"

"Kate's. E-mails and digital photos, among other things."

"E-mails can be faked. Anybody can set up a Hotmail address and fake a name. You know better than that."

"We'll subpoena the service provider's records if we have to. But I have a feeling that once this breaks, we'll have kids coming forward voluntarily, willing to tell us what really happened. Including the mayor's son."

Neil snorted, as if Kyle's word were as worthless as a dot-com stock option.

"I don't believe you." Neil reached for the door and stepped back into the kitchen. "When you guys get a warrant, you can talk to me."

Gil stuck his foot between the door and its frame. "I'm afraid you have your facts wrong, sir. This is a homicide. In the Commonwealth, we can arrest someone without a warrant. And we're not interested in talking to you in any case. At this time we'd like to ask you to wake your daughter and have her get dressed." He glanced behind him at the darkened yard. "In some warm clothes."

Neil Parsons spat a few choice phrases that, in Nick's opinion, a churchgoing man should be ashamed to say. Then he reined in his temper. "My daughter isn't going anywhere with you. She's done nothing wrong—she's been telling you that for weeks. Her friends have told you that. Whatever last-minute, Hail Mary, so-called proof you have is either a lie by a scared kid, or something made up by someone with a grudge against me. I have lots of enemies in this town, and they'd like nothing better than to—"

"This isn't about you, Mr. Parsons, as the deputy said," Nick interrupted. "This is about Kate. Please go and wake her. We're taking her downtown now."

"You half-wit, didn't you hear anything I—"

"Mr. Parsons, you can be arrested for obstructing a peace officer in the performance of his duties."

"Obstruct this!"

Neil Parsons lunged and swung at Nick, who ducked, and the blow caught Gil on the shoulder.

"Hey!"

Nick whipped the handcuffs out of his pocket, and while Neil's body was still following his fist's trajectory, Nick snapped one around his wrist, captured the man's free hand, and popped the cuff closed.

"What is going on here?"

On the other side of the kitchen, a woman appeared, tightening the belt of her baby-blue dressing gown. "Neil!"

"Mr. Parsons, I'm arresting you for assault on a peace officer. Gil, call in for another unit. We're outnumbered."

"What are you doing to my husband?"

"Mrs. Parsons?"

"Noreen," Neil shouted, twisting awkwardly with his hands behind his back, "call our attorney. Now."

"It's three in the morning."

"Mrs. Parsons, we're here to arrest your daughter Kate as a suspect in the homicide of Miranda Peizer."

"Why have you got Neil in handcuffs?"

"Mrs. Parsons, did you hear me?"

"Of course I heard you!" she snapped. "You're just not making any sense. Is this some kind of joke?"

"We're arresting your husband for assaulting a police officer, and we're waiting for backup to transport your daughter to the station for booking."

"You're all completely insane." She looked from Nick to her husband to Gil. "All of you."

"Noreen, do I have to repeat myself?"

"No, I heard you."

"Then get a move on!"

She fixed him with a glare so cold that Nick was surprised snow didn't sift down from the ceiling. "Is the attorney for Kate, or for you?"

"For Kate, of course, you idiot! I'm completely capable of managing my own defense."

What a delightful family. If this was the kind of environment that had produced a girl like Kate, she hadn't had much of a chance of turning out differently. To her, it probably sounded like a reasonable plan to threaten the kids so they wouldn't rat her out. A negotiation tactic, as it were. The fact that she'd neatly set up someone else to take the fall was most likely a cause for relief rather than guilt. Her dad doubtless talked the same kind of strategy at the dinner table when he told stories about his cases.

Even Nick could be a better parent than that. Not that he had any hang-ups about it, but getting married and becoming a father hadn't been real high on his list of life priorities, either.

Noreen had gone upstairs, presumably to call a lawyer in private, forcing him to wait. He wasn't about to bust into Kate's room like a vigilante posse and roust her out of bed, though he'd had about enough of this family. Hauling her down to the station in her jammies would serve her right.

Lights flashed out in the street, signaling the arrival of their backup. Tersely, Gil gave the new deputies a situation report and, without giving Neil the courtesy of a few minutes to get out of his nightclothes, they took him away in their vehicle.

Nick cocked an ear toward the upstairs but couldn't hear a thing. "Mrs. Parsons? Would you come down here, please?"

"We're right here."

Noreen Parsons and Kate trooped down the stairs. Kate was so pale her skin was nearly green, but she held her head high and looked at him as though he were something she'd picked up on her shoe. She was dressed in low-slung jeans, a heavy cable sweater, and running shoes.

"You just don't understand," she informed him. "It was totally an accident. I never meant to hurt her. You should be checking out Anna Hale. She's the one who was in the water with her."

Nick was tempted to say, "Tell it to the judge," but that sounded like a TV cliché.

"You'll be given the opportunity to say anything you wish in your statement," he said instead. "You have the right to remain silent."

"Yeah, yeah." She waved a negligent hand. "I get it. Anything I say can and will be used against me in a court of law. What—do you think I don't watch *Law & Order?*"

He didn't pause until he'd finished reading the girl her rights.

"I'm coming, too." Noreen fixed him with a look and barred the doorway.

"Oh, Mom, spare us the dramatics and do what Daddy said. I need a lawyer worse than I need you to hold my hand."

Noreen flinched, and Nick spared half a second to feel a little sorry for her. What a piece of work she'd raised.

"Come on, Kate."

He and Gil got her into the marked vehicle ("What do you mean, I can't ride up front? What a bunch of chauvinists!"), and as he followed them downtown in his truck he thought not of the Parsons family or even of Laurie and Anna Hale, but of Tanya.

And of how, finally, he could give her something to be thankful for.

On Friday morning, Laurie woke at daybreak and chose the silence of a run along the river path over the silence of her empty house. To her surprise, Janice hailed her a few hundred feet from the parking lot. Laurie was here only to kill time and try to find a little strength before she went home and Colin picked her up at nine.

"What are you doing here?" she asked as Janice jogged up to her, togged out in the latest fashion in sweats.

"Following your example." Her grin faded. "Or am I intruding on you?"

"There you go again, assuming it's your fault." Laurie reached out to hug her, and before she knew it, she'd burst into tears and was clinging to Janice, sobbing like a four-year-old.

"Laurie! Laurie, what is it? What's happened? Oh, honey, here, sit down on this bench and just let it all out."

And so she did, sobbing and heaving and gasping out the night's events in disjointed sentences that Janice probably had to piece together like a crossword puzzle until they made some sense. But in the end, she got the gist of it, the important part: Both their kids were safe.

When Laurie had soaked Janice's folded cotton headband with tears, she gave her face one last dab and looked up. Janice's face glowed with relief.

"Anna's going to be all right? The doctor said so? And it was Kate all along?"

Laurie nodded. Wrung out as she was, she was never going to be able to get up from this bench. But Janice had other ideas. "Come on. I feel like jumping for joy that it's all over, but that would scare the wildlife. Let's walk."

So somehow she got her legs moving and her arms swinging—and the details of the night's events into some order. "So when I realized that's what all the IMs and e-mails meant, I called Nick right away. And then I called Colin and my parents. The only person I haven't called is Tanya, because to tell you the truth, I don't think I can. Not after the things she said to me."

It seemed like years ago. But, like feuds that lasted years, she'd forgotten the details and only the bitterness remained.

"One thing at a time. I'm sure Nick will tell her. In fact, it wouldn't surprise me if he told the whole world, starting with the papers. Things are probably slow on the news front while everyone digests their turkey dinners. I bet I can convince Barrett to hold a nice big press conference tomorrow, giving Nick all the credit."

There was a time—not so long ago, as a matter of fact— when Laurie would have insisted she get some of that credit. But today she couldn't care less. She felt like a burned-out shell. Or maybe a burning lamp was a better description. A bit of glass with a tiny flame inside that had been newly lit during the wee hours of that morning.

"That would be perfect," she said.

"And as for Tanya, my advice would be to give her a break."

Laurie looked up. "Oh, I can. I just don't know how to face her again—the things she said hurt so much."

"Consider how much she's been hurt," Janice reminded her with the gentleness of a friend and the fairness of a district court judge. "The two of you will talk, I know it. You need each other—you just need to work up to it. God will give you grace."

Laurie drew in a long breath. "I hope so. I've come as close as I ever want to losing my child."

"Too close," Janice agreed. "Maybe that can be a starting place to bring you two together."

She hadn't thought of it that way. Her sleepless night had opened her eyes, so maybe it was time she started to see things differently. Tanya must have felt these emotions, too—the despair, the hopelessness, even the self-doubt and accusation. She'd once thought they had nothing in common, but now she realized maybe they did. Maybe she could see the world from Tanya's point of view. And maybe there were places where they could start to build a bridge to reach each other.

They were sisters in Christ, weren't they? And his love was a good foundation on which to build a little bridge over those scary, dark waters.

Laurie glanced up. "Thank God you joined our Bible study."

Janice's smile had all the mischief of a kid about to crayon the walls, and all the joy of a woman safe with a true friend. "You won't say that when I make you jog the next two hundred yards."

When they slowed, she saw that they were just about at the spot where the path dipped down and you could see the sandbar where Laurie had first discovered Randi's body.

"I need to tell you something."

Janice had seen her looking at the river. "About Randi? Or Tanya?"

"No, about me." She glanced at her friend. "Like that's a surprise. Is everything in the world really about me?"

"No, sweetie." Janice slipped an arm around her. "With you, it's all about everybody else."

Laurie wondered at the depth of her perception, this woman whom everyone saw and no one really knew. "You hit the nail on the head. It has been about everybody else, though probably not in the way you meant. Have you ever read Psalm 124?"

"Which one is that?"

"The one about the waves going over the soul."

"It sounds familiar. Why?"

"Last night—just a few hours ago, in fact, those waves totally swamped me. I could really understand for the first time how Anna might feel. How it would look when she couldn't see any way out. It's going to hurt for a long time that she didn't feel she could come to us for help no matter how scary Kate's threats were, but maybe we can get past that and start making some changes. If it's not too late."

"Have you ever thought that grounding her might have saved her life, if Kate really meant to carry through with what she said?" Janice walked for a few moments in silence. "I hope they get that girl some help, or we'll have a very pretty churchgoing sociopath on our hands. But what did you mean about it all being about everyone else?"

Laurie took a breath and prepared to bare her soul. "When you think of church, what do you think of first?"

"The altar," Janice said promptly. "And Vanessa Platt's voice soaring over it."

"So you think of worship." She huffed a breath that held a little self-mockery.

"Why, what do you think of?"

"The people."

"What's wrong with that? That's what a church is, isn't it? A body of believers."

"Right, but when I think of church, I think of the people in it, of committees and fund-raisers and to-do lists and charity work."

"That sounds like your life, Laurie. It's natural you would think that way. Why be so down about it?"

"It is my life. Or was. But where is God in all of it?"

Janice was silent.

"A few hours ago the waves went over my soul, and I saw

myself as I really am. Just this shell of activity all packed around an empty space where God is supposed to be."

"I'm sure it's not—"

"I've been worshipping the church instead of God, Janice. Pouring out what I thought was service when instead it was, well, a way to be somebody. I think that's the mistake the Tremores have made from the beginning. When you've been here for a century and you're brought up to think you run the town, it's all too easy to start to believe your own advertising."

"So when the wave went over your soul, you had nothing to hang on to?"

"Exactly. I had no rock. Oh, I had the promises God makes us, but I'd never proved them. I had no idea if what God said would actually work or not. I'd been feeling so sorry for myself because the church seemed to be shutting me out and protecting Tanya, and I'd lost Anna, and Colin was withdrawing, and all the nasty people were coming out of the woodwork with their accusations and their gossip. I was drowning—and that's when I realized what God was doing."

"What's that?"

"He was separating me out, bringing me close, the way I should have been all along if I hadn't been so busy doing things my way."

"I see." Janice's tone was thoughtful. "So where does that leave you now? Washed up on the beach?" Both of them glanced at the sandbar. "Sorry. That was the wrong thing to say."

"More like washed up on the Rock. The one that's higher than me, that we sing about once in a while. You know?"

"And won't the view from there be nice when the Nancy O'Days and Debbie Jackses of this world have to come and admit they were wrong?"

"The funny thing is, I don't care what they think. Two days ago, it mattered horribly. Now, I'm more concerned about what God thinks."

"People are people, Laurie. And you have some good friends at GBF. Don't write them all off because a few couldn't resist the temptation to make themselves bigger at your expense."

"Maybe. But you know what? It's a huge relief to just give all that to God and let him decide."

Janice grabbed her hands. "I feel like praying together. Isn't that weird? Out loud, right here on the riverbank, where it's forty degrees."

"Why shouldn't we if we feel like it?" A bubble of sheer joy caught in her throat. "Lord," Laurie said to the iron-gray sky above the river, the sandbar, and the leafless trees, "thank you for bringing me to yourself, all by myself. Thank you for opening my eyes and showing me where my priorities should be. Thank you for giving me a friend like Janice, who knows when to step in and tell me the truth. Help us both to get through the next couple of days. Give your strength to my little girl, I pray, and bring her spirits back as well as her health."

"Heal the distance between Laurie and Colin, Father," Janice went on when Laurie ran out of breath. "Help her to show her family the love in her heart, and help her to mend fences with Tanya and her sisters in the church. Thank you for your inexpressible love—and thank you for expressing it to us at times like this in an almost tangible way. In Jesus' name, amen."

Both women stood on the riverbank and watched the water roll by, fast and cold.

That's one thing about the wave going over you, Laurie thought. *Once it's over, it leaves you feeling clean.*

Chapter Nineteen

Saturday afternoon at four o'clock, the members of the media gathered on the steps of city hall for the mayor's press conference. Besides the stringers from the local rag, most of whom Nick knew, there were reporters from Pittsburgh and even one from Columbus. The Channel 4 News van rolled up to the curb, and Nick prepared himself for a free-for-all.

The mayor had asked him to attend in case they needed details, so here he was, boots shined, uniform pressed, and game face on.

Promptly at four, Barrett Edgar emerged from the front doors, his press secretary and two aides behind him, and walked to the portable podium.

"Ladies and gentlemen of the press, thank you for coming on such a cold, windy day. I hope you had a good Thanksgiving." He smiled at the crowd, not the plastic smile Nick was used to seeing on politicians, all expensive bridgework and what's-in-this-for-me, but a real, tired smile that spoke of long hours and long-awaited good news.

Barrett wasn't such a bad guy, as mayors went. And his wife seemed to be committed to doing what she could to make things better instead of just wearing expensive clothes and hosting a tea once a year.

"I'm very happy to be able to tell you all that we've had a break in the Miranda Peizer case," Edgar said, and the press leaned into the wind like hounds scenting their prey. "But first, let me outline the circumstances for those of you who have come quite a distance. On the night of November 7, a crowd of teenagers was on the Susquanny River Bridge just east of town, around ten thirty in the evening. Most of them were there without the knowledge of their parents. Some of them got to pushing and shoving, and Miranda Peizer went over the rail, hit her head on one of the support beams, and fell thirty feet into the water. She was unconscious upon impact, and subsequently drowned.

"Her body was discovered the next morning, and our sheriff's detectives went into action. During the course of the investigation, the detectives were stonewalled repeatedly by the teenage witnesses. Everyone blamed everyone else. No one's story could be corroborated, because every account contradicted the one before it. Numerous attempts at questioning failed to bring any clarity to the situation."

"What about Kate Parsons coming forward about Anna Hale?" one of the Glendale reporters shouted. "Has it been proven that Anna held the victim underwater, and then tried to commit suicide from guilt?"

"I would like to state here and now that Anna Hale is completely innocent," the mayor said firmly. "She and others were being cyberbullied into silence by the real perpetrator."

Nick saw heads turn as the reporters looked at one another.

"You mean like getting threatening e-mails?" one of them asked. "Like that kid in England?"

Nick remembered the case vividly, and other cases where teenagers had to face bullying not just in school hallways, but online, where the whole world could see their fear and humiliation.

"Yes. It turns out that the perpetrator had threatened a number of the witnesses, including my own son, with harm either to themselves or to their loved ones."

Oh, this was news, all right.

"The perpetrator threatened to expose me as the father of my supposedly illegitimate child, Miranda Peizer, which is utter nonsense, of course."

"But your kid believed it?"

"No, but he couldn't afford to let the perpetrator think that. Anna Hale was threatened with harm to her little brother, as was Kelci Platt, a key witness."

"That leaves Kate Parsons and Rose Silverstein," said the guy from the *Trib*, clearly no slouch in the logic department.

"Miss Silverstein is innocent as well, Mr. Taylor. We have her statement and several others indicating that Kate Parsons pushed Miranda Peizer off the bridge. She is presently incarcerated in our juvenile facility awaiting her arraignment on charges of involuntary manslaughter. Her father has been released on bail on charges of assaulting a police officer."

The reporters put two and two together and grinned at one another.

"How come Kate's not being charged with homicide?" one of them called. "She killed that kid, didn't she?"

"We haven't established that she intended to kill Randi," the mayor replied. "But she still has to stand trial for her actions." He looked to his left, and Nick braced himself. "I would like to publicly thank Deputies Nicholas Tremore and Gilbert Schwartz for their tireless work on this case. A late-night break when Deputy Tremore discovered the cyberbullying was going on led to the arrest."

Much to Nick's embarrassment, the mayor began to applaud. His aides joined in immediately, and there was a smattering of applause from the reporters. Those who weren't scuttling back to their vans to tell the story over a live feed, that is.

"Does the victim's mother know?" one of the reporters called when order had been restored.

The mayor nodded. "Ms. Peizer has been informed of our investigation every step of the way. I would like to ask that you respect her request not to be interviewed at this time. As you can imagine, this ordeal has been very hard on her. And please note that a memorial fund will be established in Miranda Peizer's name, to provide counseling services for the families of other victims of violent crime. You can call my offices on Monday for further details. Thank you for coming, ladies and gentlemen. That's all I have to say."

The reporters scattered, and Nick escaped to his patrol car as quickly as he could. Publicity made him nervous. Not only that, but it felt weird and uncomfortable to get attention that was bound to wound Tanya all over again.

Not that he'd heard from Tanya since the Thanksgiving disaster. At the restaurant, there had been a shadow in her eyes, and he could tell when he lost her attention and her thoughts went to some dark place where he couldn't follow.

As the officer on duty, Gil had been the one to tell her about the break in the case . . . and now it was Saturday evening and he'd had maybe six hours of sleep since Thursday.

All he could think of was going home and using up about twenty hours of comp time in bed, and after that he'd apply his mind to the Tanya question. Because it was clear to him that unless he made up his mind in a hurry, he was going to do something completely out of character and start thinking about a

Christian woman in a way he never had before. One that didn't involve mockery and avoidance. Life was complicated enough, wasn't it?

He put Tanya on a mental shelf, climbed into his truck, and did his best to stay awake all the way home. The silence in the house was soothing. After grilling a cheese sandwich that only partially filled the yawning hole inside him, he stumbled upstairs, pulled off his uniform, and fell into a deep, black well of sleep.

Fourteen hours later, he jerked awake with the knowledge that he was not alone in the house. An automatic glance at the clock told him it was nearly eight, and the gray sky told him that it was a.m., not p.m.

Something wasn't right. The air should not be smelling of . . . coffee and bacon?

Okay, scratch the burglary theory, and probably the stalker and the vengeful-gang-member theories, too. So what did that leave him?

Mom, deciding that he needed a little maternal TLC?

His sisters-in-law? In that case, he'd rather have the gang members.

Nick rolled out of bed, scooped a pair of jeans off the floor, and pulled on a Penguins sweatshirt dating from Super Mario's glory days. He glanced at his service weapon on the dresser and decided against it. Even if there was a gang member in his kitchen cooking up breakfast, he could probably handle it without benefit of arms.

Besides, the paperwork would be horrendous.

He'd waxed and oiled the old staircase so it didn't creak, so he managed to get downstairs and to the kitchen doorway before the person standing in front of the counter turned around.

A person with reddish-gold hair and a gift for making something out of nothing.

He leaned on the doorjamb and crossed his arms over his chest. If Tanya wasn't going to announce herself to him, he wasn't about to announce himself to her. Instead, he stood there and enjoyed the view as she moved from stove to counter to fridge. It wasn't until she stopped in the middle of the floor, as if she'd suddenly lost her train of thought, that she saw him out of the corner of her eye.

She gasped and jumped back, one hand on her heart, the other brandishing a spatula.

"Nick!"

"Fancy meeting you here," he said.

"I—I—you're not mad, are you? I knocked, honest. I knew you were home because your truck's here, and when I tried the door it opened. I thought maybe you went for a run and—"

"Tanya."

"And I wanted to—" She halted the babble of explanations with an effort. "Yes?"

"Thank you. I'm not big on surprises, but when I smelled the coffee I figured you weren't busy hauling my stereo out of here on a truck."

"I should have called, huh." She looked at the spatula in her hand as if wondering how it got there. "I forget sometimes that you're a cop. It would serve me right if you'd shot me."

The bacon spit with a sound like a gunshot, and she jumped. "Yikes! Too hot." She turned the flame down. "Sorry. Dorinda Platt tells me that forgetfulness and blanking on details are part of the grieving process. I guess I need to be extra careful in other people's kitchens."

"To what do I owe the pleasure?" He reached into the cupboard, got two mugs, and poured coffee for them both.

"I wanted to thank you. The plan was to make you breakfast, but when I figured out you were still sleeping, I thought maybe I'd make it, then leave it in the oven to keep warm, and go."

"Thank me for what?"

She threw a glance over her shoulder as she crumbled bits of herbs into the eggs. Since he owned neither herbs nor eggs at the moment, she must have brought the whole kit and caboodle for the occasion.

"As Randi would say, Duh. Your partner told me. For solving the case. For making sure Kate Parsons pays for what she's done."

"From what the witnesses say, if it's any comfort, she didn't intend to kill Randi. No one could have predicted she'd hit her head in exactly that spot on the support beam with exactly the amount of force that she did."

"And I'm glad to hear it." She poured the eggs into his only other frying pan and the kitchen filled with the scent of thyme and rosemary. "I can forgive a girl for being stupid and aggressive. I'd have a harder time forgiving her for deliberate murder. I could do it, but it would take longer. A lifetime, maybe."

"Who says you have to forgive her at all?" He saw that the oven light was on, and opened it to find biscuits baking. Just turning golden, in fact. Had she forgotten they were in there? "Let the court system take care of her."

"I don't have to live with the court system. I do have to live with myself. And if I got hit by a bus with no forgiveness in my heart, I'd have a hard time explaining that to the Lord."

"Is that all it takes to run salvation off the rails?" he asked lightly. "Scary thought."

"Jesus had strong opinions on the subject," she informed him. "I don't want to mess with what he said. So yeah, I'm glad I can forgive Kate for what she did. And we all have to live with the consequences."

"See, that's the problem I have with you Christians. Everything's always perfect in your world. Always rosy. Forgive everybody, love everybody, everybody's happy. Unbelievable."

The rosiness faded from her face, leaving her freckles in stark contrast to her pale skin. "It isn't like that, and no one's saying it is."

"You just did. You just said you forgave Kate."

"I did not. I said I'd be able to. I haven't managed it yet, but with God's help I will."

"Why? Why worry about it?"

One by one, she placed the strips of bacon on paper towels. "Do you seriously want me to live with this black lump of grief and hatred in my heart forever? What a happy thought. Thanks a lot, Nick."

That was the last thing he'd expected her to say. What happened to "Because the Bible says I should"?

"No, of course not." He sounded as stupid and awkward as he felt.

"And if I forgive Kate and God puts peace in there, and I can sleep at night without wanting to take a bunch of Tylenol myself—yes, I heard what happened to Anna. Dorinda told me that, too, when I called and asked her about counselors. If I can do that, what's it to you?"

Now he'd made her angry. What was the matter with him? "I'm sorry. I didn't mean to upset you."

"Well, you did." The threat of tears trembled in her voice as she shoveled eggs onto a plate with savage efficiency. "Forgiveness is a gift, Nick. Not an obligation, not something to badmouth just because you've never had to use it."

"In law enforcement we—"

"I'm not talking about law enforcement or how a cop sees the world. I'm talking about how I see it. And I won't have you run down something that's important to me."

"I'm not—"

"Here's your breakfast. I hope you enjoy it."

Oh, man, she was going to leave. "Tanya, don't go. Please. I was being stupid. Forgive me. There, I just admitted I needed it. That's a start, right?"

To his enormous relief, she didn't tear off the dish towel she was using as an apron over her jeans and storm out the door. Instead, she picked up her coffee mug and took a sip, then lifted her eyebrows as the oven timer pinged. She'd just remembered the biscuits.

She checked them, her back toward him. "You're forgiven," she said after a long moment in which he saw their tentative friendship circling the drain. "And I'm sorry I lost my temper. That happens when people poke at what's important to me."

She was as solid as the guys on the force, who stood by the principles they were sworn to as if it were part of their personalities. Is that what being a Christian was all about? Not the swearing to uphold justice part, but living by principles that were important to you?

"What else is important to you?" he surprised himself by asking.

"Love," she said simply, pulling the tray and piling the biscuits in a bowl. "God's love for me despite my weaknesses. The love

I had for Randi despite hers. Love's the backbone of everything. The rest of it just kind of branches out from there."

"It's easier to forgive someone you love, I'll admit that." The way each of them had just—

Now, hold on a minute. That was two friends smoothing things over, nothing more.

"Easier to forgive," she agreed. "Easier to be honest." The way she'd been with him. "Easier to be brave." Like coming here with the makings of a full breakfast, a gift from the heart from a woman who had nothing else to give, trusting that he'd take it and not push her away.

Did God do that? Sure, he knew the gospel story inside out and backward, but he'd never actually applied it to real life before. Because the truth was, he was a practical guy. Street smart. Analytical, even. And love wasn't a thing that lent itself easily to analysis. Or street smarts, come to that.

So had God come to him with a heart full of love, and he'd pushed him away? For what reason? Because he thought he could do a better job of life on his own?

Nick thought of what might have happened if Tanya hadn't had that internal backbone of love to support her. Maybe she'd have gone off the deep end, like that mother in California who had gunned down her son's molester right there in the courtroom. Maybe she'd have gotten serious about the Tylenol and taken not just a "cry for help" dose like Anna but a truly lethal one.

If not for God, maybe he'd have lost his friend.

Maybe he was lost, himself.

And suddenly Nick recognized the true nature of that yawning void inside him. He took its measure, and there was nothing left but to admit that he'd been filling it with justifications and avoidances and cynical humor, when all along the real nature of it had eluded him. The fact was, despite his close-knit family and the brotherhood of law enforcement, he needed love. He needed it, craved it, wanted it—and had deliberately deprived himself of it.

Why?

Because it means giving up your own way. Being the boss—the captain of his own soul and all that. He hadn't done so badly in the captain department, but if he were completely honest within himself, he wasn't completely happy, either.

So, to be happy, was it a case of giving up—or getting?

"This is too much for me," he muttered.

Then he realized that while he'd been locked in his own thoughts, having his little moment of truth, Tanya had set the table and put all the food out on it without saying a word.

She sat in front of the plate of eggs and waved him into his chair. "The standard cautionary preamble applies here," she said. "I know this is your house and all, but I brought the food so I'm going to say grace."

"Have at it," he said mildly. "Put in a word for me."

She bowed her head, and instead of staring politely into the distance as he'd done the other night, he bowed his, too.

"Father, thank you for this food, and thank you for giving Nick a good spirit about finding me in his house without an invitation. Thank you for revealing the truth about Randi's death, and, Lord, I hope you're taking good care of her until I get there. If there are nose rings in heaven, Lord, she's going to want one, and you need to tell her no. I pray for Nick, Father. I know you love him to pieces, and he just needs to know it, too. In Jesus' name, amen."

She raised her head, opened her eyes, and passed him the eggs.

"How do you know?" he asked.

"Know what?"

"That he loves me to pieces. How does anyone know?"

"Well, to put it in cop-speak, he let his Son be killed by a homicidal gang for your sake. If that doesn't show love, I don't know what does."

"If it happened, it happened two thousand years ago. Pretty abstract, if you ask me."

"All I can do is tell you what happens with me. He fills me up inside. It's like being loved by the greatest guy in the world—not that I have any experience there, but I can imagine it—and then multiplying by ten. He shows it in a hundred little ways. Like with Laurie and her casseroles. You and your determination to find out the truth. People stopping me in the street to say they're praying for me. He changes people, and then they show his love to other people."

"He hasn't changed me." But even as he said the words, he heard the defiance in them, and the hollow knowledge that they weren't true.

"You'd be surprised. Why else would you put up with me?"

"That's what friends do."

"It says in the Bible that he's the friend that sticks closer than a brother. I've found that to be true. Maybe you should, too."

Nick had never considered Jesus as a friend. He was the sad-eyed guy on the cross, letting people beat up on him when he could have blasted them off the face of the planet with one lightning bolt. But a friend? Someone to walk beside and talk to and get advice from? It was a little weird thinking of Jesus like that.

"I guess I don't understand a friend like that," he said at last. "He's too complicated for me."

"He's love, Nick," Tanya said softly. "And love is the simplest and most powerful force on earth." She smiled at him, and there were those seedlike dimples, and his heart squeezed and did a really strange flip-flop in his chest.

He needed to focus. Tanya was trying to tell him something important, and he couldn't think yet about why her smile kept affecting him like this.

"You like talking about him, don't you?" If he got her back on the subject of her own beliefs, maybe she wouldn't press him about not having any.

"It's natural to talk about the things you love. I love to talk about Randi." Her gaze faltered and she blinked, trying to keep the sudden rush of tears from flowing over.

He reached behind him and snagged a tissue out of the box on the counter. "It's okay. You can cry here if you want to."

She dabbed at her eyes and took a deep breath. "Dorinda tells me this is normal. You know, tears just coming up out of nowhere. Believe me, it was easier being angry."

"You? Angry? Weren't you the one just talking about forgiveness?"

"Sure, I was angry. One night I imagined the bridge collapsed and all those kids drowned. Even Anna." She glanced at him in apology. "I prayed a lot that God would help me through that stage, and he did."

In one of his courses at the academy, there had been a segment on the stages of grief. Anger had been one of them. He could imagine himself being stuck in that stage forever. Maybe Tanya was lucky to have a faith like this that would get her through it.

"I'm glad you had him to turn to."

She nodded. "He was faithful. People want to know how to help, too, you know? But sometimes what helps the most is just to talk about Randi. They try to change the subject, as if it's going to hurt me, but it's just the opposite. When I talk about her, in a strange way she's still alive, even if it's only in my memory."

"It's natural to talk about the ones we love. But when you talk about Jesus, it still seems strange to me. Like he's a real person—as real as Randi."

"He is real. And I think you're beginning to see that."

Maybe. "What's that verse about seeing through a glass darkly? He's just a shadow to me right now."

"Give him time," she said softly. "And you'll see him face-to-face."

After dawdling over breakfast and doing dishes and talking about everything from the nature of grief and the definition of healing to whether bacon was better crispy or curly, she finally glanced at the clock.

"I should go."

"Why?" It was surprising how easy it was to just be with her and celebrate the moment. He'd be happy to string all of these moments together all day, the way a kid made a daisy chain on a lazy summer afternoon.

"Because it's Sunday morning, and the service starts in half an hour."

It did? "Which service?"

"I go to Glendale Bible Fellowship. It's just on the other side of the river."

So did his family and Laurie's. "I know where it is. How about I walk you over there?"

So that was how Nick found himself beside Tanya on the river path, ambling toward the bridge. The weather seemed to have decided to prove the forecast wrong, and the snow clouds had cleared away, leaving the day sparkling bright instead of gray and damp. He wasn't into looking for symbols and meanings in things. But today, with the memory of Tanya's words still warm in his mind and the endless vault of heaven arching over them and the river whispering to itself down the bank, he could almost believe that maybe the Creator of all this was trying to tell him something.

Like he'd done something right, there in the kitchen that morning. Admitted something. Started something. Whatever it was, the world seemed to be pretty happy about it all.

When they reached the part of the path that took them past the sandbar, his instinct was to quicken his step a little and get Tanya over the painful part as quickly as possible. But she had other ideas.

"It's shrinking." She pointed at the bar. Water swirled around it, carrying it away a little at a time.

"Soon it'll be gone, and the river will make another one somewhere else. The Susquanny never stays the same for more than a few weeks at a time."

"I never thought that something like a river would change. Especially—well, especially that spot. It's kind of like a memorial for me. You know. Where she was found."

"It can still be that. But it's not the sandbar that's the memorial. It's your love for her, isn't it?"

She nodded and moved on. They walked in silence for several hundred yards, until they could see the bridge straddling the river, its awkward wooden bones dark against the bright sky.

There were people on it, just standing there looking down.

"That's where she went in," Tanya said. "Right about where those people are. You can see the support beams sticking out from here."

They were only a few hundred feet away now. Nick stopped. "Hey. That's Colin and Laurie and the kids. What are they doing up there?"

"Debbie told me Anna was phobic about the bridge. Wouldn't go on it. Wouldn't even ride in a car across it."

"Maybe. But there she is."

"They must have released her from the hospital. And Debbie must have been wrong about the phobia thing. That'll teach me to listen to gossip."

"I'd still be interested in knowing what really happened when Kyle found her standing in the water. You'd probably like to know that, too."

"I already know. She went down there to see if she could help."

"Did someone tell you that?"

"She's Laurie Hale's child," Tanya said simply. "Why else?"

He looked at her in wonder as he heard the softness in her tone. She'd forgiven Laurie, it was clear. A bit of white light now lived in her heart instead of that black lump she'd talked about earlier. And it was real forgiveness, too. This woman was incapable of playacting or putting on a face for people. She had that in common with Laurie, whose passions were right out there in the open for people to see.

Love. Forgiveness. All there for the taking.

Tanya nudged him in the ribs. "It's nearly eleven."

She sounded as though she expected him to head back to his house. As they walked, she moved away from him a little, as if she wanted to give him permission to go back. He closed the gap so that instead they walked side by side.

"No," he said. "I think I'll go with you. You never know. Maybe I'll learn something new."

"Maybe you will," she agreed.

Across the river, the bells announcing the service began to ring. It took Nick a second to recognize the tune, and when he did, he grinned. He could appreciate a God with a sense of humor.

It was "What a Friend We Have in Jesus."

Chapter Twenty

*L*aurie *glanced into* the backseat as Colin braked to approach the bridge. "Are you sure you're okay with this, sweetie?"

Anna didn't look okay. Her fingers gripped the stem of the rose so tightly that Laurie thought she'd snap it. On her right hand, a narrow bandage formed a bump over the cotton ball where the IV needle had been, and a small blue bruise had spread on either side of it. "I'll be fine."

"We don't have to do this today." Colin parked the car on the side of the road and looked at his daughter in the rearview mirror. "We can wait 'til you're stronger."

"I want to do it now. I need to." Anna got out and, wearing a determined expression, led the way to the middle of the bridge. Laurie, Colin, and Tim followed, gathering around her at the rail as though their bodies would protect her from the wind . . . and from the stares of the curious as they drove past.

They'd brought her home from the hospital yesterday, and she'd spent the day in bed. Laurie still wasn't convinced Anna should be going to church today, but Anna had insisted.

"I meant both things," Colin said. With a gentle finger, he smoothed a lock of windblown hair off Anna's pale cheek. "This and what we're going to do at church."

"I know." She looked up at him, then at Laurie. "I meant both things, too."

"Mom, it's freezing out here," Tim complained.

"We won't be long," Laurie said to him. "This is important."

Anna looked out over the dark rush of the water as Colin bowed his head. "Father God, thank you that we can stand here together as a family, whole and complete. I pray that you'll be with us this morning, and especially that you'll give your strength to Anna. Thank you for protecting her and for bringing her through this experience and out the other side. Thank you for reminding us that we can count on you, no matter what. Amen."

Laurie slid an arm around Anna's shoulders. "Father, I'm so glad that you're with us today, just the way you promised. Thank you for helping me realize that even when the water goes over my head, and over Anna's head, too, you're there with us. Thank you for loving me back to you, and for making me see that it's all about you, not about me or the church or anything else. Thank you for keeping Anna safe, and for bringing us together again. Help me go to Tanya today and ask her to forgive me for taking offense at Thanksgiving. Help me be a good friend to Janice, the way she's been such a good friend to me. In Jesus' name, amen."

She nudged Tim. "Thank you that we can be a family," he said, the way he always did when he said grace at the table. Then he added, "Thank you for bringing Anna home. Please help her be quick so we can get off this bridge and not look weird. Amen."

Anna snorted, then sobered. "Father in heaven, I'm not sure how I'm going to get through today, but I'm asking for your help. I'm sorry I was so stupid about the pills. Thank you for not letting me get away with it. Thank you for Kyle, and for my mom and dad, and even for Tim. And, Father, thank you for

Randi, too." Her voice broke, and she swallowed. "If she can see us, tell her I'm sorry, and that this is for her. Amen."

Laurie lifted her head and watched as Anna raised her arm and tossed the pink rose out into space as far as she could. It tumbled gracefully through the air, end over end, until it landed on the surface of the river. The water caught it up in a joyful swirl, like a delighted girl with a treasured gift, and ran away with it under the bridge and out of their sight.

Laurie took a deep breath, the air plunging into her lungs as clean as cold water. "Amen," she said. "Let's go."

It took only a minute to drive the two blocks to Glendale Bible Fellowship, where people streamed through the front doors as the bells rang a welcoming peal overhead. As Laurie took her seat, she caught Cale Dayton's eye while he fussed with his lapel microphone. His eyes were comforting and warm, and she let his assurance that they were doing the right thing soothe her as they sang the opening hymns. He had told her that what he'd planned would happen in lieu of their usual "prayer and praise" time after the sermon, so instead of dashing off to Sunday school, Anna and Tim stayed with her and Colin.

Was it just a coincidence that Cale's text was Psalm 124? Since she'd talked to him about it yesterday, Laurie thought not. His encouragement comforted her, gave her courage for what was to come.

When he was finished, Cale laid his Bible on the table he used in lieu of a podium and descended the three stairs from the stage so that he stood on the same level as everyone else.

"We're going to do something a little different today," he said. Behind him, Dorinda Platt began to play soft notes of praise on the piano. "In light of what you all might have read in the papers this morning or watched on TV last night, I think this congregation needs some healing. Would Colin, Laurie, Anna, and Tim Hale please come up here?"

She'd prepared the kids as best she could, but it still surprised Laurie when Anna led the way. When they'd gathered up at the front, Anna's hand found its way into hers, and she squeezed it, as though strength could flow between them.

Maybe it could.

Cale took a deep breath. "I would like to be the first in this congregation to publicly apologize to Anna Hale." He held out his hands. "Please forgive me for thinking for even one moment that you might have been in some way responsible for Randi Peizer's death."

Anna's lip trembled, and a tear tracked its way down her cheek. "I forgive you," she whispered, and was enveloped in Cale's big bear hug.

"Forgive me for the same, sweetheart," Laurie said.

Anna nodded, and Laurie folded her into her arms. When Laurie stepped back, Janice Edgar took her place.

"Please forgive me for believing that you told a lie about my son," she choked.

Anna barely got the words of forgiveness out before she burrowed into Janice's arms, hugging her tightly.

When Janice went back to her seat to cry on her husband's shoulder, with awkward pats on the back from Kyle, Tanya Peizer stood up in the very last pew near the door.

Laurie swiped at her wet cheeks with one hand as Tanya marched up to the front. She seemed to move in slow motion as Laurie's brain worked frantically. What would Tanya say? Would she take advantage of this public opportunity to repeat the things she'd said at Thanksgiving?

Well, let her. After Laurie spoke first.

She stepped forward and took Tanya's hand. "Please forgive me for offending you at Thanksgiving, Tanya."

Tanya shook her head, and from the front pew, where Maggie and her family sat, Laurie heard a gasp.

"I should never have said those things," Tanya said clearly. Her voice, which Laurie had never heard raised above a murmur, could be heard throughout the sanctuary. "Yes, I was grieving and angry and wanted to strike out at whoever took my girl from me. But I shouldn't have struck at you. I want to ask forgiveness from both you and Anna for the things I said, and to tell you that I want to start all over and be friends. Real friends, who stand by each other and support each other, no matter what."

Anna was the first one to throw herself into Tanya's arms, and Laurie's own arms stretched wide as she hugged them both. After that, it seemed as though the entire congregation needed to cleanse itself of all the suspicion and gossip and innuendo that had been seeping through it over the past few weeks.

Laurie lost count of the people who asked her for forgiveness. She was just hugging Debbie Jacks when she saw her cousin Nick step in front of her.

She blinked, gulped back her tears, and tried to speak, but nothing came out.

"I know," he said. "Big surprise, huh?"

Her throat still wouldn't produce any sound. Speechlessly, she nodded, and then the light dawned. "You're here with Tanya," she got out.

"This must be my day for learning about forgiveness," he said, and glanced at Anna, who was getting a bear hug from two of her classmates.

"Mine, too," Laurie said.

"Forgive me for having to investigate her?"

"Of course. You were doing your job."

"Think she'll feel the same?"

"You'd better ask her."

Anna chose that moment to turn, and her jaw dropped as she took in the sight of her cousin, who hadn't been in church since he was her age.

"What are you doing here?" she asked, her voice raspy from too many tears.

"I'm here for you," he said. "I want to be sure you don't hold it against me for making you part of the investigation."

"Of course not," she whispered. "You had to do it." She looked from him to Laurie. "And between you and Mom, you made it all come out right when I was so scared I couldn't say anything."

"The truth has set us free." He glanced at Laurie and grinned.

God had promised it would, and so it had.

"I wish we could do Thanksgiving over." Tanya touched Anna's hair, then let her hand drop.

"Why can't we?" Deep inside Laurie, anticipation kicked into high gear, and with it a fresh to-do list. She began to herd them all down the center aisle. "I'll pull the turkey leftovers out of the freezer, and we'll have turkey-stuffing sandwiches with all the trimmings."

"When are you going to do that?" Nick wanted to know. "Everyone goes back to work tomorrow."

"Today. Tonight. All of us—the Edgars, too." She spoke to her family, but gazed at Tanya. "What do you say?"

Tanya smiled, and Laurie realized she had never seen her smile before. "That is so like you, Laurie—and I'm thankful for it. So I say yes."

Janice finished whispering to her husband and caught Laurie's eye as they reached the door. "We'll be there. Just once, I think we can overlook the grounding rule for Kyle."

Smiling, with her friends and family knit together all around her, Laurie walked outside into the bright morning.

Reading Group Guide

1. Psalm 124 comes to mean a lot to Laurie Hale during the course of this book. Have you ever experienced the feeling of the waters overwhelming your soul? What did you do about it?

2. Laurie enjoys organizing church activities, her home, her friends, and her family. Is it possible to be involved in the church and be busy with the work of God—and yet not have a relationship with him? Has that ever happened to you?

3. Laurie didn't realize the extent of the emptiness in her soul until her daughter attempted suicide. Do you think God used this experience as a wake-up call?

4. Do you think Kate Parsons intended for Randi to die? What do you think will happen to Kate now?

5. Do you think the "mob mentality" is a reality? What would you have done if you had been on the bridge that night?

6. Tanya Peizer is a single mother doing the best she can to support herself and her daughter. Do you think she was partly to blame for Randi's being out the night she was killed? Tanya

288 ～ *Shelley Bates*

thinks she could have changed things if she'd been home. Do you?

7. Is Tanya's forgiveness of Laurie at the end of the book realistic? Do you think she will be able to forgive Kate Parsons?

8. Forgiveness is an important part of the Christian walk. Have there been times in your life when it has been particularly difficult to forgive?

About the Author

*S*helley *Bates* holds an M.A. in Writing Popular Fiction from Seton Hill University in Pennsylvania. *Grounds to Believe*, her debut CBA novel and the first book in her Elect Trilogy, won the 2005 RITA Award for Best Inspirational Novel of the Year from the Romance Writers of America. The second book in the trilogy, *Pocketful of Pearls*, was a 2006 RITA Award finalist. Shelley is a freelance marketing communications editor and enjoys playing the piano and Celtic harp, making historical costumes, and spoiling her chickens rotten.